FAIRWOOD

Also by Eli Yance

House 23
Consequence

FAIRWOOD

A Thriller

ELI YANCE

Skyhorse Publishing

Skyhorse Publishing books may be purchased in bulk at special discounts for sales promotion, corporate gifts, fund-raising, or educational purposes. Special editions can also be created to specifications. For details, contact the Special Sales Department, Skyhorse Publishing, 307 West 36th Street, 11th Floor, New York, NY 10018 or info@skyhorsepublishing.com.

Skyhorse® and Skyhorse Publishing® are registered trademarks of Skyhorse Publishing, Inc.®, a Delaware corporation.

Visit our website at www.skyhorsepublishing.com.

10 9 8 7 6 5 4 3 2 1

Library of Congress Cataloging-in-Publication Data

Names: Yance, Eli, author.
Title: Fairwood : a thriller / Eli Yance.
Description: New York, NY : Skyhorse Publishing, [2019] | Includes index.
Identifiers: LCCN 2018052466 (print) | LCCN 2018052955 (ebook) | ISBN 9781510704466 | ISBN 9781510704398 (paperback)
Subjects: | BISAC: FICTION / Suspense. | GSAFD: Suspense fiction. | LCGFT: Romance fiction.
Classification: LCC PR6125.A53 (ebook) | LCC PR6125.A53 F35 2019 (print) | DDC 823/.92--dc23
LC record available at https://lccn.loc.gov/2018052466

Cover design by Yiota Giannakopoulou
Cover photo credit Pixabay/Skeeze

Printed in the United States of America

To the real Dexter and Pandora.

PROLOGUE

She was a criminal. A thief. They all were.

But were they murderers?

As Pandora pressed the steel barrel of the Ruger against the teller's forehead, the question ran through her mind, and not for the first time. She looked into the eyes of the teller, a forty-year-old man who didn't seem to care that an attractive robber was one twitch away from decorating the bank's sterile walls with his blood and brain matter.

"If you want the money, you're going to have to kill me," the teller said with a sneer.

And so she did. She squeezed the trigger at the same moment she squeezed shut her eyes, her world turning black, a sticky web of blood washing over her features.

Annie paused. Her hands hovered over the keyboard at which she had been typing frantically for thirty minutes. She looked at the words she had written and then frowned.

"Attractive robber?" she read, shaking her head. "God, I'm so vain." She hit the backspace button and watched as as the words disappeared. "We're supposed to be sensible bank robbers," she told herself. "Not cold-blooded assholes."

She looked around subconsciously as she muttered those words, aware that if her mother heard her, she'd receive a lecture on how thirteen-year-old girls should never swear, just like her lectures on how she shouldn't play violent video games, watch R-rated films, or write fan fiction about real-life bank robbers.

But she was only having fun. And what did her mother know? She may have only been thirteen, but Annie knew there was no harm in robbing banks if no one was hurt; there was no harm in taking money from the rich. After all, wasn't that what Robin Hood did? They were views that she would never voice, because while she didn't respect her mother's overprotective standpoint and overcautious approach, she did respect her dad's, and while he agreed with her about most things, she doubted he would agree with her about the bank robbers that she idolized.

She began typing again, then stopped, a feeling of unease hitting her like a brick. She heard a car door slam outside, heard heavy footfalls approaching the house—the sound of leather soles slapping wet tarmac like distant thunderclaps after a fading storm.

She checked her watch—her dad wasn't due back for another three hours.

She heard three loud raps on the front door. The noise reverberated throughout the house and sent a chill through her. Guests weren't unusual; her mother had friends visiting all of the time and her father had an eBay habit that meant they were nearly on first-name terms with every delivery driver in the county. But something about this didn't feel right.

She could hear her mother approaching the door, could hear it being ripped open. There was a brief exchange, two voices filled with bass followed by her mother's reply. There was anxiety in her voice, trepidation, and that made Annie feel infinitely more uneasy. Her fingers, still hovering over the keyboard, trembled. She closed them into fists, pulled them to her side, sunk her head to her chest and continued to listen.

The door still hadn't been closed, the guests not yet invited in. Annie heard her mother shout, demand. This was followed by another bass-filled reply and then her mother unleashed a wail that Annie felt crawling through every fiber of her being.

At that moment she knew. She didn't know she knew, but she did.

She took once last glance at the half-deleted words on her screen. She had stopped short of deleting the first line, which now stared back at her, seemingly screaming as loud as her mother was.

But were they murderers?

She left her workstation—the computer her father had purchased for her as a Christmas present six months earlier, the desk he made with his own two hands. She left the cozy confines of her bedroom, the pink walls her father had agreed to paint when she was just six years old, the giant teddy bears he used to joke were watching him and plotting against him when he read bedtime stories to her.

Her mother's cries had faded to whimpers, the noise like a hollow echo inside her mind, filtered through rushing waterfalls of white noise that grew more intense with each step.

She felt sick to her stomach, weak, but she descended the stairs with a sense of urgency, as if each step brought with it an increased need to know, to have her fears confirmed.

At the bottom of the stairs, she turned into the living room and stopped. Two policemen and her mother stared back at her. They looked solemn, pitiful. She looked distraught.

"Annie." He mother's voice broke as she spoke. "Sit down, I have some bad news."

Annie shook her head. "Tell me."

"Please, sit—"

"Tell me!" she screamed.

The white noise had increased and her mother's words, when spoken, were even more distant than the approaching footsteps had been, even more distant than the cries of distress, as if her own mind was trying to drown out the inevitable.

"It's your dad," her mother said. "There's been a robbery at the bank. He's," she paused, turned away from her daughter, her words becoming increasingly choked as another flood of tears prepared itself. "I'm sorry, sweetie, but your father's dead."

The last thing Annie saw before she blacked out, before the rushing waterfalls in her ears reached their peak, before her knees buckled and her eyes rolled into the back of her head, was a large framed photograph of her and her dad sitting on top of the mantlepiece in between the two forlorn police officers.

It had been taken at a local fair just three days earlier. They were beaming at the camera: her holding a stick of cotton candy, him pulling funny faces. It was the last photograph they had taken together, the last photograph they would ever take together.

In the many painful hours that followed, she would see it as the last day of enjoyment life had ever and would ever provide her.

The day that her childhood died.

1

A bored beat drummed on a wooden surface with idle fingers; A monotone whistle, an emulation of an unknown pop song heard earlier in the day; A conversation, a distant rumble of baritone interspersed with the occasional laugh; The squeak of a chair on resisting laminate; staccato throat-clearing outbursts.

Dexter Bleak reacted to every noise inside the bar, his eyes flitting, his stomach churning. At the back of the room, through the haze of cigar smoke that pressed against the yellowed ceiling like layered cream, he caught the wandering gaze of a curious cowboy. His eyes, set in deep circles below pencil-thin eyebrows, stared at him from beneath the brim of a leather Stetson. He flicked his head slightly, a nod of recognition. Dexter returned the gesture and looked away.

A cowboy in northern England. He was either a long way from home or a short distance from the funny farm.

An abrupt thud and a barrage of expletives drew his wandering eyes. A youngster, no more than sixteen, was giving an antiquated one-armed bandit a piece of his delinquent mind and a feel of his tattered trainers. The youngster had been in the pub as long as Dexter; he'd watched him knock back a couple of pints and grow rapidly drunk under the peripheral, disapproving stares of the others—most of whom were old enough to be his grandfather.

The bartender, cleaning a dusty glass with an even dustier rag, shouted to the youngster: something abrupt, brash, calling him by a nickname suited more to a dog. The boy sneered at him, grimaced, turned away and returned to his seat where he mumbled into his third pint.

Dexter caught the stare of the bartender, looked away before he felt any need to exchange pleasantries. He looked at his hands, spread out on the table in front of him like he was preparing to peer into a crystal ball. A line of callouses pricked the flesh at the base of his fingers. Roughened, dry skin fleshed its way across his palms. A small cut, brown with a streak of dried blood, sketched a line across the back of his right hand.

He looked questionably at his beer. Moved his tired hands around the cold glass.

Another noise. A banging, some footsteps.

He turned sharply, pulling his hand from the moist glass as if it seared his flesh.

A door at the back of the room opened. A woman stepped through, into the smoke. All eyes fell upon her. The old men stared with inconspicuous admiration, the youngster glared with blatant lust. She was beautiful—radiant didn't even cut it. She stood out against the smoky atmosphere like a watery mirage. Bright green eyes; a diamond stud on her upper lip that caught a glisten from the dim fluorescents; a pair of equally reflective earrings that hung to her jaw; a dimpled smile that suggested she knew she was being watched.

Her hips rocked when she walked toward Dexter, her golden hair swaying pendulously. She was clad from head to toe in leather. Leather boots, buckled and belted just below the knee; tight leather pants that described the tones in her thighs and the tightness in her backside; a leather jacket, emblazoned with studs, stitches, and chains, buttoned with a single clasp, enough to allow her breasts to poke through her t-shirt underneath. Above the assortment of metal studs, just above her right breast, she wore a small bronze brooch in the shape of a butterfly. It was out of place on her chest, but few would ever notice it among the mass of metal. And no man would choose to stare at the brooch instead of her breast.

She caught the lustful gaze of the youngster and winked at him, an image he would utilize on countless lonely nights. She sat down opposite Dexter, grinned drolly—her face was constantly alight with something cheeky, something sly, something that suggested she could manipulate you in a second if she wanted to.

"You took your time," Dexter said blandly.

She shrugged passively, extended a hand, and began to toy with the edges of a moistened beer mat, bending and contorting the wrinkled corners.

Dexter sighed and looked around. He caught a few gazes, eyes that saw him with the beautiful blonde and wondered what she saw in him. Some of them had given him the same looks when he'd entered, but most hadn't paid attention until the leather-clad bombshell strolled through their midst.

Dexter was average looking at best. A hair over six-foot; his frame on the stocky side of athletic, constructed through manual labor, lazy workouts, and a poor diet. His rounded face and squared chin gave him the appeal of an action-movie star, but his short neck, pallid skin, and beady eyes dropped him some way short of handsome.

"This place is giving me the creeps." He met the eyes of the youngster who, with the blonde in his sights and intimidation on his mind, tried to stare him down. Dexter turned away, backed down; now wasn't the time to be facing off against a drunken kid.

She didn't reply, her mind was elsewhere.

"*Pandora.*"

She looked up, her blank expression shifting back to a good-humored smile. She mumbled an inquisitive reply, "Yeah?"

"What's on your mind?"

She lowered her eyebrows into an arch, "What do you think's on my mind?"

He nodded slowly, held her stare for a moment, and then turned away. The bartender was channel hopping, grunting disconsolately as a barrage of music, news, and talkshows popped onto the elevated television set.

At the back of the room, the door leading to the toilets opened and closed, buffeting a thick wave of hanging smoke as an elderly man waded through.

Pandora brightened, clucked a dismissive sound, and followed Dexter's gaze. "Problems?" she wondered.

He shook his head, watched the wading man slump into his seat with a groan. "Nothing more than usual."

"And what's the usual?"

He turned to her, grinned. He watched a wry smile grip the corners of her lips, tweaking a small wrinkle that cut across her cheek. "The usual is they're all looking at us thinking: 'What the fuck is *she* doing with *him?*'"

"Ah," she nodded. "And do you think they've figured out why?"

"Even *I* haven't figured out why."

"Maybe it's because you have a big cock."

"Do I?"

She shook her head, smiled even wider. "But they don't know that."

"Ah, right. Gotcha." He grinned and gave a gentle, self-deprecating shake of his head. Lowered his eyes to his hands.

"Cheer up," Pandora insisted. "No one here knows anything."

Dexter agreed with a nod.

He didn't look away, didn't see the channel-hopping bartender find an agreeable station; didn't see his wizened face burst into life when he saw the images of Pandora and Dexter, his two suspicious and out of place patrons, appear on the grainy screen; didn't see him attract the attention of a couple of the regulars; didn't note the awe-filled expressions or the curious way the man in the Stetson looked at them and licked his lips.

When Dexter finally lifted his eyes, met with the waiting gaze of his beautiful girlfriend, and then turned, still smiling, to the smoky room, he discovered that everyone was looking at him. The smile sunk from his face, the breath caught in his throat.

"*Shit,*" he hissed.

The bartender shared his stare between them and the television. He turned up the volume until the tinny tones of the newscaster overlapped the sound of thickening tension.

The youngster climbed to his feet, pulled up his pants, adjusted his belt, and thrust his tongue against the side of his cheek. On the next table, near the exit, a burly man with a bulging belly and a balding head rocked to his feet, knocking his chair over in the process.

Dexter and Pandora watched as their onscreen portraits faded and were replaced by a video of the exterior of a bank, its bulky facade looming over the gawking onlookers.

"*. . . today, just as the employees were breaking for lunch.*" They heard the reporter say in a serious tone, her words thumping out of the small and anachronistic television like the beat from a plastic drum. "*This sinister pair were interrupted by Mr. Earl Rodgers, a thirty-five-year-old father of one, who had worked at the bank for over ten years. Early reports suggest that the guard tried to subdue them before launching himself at the female in an attempt to pry the weapon from her hands. At this point, her partner fired twice, hitting Mr. Rodgers in the chest and face, killing him instantly.*"

Dexter's face sunk as he stared at the images of Earl Rodgers: a family portrait. He was smiling, hugging his daughter as his wife watched on.

They showed the inside of the bank, photographic stills taken years or months earlier. It was different in the photos, cleaner. The walls were painted a different color, a lighter shade, less intense—fewer splatters of blood. The floor was carpeted, fitted with thick plastic borders that traced a spiraled path to the tellers; the one he'd known was fully tiled, adorned with the petrified faces of a dozen customers and the bloodied face of a dead family man.

"*. . . is the seventh robbery in their cross-country crime spree,*" the reporter continued as the camera returned to her. She paused and lowered her eyebrows for effect, "*. . .but their first murder.*"

Dexter and Pandora had worn ski masks for their first two robberies. The first was at a post office—a few thousand notes, a hurried escape, and a story that barely even made it into the local newspapers. The second was in a bank. They had escaped long before the sound of police sirens filled the air and before panic filtered out into the street. They had ducked into a crowd of tourists, removed their masks, and walked away with two backpacks full of money.

But one of those tourists had been snapping pictures of his family on the street and he caught the moment the pair removed their disguises.

In the back of one image, Pandora could be seen removing her ski mask, her white hair falling over her face, a big smile on her face. In another, the pair were embracing.

Those were the pictures that made them overnight sensations. The ones that earned them their nicknames.

"*Known as the 'Bleak and Bright Bandits' to their followers,*" *the reporter continued,* "*this modern-day Bonnie and Clyde now have blood on their hands and an even bigger target on their heads.*"

Dexter turned to Pandora. She removed her eyes from the screen, gave him a gentle nod.

This wasn't the first time they had been in such a predicament. After their third robbery, a holdup at another post office, they had been recognized in the backstreets by a group of loitering youths. They'd surrounded them, and just when Dexter was preparing himself for a disadvantaged fight, they shook his hand and congratulated him. One of them even asked for an autograph.

Dexter and Pandora stood now, trying to avoid the gaze of everyone in the room.

Dexter doubted the hard-faced patrons in the pub would treat him the same way as the kids at the post office, and as the woman continued her monotonously toned report, those doubts were affirmed:

"Police have substantially increased the award for their capture. Anyone with any information . . ."

He put his hands on Pandora's back, gave her a firm shove, gesturing for her to quicken her retreating steps. She stumbled forward, heeded his plea, and bolted for the door. He turned, gave one last fleeting look around the bar, and then followed her, stopping when the burly man with the bald head appeared in front of the exit.

Pandora bounced into him, used her hands to stop herself from running into his bulbous belly, and then pushed herself off him when she did so.

Dexter stopped rigid behind her, turned to face the room whose occupants were closing in on him like starving men swamping the last morsel at a buffet.

"Substantial reward," Stetson said with a grin beneath the prominent brim. "How much do you think that'll be?" he asked to no one in particular.

The young drunk answered him with a sniggering grin, "Tens o'thousands, I reckon. Mebbies more." He leered at Pandora, who was trying to bridge a gap between the fat blockade and the encroaching wave of body odor and lust. "'Though I think there's sumate a lot more interesting 'ere."

Pandora grimaced at him, immediately regretting her flirtatious smile moments earlier.

The bartender stepped forward, brushing the youngster aside. He stopped a few feet in front of the couple. The pulsing throng stopped behind him, waiting like a pack of dogs for the order to kill.

"Seems like you two 'av been busy," he said with a sadistic grin that peeled apart his face like a terminal slice from a razor-sharp saber.

Dexter nodded slowly.

"They say you's 'av stole tens o'thousands," he said, crossing his arms over his chest, his smile switching to hunger.

Dexter nodded again.

The bartender glared at him for a moment, then at Pandora, then beyond them both. He looked past the bulging frame of the man blocking the door, towards the parking lot. "That your vehicle out there?" he asked with a flick of his head, knowing full well it was.

"I know what you're thinking—" Dexter began.

The bartender raised his eyebrows, gave a wry smile. "*Do you* now?"

"The money isn't in there."

"Really?" he asked, unconvinced. "I suppose you's 'av spent it all 'av ya? Handbags and dresses for your little tart, maybe?"

"Hey, fuck you," Pandora spat, receiving a giggle from the back of the pack and an amused stare from the rest.

"Feisty little bitch you got there. How's about you cut the shit, give us the money, and I won't let Rex 'ere 'av his dirty way with 'er." He pointed to the lustful teenager who was practically dripping with anticipation. "And the others, of course," he said with an appreciative glance toward Pandora. "None of us would want to pass up such an opportunity."

Pandora growled. Dexter sneered.

The bartender lowered his arms and his eyebrows, gave Dexter a quizzical nod of his head. "What do you say? Give us what you've got and we'll leave you alone, let you fuck off back to your thieving ways."

Dexter nodded softly, reluctantly. "It's in the car," he said with a lowered head.

The bartender grinned. The teenager deflated, grumbled under his breath.

"Keys," he ordered, holding out his hand.

Dexter removed the set from his pocket, tossed them toward the bartender who clasped them in his palm. The bartender grinned, celebratory, and then passed the keys to the mopey, horny kid by his side.

"Check the car, grab what you can. Be quick."

He trudged off as the others watched. He had the space to walk freely past Pandora, but he squeezed tightly past her nonetheless, brushing up against her. She scowled and stepped backward, reeling under the scent of alcohol and halitosis. Then she launched herself at his throat.

She clasped her arm around his neck, twisted and pulled until he was off his feet and up against her body, his chin dangling from her wrist. He kicked the floor, tried to right himself, to stand and defend himself, but she threw a heavy toecap into the back of his knees, bringing him back down again.

Dexter threw himself at the big man behind her. He launched every inch of his size, muscle, and strength at him, hoping the elements of surprise and size would benefit him. And they did. The big man absorbed the blow poorly; he rocked sideways, toppled into a nearby table. Dexter bounced off him just as he collapsed with a thud against the wooden top, flipping glasses into the air before slamming against the floor.

He moved for the door, which opened outwards into the parking lot. He held it open behind Pandora.

The crowd stood hesitantly, wide-eyed and uncommitted. They watched as Pandora bent the teenager over—facing the floor, his backside pressed against her groin—before sending him into them like a human battering ram. He toppled, skidding to his knees before the bartender, who stumbled over him as he tried to give chase.

Pandora turned and ran, straight out into the parking lot, straight for the car.

Dexter continued to hold the door open as he listened to Pandora rattling the keys behind him. The mob was rushing behind the toppled bartender, initially unsure how to react, then dead-set on giving chase. They clambered over the beaten teenager, over the messy floor, toward the door.

Pandora struggled with the keys, struggled to find the right one and to fit it in the lock. She flashed a worried glance toward the door, saw the mass of movement shifting toward her partner, felt her heart growing agitated in her chest.

Dexter waited until the first man, the man in the Stetson, rushed for the threshold, then he slammed the door shut with all his might. The glass panel that covered the upper-half of the door swung toward Stetson. The door met with the brim of his hat, flattening it against his face, before the glass cracked against his forehead and shattered his nose. A hail of shards exploded over his face, raining shrapnel down on him.

He screamed, wailed, and threw himself backward into the advancing army. He tripped up a couple of them, sent one of them sprawling into the bottom of the door just as another slice of glass dislodged itself, fell, and stuck between his shoulder blades with jarring precision.

They toppled over each other in an assortment of screams and curses. Dexter turned to Pandora, her face a picture of panic, her hands trembling. She had the key in the lock and was reaching for the handle when Dexter felt a heavy arm wrap around his throat.

He heard glass crunch behind him and felt himself being dragged backward, off his feet and into the clutches of his attacker.

"Don't you fucking move." He heard the voice of the bartender and felt his hot breath as he leaned in close, the top of his nose touching Dexter's cheek. "Your days are numbered, mate." His words were breathless and angry. Dexter could feel spittle and hot breath on his cheek as the bartender's arm tightened around his throat.

Dexter tried to clasp his hands around the thick, hairy wrist, but the bartender was too strong. He could hear commotion, angry voices, and crunching glass, as the patrons began pulling themselves to their feet.

"Well, that was fun," the bartender said, panting heavily.

"Don't do this," Dexter pleaded as the arm around his neck tightened.

"But we're having so much fun." The bartender laughed, his hot breath practically sticking to Dexter's cheek. "I suggest you tell your pretty little girlfriend to hand over whatever money and weapons you have in that car," he continued. "Before we change our minds and start thinking about that reward instead."

Now it was Dexter's turn to laugh, the noise choking and spluttering in his throat. He lowered his hands, stopped trying to pry the thick arm from his neck. "Why don't you tell her yourself," he said.

The bartender loosened his grip slightly and turned his attention to Pandora. She had unlocked the car, grabbed a gun from the glove box, and was now emerging with that gun thrust menacingly before her.

She pointed the weapon at the bartender, a gleam in her eye as she stared down the sights.

The bartender immediately softened. Dexter heard a whimper escape from his lips as he released him and pushed him forward.

"I don't want any trouble," the bartender said immediately, thrusting his arms into the air.

Dexter laughed again, this time in disbelief. He gave a gentle shake of his head. "Fucking asshole."

The bartender didn't respond, his sights set firmly on the weapon.

"Go back inside," Pandora warned. "To the restroom. *All of you!*" She waved the gun, gesturing to the beaten patrons who had risen to the sight of the weapon. "Wait in there until we're gone. No one follows us; no one tries to be a fucking hero. You can call the police if you like, I don't care, but if any of you try to follow us . . ." She trailed off. She didn't need to finish; the gun did that for her.

The bartender backed up into the bar with the troop of stumbling wounded behind him. Dexter waited by the driver's seat, waited until all of them, including the blood-drenched Stetson, were assumedly tucked away in the back of the bar. He then slipped behind the wheel, waited for Pandora to follow, and peeled out of the lot.

2

The rain-splattered afternoon was turning gray. It was summer, the sun was still out, yet the world was thick with misery, and an early night seemed to be descending. Max Cawley sneered at the bleak horizon. The thick build-up of cloud was so dense, it looked like the town had been wrapped in an opaque bubble. A few hours ago, when he surfaced from his sofa—where he'd slept face-down, drooling onto the cushions—the skies were lit with the promise of sunshine, an orange flare that threatened to break through the misery. After an hour, that flare extinguished, the sun gave up.

He coughed into his hand, felt a wad of spittle soak his palm. He wiped his palm on the back of his pants, took a cigarette packet from his back pocket, and stuck one of the sticks between his dried lips.

"Those things'll kill you." An obligatory warning, spluttered from the mouth of any and every pompous prick who likes to stick his nose in someone else's business. If he wanted to slowly kill himself for the benefit of a mouthful of smoke and a quick buzz, that was his fucking problem.

Max merely grinned in reply. His partner and friend, a skinny depressive woman who had never brought a cigarette to her lips but had, over the course of her thirty-eight years, drank

13

enough alcohol to drown a rock band, struggled to return the gesture.

Abigail Simpson had been Max's partner on the job for five years, and, although she could be a pompous prick, her comments on smoking had always been in jest, offered as a standing joke.

"I don't get it," Max said softly, watching as Abigail sunk in on herself, her head in her chest, her hands tucked deep into the long pockets of her rain-soaked trench coat. "Why?"

Abigail shrugged, her coat momentarily burying her neck. "I've had enough. I can't do this anymore."

Max was disappointed and annoyed. He looked around, beyond his partner's shoulders. The police cars still littered the street outside the bank, a throng of spectators gathered behind a police cordon, bracing the cold and wet day for a chance to appear on the news or see the blood spilled by the celebrity criminals. Cameramen and dole-faced reporters were packing their equipment into a series of vans that had arrived almost as quickly as the police had, baying for their pound of flesh and their headline story.

Max took a long pull from his cigarette, tossed the burning stick to the ground where it sizzled on the wet tarmac. "Five years as a detective, fifteen in the force, you can't—"

"I've made up my mind," Abigail said, lifting her head, her soppy eyes staring into those of her partner. Her friend. "It's not right. I can't do it anymore."

Max wasn't happy but he wasn't completely surprised. Abigail had problems, always had. Things started off well for her, but after her promotion to detective, after the murders, the rapes, and the dregs of society, she'd taken a fall. She had had problems with depression and alcoholism as a youth, and that all came rushing back.

"I thought I'd tell you first," she said respectfully. "I'm handing in my resignation this evening."

"You just decided this now? Give it time, think it over. What happened in there, with the security guard—"

"That's not it," Abigail said, perking up somewhat. "I mean, yeah, that's part of it. Rodgers was just a poor fucker who wanted to play hero for his kid, he wanted his moment in the sun before he resigned his pointless existence to the big, bland fucking abyss; he didn't deserve to die, but no, it's not just about him. It's about all the others who didn't deserve it: the young girls raped and beaten; the kids killed by feckless parents who can't think beyond their next hit; the bar brawls, the one-too-many drinkers who ruin their own lives and end others' because of a few drinks and a careless remark. It's about the sickness we have to put up with, the violence, the hatred . . ." she trailed off, exasperated.

Max merely shrugged, waiting for his partner to continue. Abigail finished, retreated in on herself again. She stuffed her hands in her pockets again, dropping her chin to her chest. "I can't do it anymore."

"So, what?" Max asked. "You gonna go work in KFC? Flashing fake smiles to customers who think they own you because they can afford to buy a bucket of fucking chicken?"

Abi shrugged. "Anything's better than this."

"You're a quitter."

"Maybe."

Max was annoyed, almost fuming, but he could see he wasn't going to get the heated response he wanted. "Fuck off then," he said, letting his frustrations out. "Fuck off back to your booze and your boring life. The force doesn't need you anymore. You've lost your fucking balls."

Abi lifted her head, stared into his partner's eyes. She opened her mouth, seemingly to offer a rebuttal, but she decided against it. Instead, she gave a gentle shake of her head, turned, and walked away from him.

Max watched his former partner clamber forlornly into her

car, watched her stare at herself briefly in the rearview mirror, watched her start the car and leave the crime scene. Only then did Max regret his words. He cursed to himself angrily, kicked an annoyed foot into the floor and reached into his pocket for another cigarette; the sooner the toxic sticks killed him the better.

"Detective. A word, please?"

Max sighed.

The pompous college boy with the stick up his arse. His bland demeanor had somehow won him much acclaim in the area, and he was the go-to guy for anything morbid or worthy of a primetime feature. Max hated him, had hated him since his very first job three years ago when he hounded him over the murder of a local addict, insisting Max wasn't doing his job and that the public had a right to know things that they had no right to know.

"I've told you all I know," Max said sternly as he approached, his microphone held by his side, his cameraman trailing lazily behind.

"And you've been very helpful. Thanks again," he smiled, fake, the stiffened wrinkles at the corners of his lips typically only creased to commit to his whiny and self-important speech. Max had never seen him crack a real smile—an apt idiom considering how his face broke under the strain.

Max sighed, "What do you want?"

He paused, raised his eyebrows, and then lowered his head. Scratched his chin with the tip of an outstretched finger. His attempt at casual friendliness hadn't worked.

"I want to do a feature on the Bleak and Bright bandits, an hour long—"

"No," Max cut in abruptly.

"You didn't let me finish."

"Let me guess," Max said with a cursory glance at the cameraman who wasn't filming and looked keen to pack up and leave. "You want to impress the producers, the bigwigs who, until now, see you as the annoying little prick who occasionally reports on the big stories and constantly tries to kiss their asses in exchange for a shot at the big time."

"How dare—"

"I haven't finished yet," Max said, noting the pleased grin from the cameraman who was suddenly interested. "So you want to run a show on the bandits and rope in the head detective to give a few interviews, to twist and pressure me into telling you something I shouldn't be telling you. Everyone tunes in, you impress the producers, and sail your way to national-news-anchor-cunt with your mouth dry and your dignity intact."

His mouth hung open, his eyes bulged. He snapped his jaws together, screeched a displeased *harrumph* and stormed off, barging past the cameraman who stood motionless, grinning widely at Detective Max Cawley.

"Wow," the cameraman said with a slow and impressed nod. "You're my fucking hero."

* * *

Max stopped the car outside his house. Grunted. Cursed under his breath.

His ex-wife, Sandra, was there again, trying to take advantage of the fact that he wasn't home, seizing the opportunity to rob him blind.

Her car was parked in the driveway to the three-bedroomed segment of suburbia. The trunk and the doors were open, as was his front door.

He scuppered down the driveway, preparing himself for another argument. His ex-wife breached the threshold of the front door before he reached it, a brimming box cradled in her arms. Her sleeves were rolled up the elbow, exposing the wispy hairs on her skeletal arms; a line of goose-pimples rose as she braced the cold.

"Oh, you're back."

"What the fuck is that?" he asked, edging closer to peek into the box.

She backed away, back into the house. She looked over her shoulder, toward the living room. "Johnny, he's back."

"Ah, for fuck's sake." Max grumbled. "You brought your brother? Why?"

"*Why do you think?*"

"Because you can't do anything on your own? Because you can't make your way in this world without dragging other people into your misery?"

Jonathan Meadows appeared behind his sister and placed a thick hand reassuringly on her shoulder. He was a stocky brick shit-house of a man who had barely lifted a dumbbell in his life but had been gifted with the genetics of a mutant bodybuilder.

"Hello, Max," he said with a nod of his thick head. "How's things?"

Max stared at Johnny for a moment, beheld his stocky frame, his flattened look of jar-headed idiocy. He was thirty-five and still lived with his parents. He worked with computers, that was all Max knew, although the image of the big man sitting behind a desk hunched over a keyboard was hard to grasp. He was a fairly intelligent, competent man—albeit a bit of a loner—but from looking at him, at his thick-set jaw and the blank look of idiocy that was set permanently onto his simple face, you wouldn't think he possessed the mental capabilities to tie his own shoelaces.

"What're you stealing from me now?" Max wondered. "What's in the box?"

"My things," Sandra said with a jerk backward, inching away from her former husband.

He hadn't beaten her, had never laid a rough hand on her,

yet she had been playing the victim since their breakup. It was a show; for her brother, for her father, for everyone. She couldn't tell them what an abusive bastard he was when he wasn't, but she could play the pitied victim in front of him and let them form their own conclusions.

"Your *things*? You don't have any fucking things left," he spat. "Nor do I, for that matter. You took everything. You took my television—"

"—*our* television."

"—You took my computer—"

"*Our* computer—"

"You even took my fucking bed!"

"It was *our* bed."

"What, so everything that was *ours* is now *yours*?"

She didn't answer; she just gave him a blank stare, which she eventually shrugged off. With her brother behind her, she moved past Max, dumped the box in the trunk of the car, and then stood by the open door, looking toward the house, toward him.

"I'll be back for the rest," she said.

"The rest?" he looked dramatically at the house. "You mean you *left* something?"

"Goodbye, Max," she said, lowering herself into the driver's seat.

"Fuck off."

Jonathan paused before slipping into the passenger seat; he gave Max a disapproving frown, surely thinking about commenting, but then dipped inside the car. Max watched her drive away before walking inside his empty house and slamming the door angrily behind him.

He had met Sandra when he was twenty-five and she was nineteen. He was a young recruit, happy with his job and happy with his life. She was fresh out of university and fell for the rugged copper with the optimistic outlook and the bright sense of humor.

After fifteen years of marriage, the cracks began to appear. She wanted kids, he didn't, and what she wanted she usually got. He gave in after a year of nagging and they tried to have children, only to find out that he was shooting blanks and she was barren.

They tried fertility treatment for a couple of years, but their marriage was in freefall. He stayed at work for as long and as often as he could. He did his best to avoid her, tried everything short of having an affair. He was an asshole, not a bastard.

She was thirty-nine and desperate for a few little smiling faces to light up their house. He was forty-five and confident that he never wanted the screaming, shitting monsters in his life or his house. The tension, the anger, and the arguments came to a head just a few days after her thirty-ninth birthday.

The topic of infertility had been broached. She had stood in front of him. Her fists clenched into tight balls and thrust into her hips, the stance of a pissed-off woman.

"I told you, we could adopt."

Max sniggered derisively. "Fuck that. I don't want some mail-order rugrat from fucking China."

"What?" she said in disbelief. "That's not how . . . *what the fuck is wrong with you*?"

He didn't know what was wrong with him. He started arguments for the sake of arguing and interspersed them with as much absurdity as he could. It wasn't just because he knew it annoyed her—which it did—nor was it because he believed any of the nonsense he spouted. He had just tired of the typical, bored with the usual. They had been arguing about the same things for what seemed like the majority of their marriage; it was a story he had read countless times and one that never had an agreeable ending. He was just spicing up the narrative.

"I'm not getting any younger," she said, trying to calm herself down. "I want a kid while I still can. We need to come to a decision."

A decision. He liked that. What she actually meant was *you need to start agreeing with me.* That annoyed him, riled up what was left to be riled.

"Otherwise," she had continued slowly, preparing for an ultimatum, "I think we should get a divorce."

"Fine," he had said, perhaps too quickly. She had pissed him off and he was speaking in the heat of the moment, he knew that, but it felt good. "A divorce it is," he continued placidly. "We both need a new start, a new life. You're right."

She had opened and closed her mouth several times. She lowered her hands by her side, clenched and unclenched her fists, made a choking sound with her throat, and then stormed out of the room.

That wasn't technically the end of their marriage, but that was the final straw. She moved out, back into her parents' house, and started divorce proceedings before he could apologize and beg for forgiveness. He hated to see her go and part of him wished she hadn't, but only because he was used to having her around. He was accustomed to the noise, the screams, and the fighting. He also still remembered the woman he had fallen in love with, the woman who he had seen brief glances of through the difficult years.

3

The radio fizzed with a static wail, a banshee screaming through resisting airwaves. It heightened and faded as the semblance of music and chatter was discovered and then released. It settled on a distant, buzzing station—a somber-toned man with a hypnotic drawl was reciting the weather.

Pandora released the knob and sighed. She reached into the glove box, dug around through the dated collection of CDs, but failed to find one she liked. She squeezed a hand into the pocket of her leather pants, which hugged tight to her thighs. She clasped her phone with her fingertips, pulled it out with the sound of a blade leaving a leather sheath.

The phone was dead, had been spluttering on its last legs when she last checked, and had slipped into oblivion at some point over the last few hours.

She cursed under her breath, shoving the device into the glove box, which she closed with force. She looked across at Dexter who was watching the road with the distant eyes of a man who had other things on his mind.

She gave his profile a half-smile, a look of compassion and pity. She had known him for a long time, eight years in fact. When they met, she was a seventeen-year-old desperate to shake the clutches of her mundane life, of college, textbooks, weekends out with friends, and parents who trapped her in the purgatory of middle-class suburbia.

She had been with her boyfriend at the time, a bassist for a local punk band whose music and personal hygiene was an assault on the senses. He had dragged her to a gig in which he performed a short, sweaty, and frantic show with his band. After the gig, she had gone in search of him, only to find him with his lips locked with one of her best friends outside the club.

The argument that followed was as violent and as loud as the gig, only this time she had been the one standing center stage. She lashed out in her anger, he fought back, and she ended up on her backside on the pavement, her boyfriend looming aggressively over her and her friend keeping her distance behind him.

The anger and the fear that she felt quickly changed to adoration when Dexter, who had been working security on the door, dragged her boyfriend away. He was cool, calm, collected, and when the wannabe rockstar started wildly swinging, he handled the situation with just as much serenity, twisting her boyfriend's arm behind his back and pinning him against the wall.

There was no arrogance, no bravado. He didn't even seem interested in being a knight in shining armor, because after watching the bassist leave and helping Pandora to her feet, he merely returned to his post without saying a word.

She always felt it odd that she could feel so close and so connected to someone, even back when they had only known each other for a few months. She had spent a lifetime with her friends and her parents—who were too tied up with their careers, their two-bedroom house, and their middle-class tedium to bother with the little girl who wanted to rebel—but after just a few months with Dexter, she had felt closer to him than she had with any of them.

Pandora had chased Dexter for weeks after their initial meeting. She returned to the same bar night after night, each time trying to get his attention, trying to win his affections with the same flirtatious moves that had caused so many teenage boys to go weak at the knees. But he was in his early twenties, much older than the boys she was used to, and seemingly much more experienced.

After enduring more of her former boyfriend's gigs, not to mention his drunken apologies and come-ons night after night, Pandora finally found the way into Dexter's heart when she gave up on the hair twirling, the giggling and the pouting, when she stopped acting like the pretty girl she knew many other men wanted and started acting like the woman *she* wanted to be, and the woman, it turned out, that Dexter wanted to be with.

She felt like she knew more about him than he knew about himself, and she knew he wouldn't hurt a fly. He was an outlaw, that part of him excited her, but he wasn't a murderer.

She had always been the reckless one. He was the one who worked hard, the one who tried to make a life for the two of them. She had been the one who took what she wanted when she wanted it, the one who shoplifted from clothing and jewelry stores and generally lived life on the edge.

She knew that if it hadn't been for her desperation, her insatiable need for excitement, they would have never robbed those banks and post offices, they would have never been fugitives and he would have never killed that security guard.

She turned away from her lover, feeling ashamed, guilty. She looked out toward the road, a chipped backroad that cut a winding path through the green country side.

She knew he hadn't intended to do it, had rushed to pull the trigger when he felt Pandora had been threatened, but he had done it nonetheless. She could live with it, she could accept it for the mistake it was, but she doubted he would ever be the same.

"No decent music in there?" Dexter glanced across at her, his eyes half on the road, his thoughts back on the present.

She shook her head.

"I could sing for you if you want?" he offered with a dimpled grin.

She sniggered, shook her head. "I'll pass, thank you."

"You're missing out."

"I'm not. I've heard you in the shower," she sighed heavily, gave him another brief giggle as he turned a grin toward the road. "Where are we going then?"

"Like I said and like we planned: somewhere to lie low."

"But, where?"

He shrugged, scrunched up his face. "There's bound to be somewhere around here."

"Another place like the bar back there? With a dozen dumb-fuck locals looking for rape, torture, and reward?"

He shrugged again.

"Hm," she glared at him.

"I wouldn't trust anyone to hole us up with such a big reward hanging over us," he paused, contemplated. "Not this time."

After the incident outside the post office, they had let their guard down and began enjoying their notoriety somewhat. There were groups of people out looking for them, snapping pictures of strangers they thought were them and telling stories of meeting them, most of which were fabricated.

Social media was rife. The *Fans of the Bleak and Bright Bandits* Facebook page had more than a million followers, with everything from fan fiction to artwork posted daily; #SupportBleakandBright trended on Twitter after every new robbery.

They had gotten close to being caught on two separate occasions. The first time, they were lying low in a backyard, sirens screaming throughout the suburban streets, when an old couple strolled out, greeted them, and nonchalantly invited them in for tea and scones. They regaled them with tales of their youth and even offered to put them up for the night. The fugitives thought they had been mistaken for family members, friends, neighbors—anyone but who they actually were. But as they bid their goodbyes and prepared to venture into a night that was now devoid of sirens and panic, the kindly old woman informed them, "And don't worry about those bastard pigs, they're useless. They couldn't catch a cold sore from a hooker. You'll be fine."

The second time they had been saved by a drug addict. They had seen a police patrol car after venturing out one night, and as the car slowed down alongside them, they panicked. Pandora ran, Dexter followed, and seeing two suspicious citizens suddenly sprinting at the sight of a Panda car, the police followed as well. They ran straight down an alleyway, into a dead-end, and two police officers followed, jumping out of their car and shouting vociferously into the cacophonous alley.

They passed a seemingly unconscious drug user who awoke at the sound of their heavy footfalls and then carefully digested the scene—the advancing police officers shouting loudly, the panicked bandits looking lost. He guided them through a back door, into a squat, and as they carefully worked their way from one side to the other, they could hear the drug user shouting, arguing, and eventually fighting with the police, buying them more than enough time to escape.

They knew that their status as national celebrities, as lovestruck partners in crime—and as all the other idealized versions of themselves that their celebrity had created—was enough for even the most destitute of citizens to overlook the meager reward. But now they had been branded as killers, the reward had grown, and their status had changed.

Pandora looked lost, disappointed. "There must be somewhere we could go," she said hopefully.

Dexter turned to her. "I don't know what you want me to say."

"How about, 'I've arranged a flight out of here,' or 'I have a friend who's going to let us stay at his place until things blow over.'"

"Unless you have a light aircraft that I don't know about then we can't fly, not when every security checkpoint in every airport is looking for us." He sighed and then added, "And I don't have any friends."

A smile fought annoyance on her face and eventually won. "Fair enough," she conceded. "A drive into nowhere it is then."

* * *

She'd fallen asleep. She dreamed of something unreachable; a desperate urge to grasp that which couldn't be held. She had no idea what, she thought it might have been human, might have been someone she loved—probably Dexter—but she couldn't remember a thing when her eyes opened.

She felt like her first boyfriend, Steve Rowling, had been there. She wasn't sure it was him, but what little images she retained when she woke reminded her of him. His pimpled face pleaded with her, begged her, teased her, and then tried it on with her. He had always been a strange one and she'd never been sure what she saw in him. She was young, fifteen bordering on sixteen, and desperate for her first dip into the dating pool. He was the first boy that came along, the first boy to truly appreciate her newfound curves and the beauty that had blossomed from a fairly average face. He was two years older than her, spent a lot of his time drinking and taking drugs, but he doted on her, and she found his wild side—the drug-taking, heavy-drinking side that often saw him arrested for reckless behavior—intriguing. The perfect antidote to a bland adolescence.

But she had never loved him. She thought she had, but only because she had nothing to compare her feelings to and thought that the mild attraction and interest she felt was as good as it got. Not until she met Dexter did she really begin to understand what love, lust, and pure attraction were.

Steve had returned years later. She was nineteen and had matured a lot, and he was twenty-one and just as stupid and childish as he had always been. He bumped into her on the street one morning, and although he initially tried to be charming and sweet, as soon as she let her guard down, he had tried to grope her.

She hadn't let him touch her when they were together and had no intention of doing it then either. Their meeting ended with her kneeing him in the testicles and punching him in the face. The anger and the rush she felt after that incident was one of the things that led her to shoplift for the first time just a few hours later, and from there she found a release that she would go back to time and time again.

* * *

She woke when the car thumped heavily over a broken swatch of road. Her body jolted, her mind snapped away from the ethereal images, back into the gray reality. She mumbled something, probably something from the dream, but when it departed her lips, it vanished from her memory. She caught Dexter looking at her, frowning with tilted eyebrows that looked like colliding swords.

"Strange dreams?"

"You could say that." She stretched, touched the roof of the car with the palms of her outstretched hands. Yawned deeply. She looked out through the windscreen; the road was patched and potholed, a carnage of small craters and pockmarks, like the face of an acne-ridden teenager. The road was barely big enough for two cars to squeeze alongside each other and was flanked either side by thick hedgerows, beyond which lay an abundance of fields.

"Where are we?" she asked.

He shrugged. "I checked the map a while back," he said with a nod to the back seat where an Atlas lay strewn. "I stopped to have a look while you were muttering to yourself. Couldn't really figure out where we are."

"I said you should have brought the GPS," she said.

He glared at her and she looked away, understanding. He had always hated it, and every other gadget they owned. On several occasions, he had regaled Pandora with lectures on how the world was a better place without the distraction of technology, reminding her that this particular piece of technology had twice led him to the middle of nowhere and once told him to take a shortcut across a lake. She loved gadgets, but he wasn't a gadget man. He had a mobile phone but not one capable of doing anything more than making phone calls or sending messages, and even that was a stretch. He had a laptop as well, upon Pandora's insistence, but he never used it.

Pandora didn't know a great deal about his upbringing, except that it was far from pleasant and enough for him to reject his family as soon as he was old enough to live independently. He had grown up in abject poverty on a crumbling farm. His mother a homemaker; his father an asshole. He had brothers he didn't speak to, an education that stopped after high school, and a knack for mechanics and manual labor. He approached a computer like it was wired to a nuclear bomb and a single mistake would detonate it. The first time Pandora gave him her phone, he pulled out the attached stylus and then apologized for breaking her antennae.

"There'll be a town around here somewhere. A little village perhaps," he said confidently. "Somewhere to keep our head down; figure things out."

"How are we going to keep our heads low?" she asked. "This is the twenty-first century and not everyone is as backward as you, you know. They have televisions, computers, even radios. Our names, descriptions, and faces will be everywhere."

"Things are different in these places," he insisted. "They're farming folk. They don't have this fancy broadband internet—"

"*Fancy broadband internet?*" she guffawed. "Oh my god, you're like my granddad. This is like the Twitter thing all over again, I can't believe you thought a hashtag was something from the McDonald's breakfast menu. I mean, we're famous, but not famous enough to be sponsored by Mickey D's."

"The lines aren't installed this far out," Dexter continued, unperturbed, ignoring her recollections.

"But they have television, phones . . ." she trailed off.

He shrugged again. "Then we cross our fingers and hope they don't watch TV and don't phone the police if they do."

"Hmm," she mumbled, unconvinced.

"Do you have a better idea?" he wanted to know.

"We could at least try a disguise," she suggested. "A wig, some makeup, some hair dye . . . anything. It worked in the past. I mean, we're wearing the same clothes in the recent photos they have of us. Hardly master criminals, are we?"

He looked at her, gave a sharp nod of his head. In the past they kept low, using disguises where they could, but ultimately they relied on the fact that they rarely ventured out in public, always wore masks to their robberies, and had a fanbase that adored them as opposed to feared them.

"We'll see what we can do."

* * *

They had been driving for a couple of hours before they stopped. A bright afternoon had steadily given way to a dull evening, and now the skies were gray and ready for rain.

They stopped at a gas station, a grim and dilapidated specter of a building that wedged itself unceremoniously against the green and glorious countryside. The wheels bounced uncomfortably over the uneven entry as they parked by the pumps,

30

watched through a large screen window in the building ahead by an apathetic youngster in a baseball cap.

"Is it just me or does this feel very . . . *Deliverancey* to you?" Pandora wondered, her eyes on the man who watched her with his blank and empty eyes.

Dexter gave her a quick grin. "Wait in the car," he told her. "But if you hear banjo music, run."

She scowled at him. "Fuck you. I'm coming with you."

He laughed softly and clambered out of the car with Pandora behind him. "You fill up," he said, nodding to the pumps, "and meet me inside."

He found a wealth of crap inside the petrol station, from ready meals and flowers to books and deodorant. He also found a selection of hats and, in case that failed, a large pair of scissors. They'd never recognize Pandora without her gloriously golden locks, but it would take a skilled mortician to recognize *him* if he told her to cut them off.

They had been reckless, they could both concede that, but they had never set out to be famous and both had been guilty of letting that fame go to their heads. After the first two robberies, and those now iconic pictures, they took to wearing cheap plastic masks of fictional couples—the Joker and Harley Quinn, Batman and Batgirl—playing to their notoriety with whatever they could find in stores.

They had also changed their appearances several times, but the only time it mattered was just before a robbery or during the getaway, because every minute in-between was spent holed up in a hideaway, from the two months they spent in a rundown former factory on the outskirts of the city, to the two weeks they spent living in a drug squat, and the countless B&Bs in-between. The rest of the time, they were on the road, sleeping in a car, a van, or in parks.

It wasn't the life Dexter had wanted. He did it for her; everything he did was for her. But even she had seemed to lose heart. The former wild child who did anything for an adrenaline rush was slowing down. He had sensed it, and now that they had taken a life, their fame would turn to infamy, their adoration would turn to hatred, and they would be given the get-out clause they had both been secretly hoping for.

There were only three aisles inside the gas station, crammed with all of life's un-necessities. He kept his head turned away from the clerk as he slalomed through, making sure to look the other way whenever in sight. It didn't really matter; he would have to pay for the gas soon enough and would be seen. He was just buying time, praying that the dim-witted clerk didn't recognize him.

He heard the jangle of the door opening and closing, felt Pandora creep up behind him. "You can put those fucking scissors back," she whispered hotly in his ear.

"What about the hats?" he wondered, doing a quick model for her. They were all cheap and tacky; the fedoras wouldn't suit even the most style-less of gangsters and the baseball caps were emblazoned with promotional and marketing logos.

Pandora scrunched up her face, clearly not happy with the notion of being a walking billboard for a local hardware store. But she eventually conceded, shrugging her shoulders.

Dexter picked up a handful and bought some cheap prepared meals. They hadn't eaten since the morning, before setting out from the bed and breakfast that had been their home for a few days—owned by an old couple, crazy and senile enough not to realize they were harboring criminals. He sent Pandora back to the car while he strode up the register. She would be recognized, he wouldn't.

The clerk watched him as he approached. He seemed to be weighing him up, admiring his height as his disinterested eyes traced every inch of it. Dexter smiled at him as he placed the items on the counter. The youngster held his smile, didn't return it. He looked down at the items, then at Dexter.

Dexter felt his heart quicken. The kid knew who he was. He was moments away from outing him, from ripping out a weapon and threatening to hold him until the police came.

Dexter clenched his fists, prepared for another confrontation. He squeezed his eyes shut, saw the world turn red beyond the tightened lids, and then sprung them open again, ready to launch on the defensive.

The kid was calmly running the items over the register's scanner. His eyes no longer on Dexter, his attention back on his own bland thoughts.

Dexter released a long sigh, then decided to test his luck. "Do you know if there's anywhere to stay around here?"

The kid paused, looked up suspiciously. Dexter immediately regretted speaking. He wanted an answer to his question but part of him also wanted to test the youngster and his own innocence, as if by starting a conversation in a gas station he was officially declaring to the world that he wasn't a fugitive because that's what normal people did.

The youngster held his eyes a moment longer then looked back at the goods, continuing to run them through. "There's a town a few miles down the road," he said with the enthusiasm of someone who hated every moment of their job and every person it forced them to interact with. "Fairwood. Small, can't miss it though."

He bagged the items, left the bag on the counter, and pushed it across to Dexter. "Perfect place for you," he added.

Dexter held his stare; the youngster's eyes suddenly appeared more intense, more alive than before. The corner of his mouth hooked into a smile and then creased back into a straight line. It looked like he'd found something interesting in Dexter, in his own words. Then his eyes returned to a bland state, and any sense of a smile disappeared from his face.

Dexter stared at his emotionless face, shrugged off any peculiarities. "They have a bed and breakfast there?"

The youngster gave him a long and tired stare, followed by a nod fueled with all the exaggeration of youth.

Dexter took the bag and left a weak smile with the bored idiot.

4

Pandora used the overhead mirror to cram her lustrous locks into a tight wad before slipping one of the baseball caps over the top. It gave her a much more youthful, sporty appeal; an almost boyish attractiveness.

They saw the sign, blazoned onto a rusted slab of metal and held three feet off the ground on rusted poles: **Fairwood.** The road that led to the town itself was a narrow and twisted path, bordered by thick and overgrown hedgerows that stretched bare, ghoulish branches toward the chipped tarmac.

They didn't expect much: a scattering of houses, a farm, a shop maybe, but they were pleasantly surprised when the road widened, the hedges vanished, and a pleasant, almost picturesque, town exposed itself. A farmhouse on the left, advertising fresh produce via a wooden sign that rocked on free hinges; a stable and a field on the right with wary and inquisitive horses poking their heads through the fence to inspect the visitors.

Beyond the farmhouses, further down the road, an unidentifiable sculpture sat on a roundabout island. The grass around it was well-manicured and a beautiful shade of green, the border—gray cobbles—was built to a perfect sphere.

There were no other cars in sight, so they took the mini-roundabout slowly. To their left was a long lane—flanked by cobblestone houses that led back into the countryside. To their right: a couple of shops, a large pub, a dead end. They went straight over at the roundabout, passed a couple of large detached houses. They saw parked cars, signs of life through flickering curtains. At the end of the roundabout, sitting on the curb and watching them intently, was an elderly man, squinting through the gray to see them as they approached and stopped the car.

He looked up, didn't attempt to climb to his feet or acknowledge them. Dexter rolled down the window, stuck his head out, and peered down at the man. He was skinny, rough around the edges: his face heavily tanned, almost leathery; his hands worn to thick calluses.

"Hello there," Dexter called merrily.

The old man looked up, acknowledged him with a gentle flick of his head, and then turned away.

"We're looking for a place to stay for the night," Dexter continued. "Do you know if there are any—"

He didn't finish. The elderly man thrust out his arm, pointing across the road. Dexter stopped, swallowed his words, and ducked back in the car, looking across Pandora and out of the passenger-side window. One of the large detached houses—a cobblestone exterior, Victorian windows, a garden brimming with color—was marked with a hand-drawn sign declaring it to be a bed and breakfast. Dexter turned back to thank the man, then decided against it, not sure if he would hear or care.

He parked the car further up the road, next to a tall fern that drooped over the fence from a nearby garden, its green claws grasping at the roadside.

Pandora looked around as she climbed out of the car, her eyes on the immaculate gardens, the rows and rows of pristine flowers and lawns. She nodded approvingly. "This place is cute."

Dexter mumbled unsurely, his eyes on the old man on the

corner. He had twisted his wizened body to stare at them and was doing so without any shame, openly glaring. Dexter tried a pleasant and uncomfortable smile; the old man didn't flinch and continued to stare. Dexter turned away and raised his eyebrows at Pandora, who hadn't noticed it.

"I could live here," she said, still glancing around.

"*You. Here?* You're a city girl. Bright lights an' all that. There's none of that here."

"I could manage. I could get quite comfortable here." She looked at him intently. "City girl or not, I've always liked the idea of settling down in a place like this, maybe starting a family."

Dexter nodded. "Maybe buy a farm, some animals—"

"Don't spoil it," Pandora joked. "I want to live near animals, not be responsible for them. Kids will be enough for me. A nice little country house, white picket fence an' all that."

Dexter knew she wanted kids. He did too. But they were fugitives, criminals, outlaws—they couldn't have it both ways And even if they did want to change and leave their criminal ways behind, they were in too deep to give up easily. He also doubted that she would settle for a life in the country. She had a way of falling in love with things as soon as she saw them, but she usually quickly fell out of love again, just like she'd fallen out of love with their last car, their last apartment, their last computer, or even with the idea of buying a dog. She hadn't fallen out of love with him yet.

A white wooden gate on smooth hinges opened onto a cobbled walkway that cut through the green surroundings and traced a path to the door of the bed and breakfast. They tried the door and were surprised to find it locked. They exchanged a look of bewilderment, double checked the sign, and then rang the bell.

They could hear the tinny sounds of the tubular bells echoing beyond the door. On the fifth note, a grinning old woman in a flour-stained apron opened the door.

"Hello!" she beamed with a joy that didn't suit the dreary day. "What do we have here?" She looked them up and down.

"I'm Andrew," Dexter said. "This is my girlfriend Susan. We're in the area seeing family, had a few problems back home," he said with a somber note that needed no further explanation. "I know it's short notice and we didn't phone in advance, but do you happen to have any rooms available?"

He didn't think it was possible but the beaming smile on her face stretched even further, cutting a morbid slice through her ruby-wrinkled features. "Of course! Come in. Come in."

They entered to the smells of baking: fresh warm bread, cinnamon, sugary delights. An instant warmth covered them and wrapped them in a narcotic blanket. The house was bright and cosy, like walking into a favorite grandmother's house.

"This is gorgeous," Pandora said with glee. She liked loud and dark clubs that played screaming heavy metal and were populated by pierced, sweaty men in leather; but her guilty pleasure was a taste of home, a reminder of her own grandmother, a woman who had doted on her more than her parents, a woman whose death during her adolescence had affected her more than the death of her parents. Her butterfly brooch was the one thing she retained from her youth, the one thing she owned that reminded her of her former life. It had been her grandmother's; left to her in a will that didn't have much to give. It was worth very little, but its sentimental value was priceless.

Dexter saw the delight on her face and smiled. She danced up to an antique table adorned with a crystal vase and freshly cut flowers. A heavy gilded frame, a portrait of an unknown ancestor, hung above the table.

"This is so lovely!"

"Thank you, dear," the old woman said proudly. "Now, you'll be wanting twin beds, right?"

Pandora frowned, looked at Dexter before answering. "A double, please."

"But you two aren't married," the woman said, looking a little appalled. "I can't allow that."

"Oh," Pandora looked taken aback. The delight had been sucked out of her face, leaving the grim expression of a child who just realized that Santa doesn't exist. "Okay then, I guess—"

The woman laughed, a joyful and cheery sound that seemed to emanate through every inch of her short and merry frame. "I'm just playing with you, love!" She gave Pandora a playful shove on the arm. "A double bed is fine. They're your bodies; you're free to do as you want with them." She hushed her voice, spread a cheeky grin. "Just try to keep the noise down, I don't want my Eric getting jealous." She winked.

"Is Eric your husband?" Pandora asked.

"Yep," she put on a proud and determined stance, like the one adopted by veterans of life and love about to tell you how old they are, or how long they've been married. "We've been together forty-four years this August."

She directed the announcement to both of them. Dexter never knew what to say in such situations. "*Well done*" didn't seem appropriate. Thankfully Pandora did the talking for him.

"He must be a lucky man."

"Damn right," she said with another wink. She assumed a look of exaggerated shock. "I never told you my name, did I? How rude of me! *I'm Dorothy.*" She shook both of their hands. "Can I show you around, get you settled in?"

The rest of the house was just as inviting: a large sitting room fitted with cozy leather furniture and an open fire; a kitchen complete with a stove and stenciled designs of pottery and cutlery on its warmly decorated walls; a backyard that caught the fall of the day. On the second floor was five rooms in total. The largest was for Dorothy and her husband. Two of the others were small—"boxy" was how Dorothy had honestly described them—perfect for a single occupant. The other two were expansive with four-poster beds.

"The lack of an en-suite is a pain," Dorothy informed them with another dose of honesty. "But this is the sticks out here, the middle of nowhere. Think yourself lucky you don't have to potter outside to use an outhouse. You'll have to use the guest bathroom, but as there are currently no other guests, you can consider it yours."

"Are you usually busy out here?" Dexter asked when they'd been shown to their room and Dorothy was lingering near the door.

"Not really. Not much out here for the tourists. It's pretty remote. The last couple that stayed over nearly went mad; they were near death when they finally left," she declared, amused. "I think it's the lack of a mobile reception that does it," she added.

"No reception at all?"

"Afraid not."

"Where's the nearest supermarket?" Pandora asked.

"A good thirty or forty miles in either direction," Dorothy informed her with an apologetic smile. "We have a local shop; you can get some essentials from there. There's a pub as well. *Oh!*" she said, snapping her fingers in the air. "Tomorrow night is quiz night, like a trivia night. You'd like that. They hold a quiz and a raffle, *everyone* gets involved."

Pandora didn't look too impressed but did her best to hide it. "Thanks," she said with a distant nod. "We'll check it out."

5

Detective Superintendent Clarissa Morris was the devil in human form. She was a frail figure of a monster with imposing eyes, a slender, breakable frame, and an uninteresting face. But as soon as she opened her mouth—tested those vicious, sometimes callous and often insulting vocal cords of hers—any suggestion of frailty vanished.

She was despised within the division, but she was also feared. She was as revered as any ball-crumbling god should be revered. She had the power to reduce butch, chauvinistic coppers to whimpering childish wrecks and she rarely broke from her toughened, iron-lady facade.

Max had a lot of respect for her. He liked strong women, if not only because nothing satisfied him more than watching a macho man being reduced to a puddle of pity and apologies in front of them. But they were at war, and that's the way he liked it. It wasn't that he thrived in a hostile environment, but that he had become so accustomed to living in chaos that anything else felt alien. He also hated her personality, and the attitude she had toward him.

Max had seen a different side to her once. It was just after the office Christmas party, when the early-nighters and the weak-stomachs had retired and left just a few of the experienced drinkers—the borderline alcoholics—to their vices in the early hours of the morning. Clarissa hadn't started drinking until most of the others were already drunk, making sure she had the upper hand even during times of joviality.

She'd loosened up, become a different person. She was still a bitch, still a little loose with her insults and her uptight, headmistress attitude, but she geared it down a few notches. The others hadn't noticed; by then the handful of drinkers were too drunk, tired, or distracted with trying to get off with each other to notice that their typically satanic boss now resembled something half-human.

Max found himself stuffed into a corner talking to her—a tumbler of whiskey in his hand, a bottle of beer in hers. They remained until the others filtered away, the last to leave being a May to December pair who would wake up the following morning in the backseat of a car with blistering headaches and deep regrets. Clarissa was almost strewn out across one of the desks, her legs—tight and pale flesh wrapped around thin bone like loose skin on a frozen chicken carcass—dangled over the back seat of a chair.

He was drunk, and he was arguing a lot with his wife at the time. His boss was beginning to look like an attractive catch, despite how unattractive she was, but he maintained enough sobriety to remind himself just how evil she was and just how awkward things would become, so he had no intention of trying anything. She had other ideas.

She threw one of her legs towards his crotch, grinning as her naked foot played with his groin. He tried to ignore it, to shift casually away, but her bony toes followed him like the persistent fingers of the grim reaper. He tried his best to change the subject, he checked his watch, mentioned that he really should be getting home to bed. Then she launched herself at him.

Before he knew what was happening, she had her beer-scented, musty mouth pressed against his and was trying to stick her slimy tongue down his throat. He played along, hoping it wouldn't progress, but then she tried to undo his pants, simultaneously slipping a hand up her skirt to remove her knickers.

He pulled back, so did she. She moved to the desk, splayed out like a drunken hooker: her legs open, her eyes lustful. He felt the contents of a night's worth of boozing fight its way to his throat, threatening to unleash itself over her.

He shook his head slowly. Remained standing, staring. After a while she propped herself up on her elbows, looked at him with a stern annoyance—the same look she gave him a few weeks earlier when he'd failed to secure any evidence against a prolific burglar he'd been forced to release.

"What's wrong? Can't get it up?" she asked bitterly. She propelled herself forward, grasped a rough hand around his crotch, squeezed. Her eyes looked skyward thoughtfully like a doctor examining her patient. She released, gave him a distasteful grimace. She dropped down, pulled her knickers back up, growled at him, and then left.

He had escaped an inhumane fling with a succubus, but after that, Clarissa treated him with even more disdain than before. She often singled him out and made no effort to disguise her contempt toward him. The disguised respect that he had initially felt for her began to fade, replaced by a growing contempt. He still enjoyed watching her tear through his colleagues; he still enjoyed the moment when, every now and then, a new officer would start work, make a throwaway sexist comment about Morris or women in general, and would then be metaphorically castrated in front of everyone when she found out. But he didn't like being in her presence, and whenever he was the one being berated, he couldn't help but bite back.

"Simpson's gone," was all she uttered in regard to Abigail's resignation. Max had been called into her office the morning after the robbery and shooting, the morning after Abigail

Simpson had left him in the lurch, choosing to find answers at the bottom of a glass rather than in the job that had been her second home.

"So I heard," Max said softly, still bitter over the incident. He told himself that the bitterness came from pure resentment, resentment that his partner had abandoned him, that she had taken the easy route—preferring the solace of alcohol to the cold, hard reality of everything else. The truth, although he would never admit it, was that he was envious. He was beginning to despise his job and he felt a certain degree of respect for Abigail to have the courage to stand up and fuck off. He still enjoyed the parts of the jobs that he'd always enjoyed—he liked to catch bad guys, to feel like he was making a difference in the world—but the positives that had so blatantly been etched in white at the beginning of his career had grayed around the edges and were now dimming to a mottled black. He was too accustomed to it, to understanding that he never really caught any bad guys, that he spent his days arresting teenage delinquents who were given a slap on the wrists and sent back into society to turn the cogs of a repetitive system that would lead them straight back to him.

His home life also played a big part. At the beginning of his career, it didn't matter that he was so heavily work-oriented. He was starting a life. He had bills to pay, a house to buy, a wife to enjoy. That was dwindling now, and he'd spent so long in the rut of work, of a life as a copper and not a human being, that he was struggling to dig himself out. He could never find another woman—he wouldn't know where to begin, wouldn't know what to do with her when he had her—and he couldn't spend the rest of his days alone and bitter. The force had sucked the life out of him, and it was too late to breathe any back in.

"You're on your own now." Clarissa hadn't looked up from her computer screen since Max walked in. She wasn't busy; Max knew she would be playing a hand of solitaire, spying on her sergeants' Facebook pages, or reading the latest copy of *The Satanic Bible*. She just wanted him to know that this career-affecting change didn't bother her at all.

"So, who're you going to set me up with?"

She raised her eyes. Her brow tweaked. "*Set you up*? This isn't a dating agency, Cawley."

He sighed inwardly. Hated the way she toyed with him, played on everything he said, no matter how trivial. "Who's my partner?" he pushed.

She grinned widely, gave a gentle shake of her head and then returned her attention to the screen. "This isn't an American cop show; this isn't the NYPD. You don't need a partner. You'll manage, I'm sure."

He thought he sensed a hint of something else in her words. Did she know about the impending divorce? Was she fucking with him? It could be paranoia—just because something affected his life so deeply didn't mean the rest of the world gave a toss about it—but she was evil enough, malicious enough, and omniscient enough to know everything about his life and use it to mess with him.

"What about Matthews?" Max offered. "She doesn't have—"

"You want to hook up with the office hottie, Cawley, is that it?"

Rebecca Matthews wasn't much of a looker, but she was the darling of the office, which said more about the office than it did her. Max wasn't interested in her looks, but he liked the fact that she was calm, happy, devoid of drama.

"No," Max affirmed honestly. "I just—"

"Forget it, Cawley," she snapped. "She's taken. She has a husband, a kid."

Max growled, swore under his breath. His boss heard and smiled slyly at the reaction.

"So I'm on my own," he stated.

"You got a problem with that? I figured it would suit you."

He opened his mouth to object but slammed it shut. She wasn't worth it.

She finished on her computer with a flourishing tap. She gesticulated to a notepad on the desk where someone had scribbled a series of hasty notes. "I need you to check this out," she said. "Last night at a place called Grubbies, or Stubbies or some such nonsense, about thirty miles north, there was a sighting of Bleak and Bright. We had an anonymous call that they were there. Bartender by the name of," she paused, checked the notes, squinted to read the writing, penned by an officer who had taken the message, "Sellers, confirmed it. Said they came through, trashed up his pub, and then left."

Max shrugged indifferently. Since the bandits had made the headlines a few months ago, the department had received hundreds of suspected sightings, the vast majority of which were nonsense calls, hoaxes, and popularity seekers, even people who called just to ask the arriving detectives how the case was progressing. Now that a large reward had been placed on their heads, the calls would only increase, as would the absurd claims.

"Why me?" he wondered. "Can't you get the local bobbies to check it out? Probably a far-fetched insurance claim, someone looking for some publicity for his pub."

"You think I didn't think of that?" she said with a glare. "They checked it out this morning, an hour or two ago. They said it had some promise, this Sellers chap seemed a bit beaten and reluctant, they reckoned he was hiding something."

"The truth is what he's hiding," Cawley suggested.

"Possibly, but this Sellers probably knows something; certainly more than he's letting on," she stated. "If he did see them, great; if not, then he's up to something."

Max groaned, retrieved the note from her desk, and exchanged one last contemptuous smile with her. "I'll check it out."

6

T he county was full of tiny holes, pockets of nothingness where small villages flourished. Most began as farming or mining land—small outcrops built around busy farms and busier mines—but over time, the mines closed and the farms expanded around the villages like green plumes of smoke. The occupants tended to be those who were old enough to still remember the days when the village flourished—old enough to look back on the past as something resembling perfect, a utopia where no one stole anything, no one killed anyone, and no one committed a crime, not like the inner-city yobs of today. Of course, these also tended to be the times of world war, of rampant murder on a global scale, of hunger, starvation, of parents stealing to feed their families, and of chronic suffering. Time has a way of blurring the edges of truth.

Stubbies, a working man's pub for the chronically unemployed, was on the fringes of one of these pockets of nothingness. It used to be a mining town, the mines long since closed, the work long since dried up. In the recent past, the dwindling populace were primarily the direct descendants of those that had toiled the mines; they struggled to work like their fathers did, struggled to scrape a meager existence, and often resorted to living off the state. The current populace were made up of *their* descendants. The second generation without a job, the first that didn't give a shit.

Detective Cawley worked this county, knew these people well. His own backyard was a touch more urban, but he had plenty of run-ins with the wave of jobless youth who plowed the streets and littered the cells.

One of them was in the pub when he arrived. A feckless and scrawny thing who propped up the bar with the experience of a veteran alcoholic.

"I'm looking for Sellers," Cawley said as he eyed up the youngster, struggling to hide the distaste on his face as a waft of body odor leaked into his nostrils.

The youngster spun on his stool, looked Cawley up and down, gave a questionable flick of his head. "Wha's 'e to you?"

Cawley regarded him with contempt. He nodded toward the half-empty pint glass on the bar in front of him. "Should you be drinking that?"

The youngster's eyes flickered from the glass, back to Cawley. "Wha's 'e to you?"

He showed him his badge, delighted in the fear he saw light up the rat-like face in front of him.

The youngster hesitated, Cawley could almost hear his mind whirring like the spitting, clunking engine of a battered car. "So—*so?*" he said anxiously. "You're a copper, so what? I'm sixteen, I'm allowed to be 'ere. I'm allowed to drink."

"The drinking age is eighteen." Cawley nodded toward a sign above the bar that validated his response.

"Oh." He paused, looked up and down, lowered his face and his tone, then snapped into the defensive posture of a stubborn idiot that Cawley had seen on every accused kid he'd ever had to arrest. "So what? Ya wanna arrest me? Prove it. Prove that I bin drinking. You can't, can you, eh? I bet you—"

Cawley held up a palm, asking the kid to halt his bullshit. "I don't give a shit. Just tell me where Sellers is." He couldn't do anything to the kid and had no intention of arresting or charging the bartender who *could* be prosecuted; he didn't care either way. Without a pub to drink in, the little waster would be pissing it up in the gutter on cheap cider or stolen spirits. It didn't matter where he got his booze; he was always going to get it.

The teen aimed a shout behind the bar where an open door led into a small hallway—a couple of rooms either side, a staircase visible at the back. He drained the last of his pint, his eyes on Cawley the whole time, and then departed with a hitch of his pants and a throat-clearing snort.

Sellers emerged through the door—a short and stocky middle-aged man with a prominent brow and a perpetual look of suspicion on his face. He nodded at Cawley, a quizzical inflection of his dumpy little head.

"Detective Inspector Cawley," he answered, flashing his badge. "I've come about the sighting of—"

"The Bleak and Bright bandits," Sellers cut in with a knowing nod.

Cawley sighed as he stuffed his wallet back into his pocket. He hated that name. The police had identified the bandits, initially spotted by TV, then made famous by a few opportunistic tourists' snaps. They gave their names and pictures to the press. They were the perfect targets for national news and their names and faces wrote the headlines: Dexter Bleak, bleak by name and nature; Pandora Marsh, beautiful, radiant, the beauty to his beast.

The public thought of them as a modern-day Bonnie and Clyde. Heroes. A few of those opinions would change now that they'd taken their first life but most would remain the same. People had a way of glossing over details they didn't like. In Cawley's eyes, they'd never been the heroes. He appreciated their brazen style, could admire their confidence and their nonviolent and somewhat Hollywood approach—more about the style and intimidation than brute force—but criminals that carried guns and lived on the run often crossed the line. It was only a matter of time before they killed someone, and now, while the public sang their praises, he was counting down the minutes until they killed someone else.

He had been on the case since the beginning, before the public jumped on the bandwagon, before it became global news. The first robbery hadn't been glamorous enough for the media, but it was an armed robbery nonetheless, so the police had taken it seriously. Leads had been few and far between. They relied on the public to provide them with information, but most of them seemed to be siding with the bandits and none of them were helpful.

"Yes," he grumbled. "Them."

"They were in here yesterday afternoon, messed up the place," he gestured toward the door. From the outside, Max had just seen the large wooden board that someone had nailed over the front, but from this side, he could see a line of broken glass jutting around the border of one of the panels. A large slice of it still remained at the bottom, pointed upward like a jagged tooth.

Cawley removed a pen and a notepad, for appearance sake if nothing else. He doubted that the bartender would have anything noteworthy to say but he wanted to at least make it look like he was interested in hearing it. He had taken hundreds of reports since the spree began, and he always seemed to be at the back of the line. On several occasions, they had been chased by local police officers on their rounds, once they had an armed response hunting them down. And every time Cawley had heard those stories, he had prayed for them to get away, because as much as he disliked them and the perception that the public had of them, he wanted to be the one to catch them. It wasn't just about getting them off the streets, or even about ending this crazy national obsession, it was about giving him purpose, giving him the satisfaction of being a hero to the police and an anti-hero to the public, and about showing his wife, his boss, his friends, and his colleagues that he wasn't finished, he wasn't washed up.

"What time did they arrive?" Cawley asked.

The stocky man shrugged, glanced around in a moment of recall. "Early afternoon, maybe one or two."

Cawley lifted his eyes from the pad where he was doodling; he raised an eyebrow at the bartender. The robbery at the bank had been around twelve. The cameras clocked the culprits leaving just after twelve-thirty. A thirty-minute drive northwest, along the winding country lanes that peppered this part of the country like snakes in wild grass, would put them at approximately this location.

"And what time did they leave?" he enquired.

He shrugged again, looked distant, mischievous. There was something he wasn't saying. "They weren't 'ere long. Ordered a couple o' drinks, used the toilet and then left," he seemed to be finished, and then added: "after trashing the place."

Cawley raised his eyebrows further, asking for clarification. When it didn't come, he asked, "They just smashed the door and left?"

A pause, a look in a false memory, and then the bartender answered, "The report about the robbery came on the television," he shrugged. "They panicked, I guess. One of the lads tried to stop them, calmly ya know, then the guy went ballistic. He hit him, shoved 'im against the door," he nodded towards the paneled door. "Then 'e pulled out a gun, ordered us all into the toilets whilst 'e escaped."

Cawley flipped to the previous page in the notebook; he'd spoken to the officer who had taken Sellers's call and made a few notes. "This happened yesterday afternoon?"

"That's right," he said with a half-smile of cooperation.

"And yet you never phoned the police?"

51

The smile disappeared from his face, was replaced by a look of anxiety.

"We wouldn't have found out if not for an anonymous call yesterday," Cawley informed him. "Why?"

"I was a little shaken, I guess. He pulled a fucking gun on me, ya know."

"So you said. And the others, like the one they hit, none of them thought to call us?"

He shrugged, tried to avert his gaze.

"Do you have any idea who might have phoned us?"

Something glared behind Seller's eyes, his features twitched with an instinctive, uncontrollable disgust. He shook his head and denied knowledge; Cawley knew he was lying but that didn't prove anything. The call had probably come from a drunken patron after watching the story on the news, something that Sellers wasn't willing to admit.

"Okay," Cawley said long and slow. The bartender was clearly hiding something. If the bandits had been in his pub, he had nothing to hide. He wasn't harboring them; the officers had already checked out the building and the bandits weren't dumb enough to hide in a shit hole run by someone who would sell them out in a heartbeat.

"What're you not telling me?" Cawley persisted.

"What do you mean?" Sellers wondered without conviction.

Cawley sighed. "You're hiding something. You're lying to me."

"Why would I make up a story like this?"

"You tell me."

Sellers groaned and grumbled, looked around the room with the air of a troubled soul. "Okay," he said, softly and resolutely. "The truth is, things got a little heated. We had a full house, usually do . . ." he paused, checked for the dozenth time that no one else was in the pub.

"Go on . . ."

"The boys got a little rough. They saw the television report. They just wanted to bring 'em in, do the right thing."

"I bet the reward helped."

He nodded. "It happened as I said, only they didn't throw the first punch, we——the others, that is——did. We tried to restrain 'em, but they got the better of us. They escaped, we followed 'em to their car, but 'e pulled a gun on us. That's it, God's truth."

He had a pleading look in his eyes when he finished, a look that begged to be understood and accepted.

Cawley nodded, he could see the desperation in the bartender's eyes. He had dealt with enough liars, cheats, and criminals to know when someone was lying or when someone was trying to feed him a false series of events. He felt a little better at the explanation, things fit into place.

There was a good chance that the pair had passed through. He was on the right track.

7

They awoke in silence, a silence interrupted sporadically by the careful clatter of cutlery from a distant part of the house. Pandora rose first, smiling and stretching after what had been a long and pleasant sleep, the best she'd had in a long time.

She climbed out of bed, dressed in her underwear, and peeled back the curtains to greet a warm and glorious sun. She boiled the kettle in the room and sat on the window seat, her legs pressed up against her chest, her face turned to the heated day. When Dexter woke, more noisily and cumbersome—he wasn't a morning person—the sounds from downstairs had dissipated and were replaced by the smells of freshly cooked breakfast.

"Do you think that's for us?" he wondered, sniffing the air loudly.

It had been a while since they'd eaten properly; they'd snacked on sweets, crisps and pre-packed sandwiches that tasted more like plastic than the crinkly triangles that encased them, but they hadn't had a cooked meal for weeks. They'd been too eager, excited, and nervous to take advantage of the breakfast offerings on the morning of the robbery, had been too preoccupied since then.

Pandora gave a shrug and beamed a wide smile that stretched even further across her sun-drenched features when Dexter traipsed his way over to her. He wrapped his arms around her, planted a kiss on her hair—the scent of sweet shampoo long since faded, replaced by a thin veil of must and smoke. He brushed a strand of hair from her forehead, kissed her head, her cheek, and then her lips. He traced a hand up her leg, from her tight and outstretched calf, over her bended knee, and down to her thigh. The tip of his finger heated as it worked its way south.

She stopped his hand before he could go any further. He grumbled, tried to push it further, but was met with resistance. She pulled away from him, having to tilt her head backward to maintain a distance from his lustful mouth.

"I need to shower," she warned. "I stink."

"I don't mind."

"I do."

He sighed, met her adamant stare, and grumbled again, turning away.

He had left his clothes hanging over the back of the only chair in the room, a hardback antique that sat before a dated and dusty dresser. He picked them up, began to shuffle his way into them as Pandora stared out the window. The room was at the back of the house and looked out onto the backyard, alert and awakened to the bright day. A large wooden deck peeked onto a lush green lawn interspersed with flower beds and vegetable patches and interwoven with a labyrinthine cobbled path that disappeared into a cluster of lush hedges and ferns.

An elderly man appeared on the decking. She watched, staring down at his back and the top of his head, as he stood and stared out onto the field of green. He turned slowly, back toward the house, and then stopped after taking a single step. He craned his neck, peered upward, toward Pandora.

She felt a startled cry trigger her nerves, felt a little creeped out and uncomfortable. She didn't attempt to hide or to cover herself but expected him to turn away, to avert his eyes in embarrassment or shame. He didn't. Once his eyes locked onto her, he didn't seem to want to move them.

He was older, possibly seventy, maybe more. He had a wrinkled and almost ageless face that would suit a haggard, wheelchair-bound centenarian. His skin was rough, hardened, yet hung loosely from his bones. In the sunlight, his eyes seemed almost gray, like little balls of dwindling ash.

After a few moments, she gave him a little wave, pretending that she'd been gazing out at the garden in a daze and had only just noticed him. When he didn't return the gesture, she wrapped her hand back around her shins and shifted into the fetal position, suddenly very cold despite the warmth of the morning.

"I'll go and see if that food's for us," Dexter said, zipping up his pants and shaking out the creases. "Come down when you're ready."

Pandora turned sharply, almost forgetting he was there. She nodded distantly. He didn't notice the unease on her face as he gave her another kiss, left a warm hand on her shoulder, and then departed.

She turned back to the window, expecting to see the old man still staring, but he was gone. The yard was back to its trancelike state, peaceful and empty. Pandora didn't feel it anymore though; she climbed off the windowsill and headed for the bathroom. She needed a shower.

* * *

Dexter followed the scent of food downstairs, like a wide-nosed cartoon dog tracking the trail of delectable delights. He passed portraits and landscapes, a littering of pictures gilded and hung to keep guests entertained as they climbed and descended the twisting staircase that led from the second floor down onto the entrance hallway.

He followed the smell to a dining room where three tables lay in wait, only one of them set with the implements of breakfast: toast rack, cutlery, plates, a selection of jams and butters. He caught Dorothy rearranging the plates so they sat in perfect alignment with one another.

"Good morning," he said with a nod.

She turned quickly, instantly broke into a beaming smile when she saw him. He stopped in his tracks, prepared himself for a joyous greeting.

"Good morning, love!" she called merrily. She opened her arms, indicating the empty spread in front of her. "You'll be having breakfast I hope?"

He paused as if to give this some thought. "Sure." He directed his attention to a buffet table at the other end of the room, where a toaster, a kettle, and a series of cereals awaited for the continental offering.

"Excellent!" She made a scene of looking behind him. "Your beautiful other-half not awake yet?"

"She'll be down soon." He looked toward the kitchen, the scent of cooked food still making his mouth water as he picked at a few slices of melon. "That smells gorgeous," he noted, hinting.

She winked at him. "Full English breakfast, all part of the deal, my love. Give me a shout when she surfaces and I'll come and take your order."

* * *

"So, dears," Dorothy exclaimed, pressing her hands together in front of her waist and beaming broadly at Dexter and Pandora. "What'll you be doing today then? Got anything planned?"

Dexter and Pandora exchanged a glance. They hadn't

planned to do anything but keep out of sight for as long as possible. Pandora scrunched up her face and reached for a slice of toast, keeping herself occupied and letting Dexter do the thinking and talking for both of them. She was perfectly happy to have a wander around town, see the area, have a drink or two at the local pub in the evening, but she doubted Dexter felt the same way. He would want to be secure, would probably want them to hole up in their room and avoid any contact with anyone but the smiling B&B owner, who clearly didn't recognize them.

"What do you suggest?"

She was staring absently at the toast in her hand when she heard Dexter ask. She assumed he was talking to her, that he was offering her the question purely for Dorothy's benefit, expecting her to burden the responsibility of avoiding the town—perhaps by blaming woman's troubles or a headache—but when she looked up, deflated and ready to answer, she saw that Dexter was looking at Dorothy, returning her smile.

The bubbly woman shrugged, looked at each of them in turn. "You could go for a walk into town," she ventured. "There's not much to see, not many shops and not many people, but it's . . ." she lingered in search of the right word. "Quaint, I guess."

Dexter turned a quizzical eye to Pandora, who was grinning back at him, happy to do whatever he wanted if it meant she didn't have to spend the next few days locked up inside.

"Sounds good," he said.

Dorothy reached for their plates, piled one of top of the other, and slipped them onto her left hand before grasping cups and saucers with her right. "Oh—" she snapped, suddenly remembering something. "And don't forget the quiz tonight," she remarked. "We'll all be there."

Dexter nodded, implying they would be there as well, although Pandora knew he had no idea who "*we*" were. The only other person he had seen in the town since they'd arrived was the belligerent old man who'd pointed them in the direction of the bed and breakfast.

"So . . ." He stared across the table at Pandora, obviously delighting in the childish smile of glee plastered on her beautiful face. "Shall we go?"

8

The bandits were still on the news, they always were. It didn't matter if it was the local news or the national news—even the worldwide media were sticking their eager noses in—everyone wanted a seat on the bandwagon. They had been reporting the news of the latest robbery for two days straight. Throughout the day of the robbery, they spoke to the family of Earl Rodgers, the murdered security guard. They ran interviews with everyone from the grieving widow and her kid through to the old couple who lived across the street and occasionally waved hello to the recently deceased. The following day, the news stations ran repeats of the previous day, alongside analyses from psychiatrists, psychologists, criminologists, and anyone with a vaguely connected PhD who wanted to earn a few bucks.

The morning after that particularly bland and repetitive news day, the media had a break. Rodgers' thirteen-year-old daughter had killed herself. The troubled girl was a recluse who had spent several years of her young life suffering from depression. She was also a daddy's girl who, like so many other youngsters in the country, had treated the Bleak and Bright Bandits with respect they didn't deserve. It was the perfect storm, too much for her young mind to take—she'd taken a handful of her mother's painkillers. A suicide note had been left on her computer declaring how sorry she was, how she believed it was partly her fault, and how she had no other choice.

She had seemingly expected to go quietly. The bed had been made, a photograph of her and her father placed alongside it, the song "Lust for Life" by Iggy Pop—a seemingly ironic choice that had apparently been her and her father's favorite song—played silently on repeat. But her final moments hadn't been pleasant. Her mother had woken from a self-pity induced drunken stupor to find her deceased daughter curled into a ball at the bottom of her bed, dried vomit on her chin, her hands clutching her stomach, a pained expression on her cold face, the background music an ear worm that would haunt the mother at every play.

The inevitable tabloid reports that followed claimed the Bleak and Bright Bandits had taken their second victim. It was media hype as far as Cawley was concerned. Reporters had hounded the young girl and her mother from the moment they heard about the death of their father and husband. They had plastered their faces and their stories all over the newsreels and the front pages, begging for sympathy, for viewers and readers. Cawley knew as well as they did that they were as much to blame in the little girl's death as the bandits were. He also knew that after spending a few days squeezing every last angle they could out of her death, they'd tire and return to bent politicians and promiscuous footballers, waiting for the bandits to strike again. The good thing, as far as Cawley was concerned, was that it would give the public another reason to turn against the fugitives.

Cawley discovered the news on his way to the office. It had been playing on cycles all morning on one of the local radio stations. They said she was an aspiring writer, a girl who had the world at her feet. It sickened him, and further fueled his hatred of the bandits, but he knew what the media refused to admit: it wasn't their fault.

Detective Superintendent Morris called Cawley into her office when he arrived. She was annoyed; she always looked annoyed, but now she had a reason.

"You didn't report back to me yesterday," she said, her nostrils flaring. "May I ask why?"

Cawley stood near the closed door. He had no intention of sitting opposite her, no intention of going anywhere near her. He gave her a simple shrug.

"Well?" she snapped. "Are you just going to stand there or do you want to do your fucking job and tell me what happened?"

He had to force himself not to smile. He loved to see her angry. It was in that anger that he saw something he actually liked, a strength he respected, even when it was directed at him. He took great pleasure in making her that way, felt something innately beautiful and pleasing inside of him whenever he knew he'd pissed her off, and not just because he liked that side of her,

"Nothing to it," he said softly. There were easy ways to annoy her, but he had to maintain a tone of professionalism, give her no reason to sack him. "The bartender is lying. He's up to something."

"What?"

Cawley shrugged. "God knows, but I don't think it concerns us."

She seemed to calm down a bit. Cawley sighed internally; he was looking forward to watching her pop her skull like a microwaved egg.

"Anything else?" she demanded.

"There's a potential lead on the outskirts of town. A woman reckons her neighbor was harboring the bandits until this morning."

Clarissa looked alert again, her hairy nostrils beginning to flare. "And I'm only just finding out about this now?"

Cawley shrugged, briefly wondered just why he enjoyed

rattling her so much, why he enjoyed the anger, the hatred, the drama. It hadn't always been like that, nor had it been so with his wife. He used to give a shit; he was once desperate to please, desperate to be liked. He loved his wife, and even though he didn't want kids, if he was honest with himself, he would have been happy to have them. But then he found the emails, the pictures—he had never spoken of it, he had never approached her about it, but he knew she had cheated on him. That broke him more than she could have ever known. The evil, mean-spirited demon in front of him probably didn't help him out either.

"I only just found out about it myself," he said.

She nodded, seemed happy with that. "Look into it. Hurry up, we have no time to waste."

Cawley nodded, left the room without saying anything further. He didn't mention that the woman with the report was Mrs. Barnes, a legend in the police station. A woman who had once claimed, rather vehemently, that she had seen Elvis stealing a loaf of bread from Tesco. A woman with a shitload of cats and very little grasp of reality. It wasn't Cawley's prerogative to see her; it didn't matter if *anyone* went to see her. In a few days, she would forget about her claim and move on to the next insane delusion, but Cawley felt like a change of pace. He needed some time away from the stress and the pressure, some time away from vindictive women and evasive fugitives. A mentally unstable woman with no grasp of reality wasn't ideal, but it was certainly a break from the norm.

9

Dexter felt good. The sleep and the breakfast had done wonders for his plagued mind. He felt cleaner, better, more human. He felt like he was waking up to his first week of sobriety following a massive binge, and, in a way, that's exactly what it had been. They'd both been caught up in the adrenaline and the excitement. They were junkies, craving more, doing riskier things. After the murder, things had taken a different turn. That was their comedown, their crime spree was over. Now they were waiting for the hangover to dissipate so they could get back to normal, if normal could ever be attained after what they'd gone through.

They both sensed that this was the end. They still loved each other, possibly more than ever, but they didn't need that adrenaline to fuel it. Never had. It had just been a drug they couldn't resist. They had a chance to start a family, to get clean, to stay out of the limelight. Dexter didn't care what they did, as long as she was by his side, and he knew that Pandora felt the same way.

They stopped at a local shop, a quiet little hut of a building parked opposite a residential street. Pandora waited outside—resting up against the exterior wall, one foot behind her, her arms crossed over her chest, bathing in the sunshine—while Dexter ducked in to pick up a few supplies.

The shopkeeper eyed Dexter as soon as he entered. He was a hunched, haggard old man with tired eyes and failing skin that drooped off his neck like a punctured football. He looked ready for death, not just because of his dwindling years—the reaper was certainly around the corner—but because of an attitude that suggested he was ready, that he had given up on the few things life had left for him and was ready to bid it farewell with one last cynical sneer.

Dexter didn't even try to acknowledge him. It always paid to be friendly, especially when you needed the world on your side, but with some people it wasn't worth the effort.

The shop looked like a newsstand, but there were no newspapers or magazines, a relief for Dexter, who didn't have to wonder if the grumpy old git behind the counter was waiting to supply the town with pictures of him and Pandora at their worst.

A scattering of items littered the shelves. Dorothy said this was where the locals did their shopping, this little hovel that was barely big enough to hold its sour-faced owner and his antique till, was where they all came to acquire life's essentials. They stocked stacks of toilet paper in the corner, like bales of hay in a farmer's field. Crates of pop, juice, water, and milk sat in the other corner—Dexter had to be careful to avoid standing on them when he scoured the shelf, reaching up to pluck some chocolate bars and a couple of bags of chips.

He didn't crack a smile when he laid the items down on the counter, wasn't expecting the old man to talk to him.

"Pretty woman you have there," he said in a voice that crackled like an out of tune radio. He nodded his head toward the window, through which Dexter could see Pandora's shadow as she stood in the sunlight, talking to a little girl on a bike.

He let a curious expression cross his face but didn't reply to the old man. There was something sinister behind his gray eyes.

"You want to keep an eye on her," he pushed, not making a move to tally the items on the counter.

"What's that supposed to mean?"

The gray eyes bore through him. A soft cackle spilled out of his thin blue lips; a smile curled half of his face like a stroke.

Dexter held his stare, shook it off. He looked down at the items on the counter, raised his eyebrows to indicate them.

The old man put his hands—skeletal specimens poorly wrapped in loose-fitting skin—flat in front of him, slapping the counter with a hollow, fleshy thud. They trembled as they moved with an arthritic stutter across the counter; Dexter began to feel sorry for him, seeing the struggle and the pain he suffered.

The wrinkled hands violently shoved into the chips and chocolate, forcing them away. They tipped off the edge, spilled around Dexter's feet. The old man snarled like a hairless pit-bull, spat a stuttering snigger that seemed to rise through his entire decrepit body before cackling out of his throat.

"Take your goods and fuck off."

Dexter held the sinister gaze, felt weakened in its grasp. He ducked out of sight to pick up the items, stuffing them into his pockets. When he returned, an annoyed rebuttal on his lips, the old man had turned around. His hunched back, clad in a cardigan that clung tight enough for his protruding spine to poke through, faced Dexter.

He swallowed his words, gave the old man's back a sneer of his own. He left a few coins on the counter, more than the goods were worth—the least worthy tip he'd ever given—and left the shop, keeping his frustration to himself.

* * *

Outside the shop, Pandora stood surveying her surroundings. She thought she could get used to a place like this. Everything shone with an idyllic glimmer. Everything seemed neat, tidy, and clean. The sort of place that seemed devoid of criminals, of the lower side of the human psyche.

Pandora knew that wasn't true, even without the presence of her and Dexter. Society as a whole was rife with perversion, sickness, and evil, whether that spilled out onto poverty-stricken streets—where the youths were jobless, hopeless, and desperate and life was extinguished with overdoses, malnutrition, foul play, and stupidity—or whether it was hidden behind closed doors; clandestine evil polluted perfection with domestic violence and murder. The perils of society were everywhere, but at least in Fairwood they were kept off the streets.

The sun cast an illuminating beam on the houses over the street, on the emerald green lawns surrounded by a bounty of flowers and bordered by a picket fence that stretched across the terraced houses like pearly veneers.

It was quiet, still, peaceful. The only sound was that of a distant lawnmower chopping up the summer grass, spewing scents of freshly cut turf into the tepid air. There was no noise pollution, no roaring engines firing fumes or bouncing bass-laden tunes into the silence; no birds yapping to each other with high-pitched, piercing shrieks; no shouting, talking, yelling, or arguing.

A small squeaking noise entered the silence, broke through with a jolt. A rolling, turning sound of mechanical sufferance. Pandora turned to see a young girl approaching on a bike, her legs lazily working the pedals, which turned a wheel fitted with frilly spokes and a bright pink light that failed to declare its presence in the sunshine.

She was no more than eight or nine, a pretty little thing with an indifferent and distant look on her face. She wore a flowery dress—hitched up to stop the skirt slipping into the spokes—cream sandals and pristine white socks up to her knees.

The bike twitched along the road ahead of Pandora. The little girl had flowing brown hair that lifted and splayed in the wind. She didn't lift her head to acknowledge the blonde woman waiting outside the shop.

Pandora pushed herself off the wall. The sound of her shoes grazing against the brick broke the mechanical whirring of the bike and alerted the little girl. She slowed down but still didn't move her head.

"Hello there," Pandora said joyfully.

The little girl stopped the bike, the silence returning to the morning air. She rested her feet on the ground to save herself from toppling over, looked at Pandora with the same blank stare that she had previously been offering the empty street.

She didn't say anything, didn't smile or acknowledge her.

"What's your name?"

The girl continued to stare for a moment, then she answered in a soft and ambiguous tone. "Susie."

"Oh," Pandora put on a bright smile, "that's a nice name." She never really knew how to act around kids, wasn't sure if the childish tone was appropriate for a maybe eight-year-old or if she would consider it condescending. The little girl didn't flinch so she kept it up. "Do you live around here?"

She nodded slowly, maintaining eye contact. Pandora moved forward a couple of steps, saw the child's blazing blue eyes watch her shuffling feet.

"Do you like it here?"

Susie shrugged indifferently.

"It's nice, isn't it?"

She didn't answer.

"Are you out by yourself?" Pandora wondered. "Where are your friends?"

"I don't have any."

"Oh." Pandora could empathize. As a little girl, she had spent most of her playtime by herself. She would play with her dolls, ride her bikes, watch her television and play her computer games without the company of kids her own age. She was shy, a cautious only child who suffered under her parents' distant and protective hands and didn't know how to function around the children who were allowed to stay out late and owned the latest toys and games. "That's a shame," she said softly. "What about your parents, your mum and dad?"

"What about them?" the girl asked simply.

"Are they around?"

"My mum is at home. I don't have a dad."

"Oh, I'm sorry."

"Why?"

Pandora frowned, gave a gentle shrug of her shoulders. "I don't know. It's just that, well, it must be hard not having a dad."

The little girl didn't answer. She looked Pandora up and down, concentrating on her beautiful eyes, studying her features in detail. Pandora felt like she was under the studious and knowing gaze of a doctor or a psychiatrist. She became uneasy on her feet, in her own skin.

"*It is*," the little girl said eventually. She lifted her feet, gave Pandora one last bland stare, and then pedaled away, her legs working methodically as the bike crept out of sight along the empty street.

Dexter appeared moments later, looking equally bemused.

"Everything okay?" she asked.

He nodded and asked her the same question, seemingly noting that she was no longer smiling.

"I suppose so," Pandora said, looking off in the direction that the young girl had traveled. "But you remember when I said I wanted kids?"

"Yes."

"Well, I changed my mind."

She looked back at Dexter, at the picture of confusion on his face.

"Only joking," she said, hooking her arm in his. "Come on, let's get out of here."

10

Cawley was hit by the musty stench of piss when Mrs. Barnes opened the door. He flashed his badge and struggled to tell her his name while trying to hold his breath.

"I've been expecting you," she told him with a sinister and gleeful smile on her cadaverous face.

He rolled his eyes, stuffed his wallet back in his pocket, and took a step backward, keen to avoid the smell. He wasn't sure if it was coming from her or from her house, but he was sure it was more criminal than anything she was waiting to tell him. If he could, he would arrest her for assaulting a police officer with a disgusting smell, or for the intention to incite vomit, because when she grinned at him—exposing rows of yellow teeth, wedged into blackened gums like burnt-out and boarded windows on a dilapidated tenement—he felt the need to unleash the contents of his stomach.

He hadn't exactly rushed to the crazy old woman as he told his superior he would. He stopped off for breakfast first: two fried eggs, three slices of bacon, and a slice of dripping fried bread, all swimming in a pool of grease and canned tomatoes. The owners at the local cafe were happy to give him the extra portions, perhaps thinking that if they didn't he would arrest them for cooking up heart attacks in kitchens where only men in Hazmat suits should venture. They didn't like him; they were all smiles and greetings on the surface but, underneath that, he felt an air of distrust, sensing that they were on edge because of their poor food hygiene, the stacks of pirated DVDs, snuff films, drugs, or whatever they kept hidden away in their one-bedroom apartment above the cafe. They probably spat in his food as well, but he didn't care; the saliva would be neutralized by the oil, the fat, or the e-coli.

"Come in," Mrs. Barnes said, stepping aside.

He smiled, burped a noxious waft of fry-up fumes into his hand. "I'd rather not," he said softly.

She gave him a curious and suspicious look. "I'll make us a cup of tea," she said, as if to sweeten the deal.

He had every intention of letting her waste his time inside her hovel, but he hadn't remembered the smell. The last time he'd been to her house was a few years ago when she said she'd been burgled, apparently by the least picky burglar in the world. She hadn't lost anything but was sure that she had one fewer useless pile of shit than she usually had. The smell wasn't so bad then, but it had been putrefying ever since.

"No, thanks," he said, taking another step away from her.

She looked both offended and suspicious, as if unable to work out his refusal, like he had just passed up the opportunity to bed a twenty-one-year-old supermodel with tits the size of his head.

She folded her arms, leaned against the doorframe. She poked her head out, looked this way and that—Cawley took another step back when he saw something move in her hair—and then looked at Cawley with eyes that suggested she knew something that he didn't: possibly the source of the rancid smell, but he doubted she even knew it existed.

"I know where they are." Her rotten breath hissed into the wind.

"Really?" Cawley said, trying to feign enthusiasm but dealing exactly the amount of sarcasm that he felt.

She nodded, oblivious to just how little he cared. "I saw them."

Cawley nodded and tried to look interested. He regretted paying a visit to the crazy woman. It was still better than sitting in his office, doors away from his demon boss and her many minions, but only just. He needed a break; he needed to get away from things for a while; away from his wife, from his boss, from his job. He hoped that he could catch the bandits and feel alive again, feel like he wasn't just a worthless piece of shit in a pointless machine, but there was no chance of that. They'd already gone, onto another district, another country maybe. Everything he did from now on was just routine until the bandits were caught and he went back to arresting delinquent kids and drunken idiots.

"They were out at Rosie's Point," she told him, looking over his shoulder to make sure no one else had heard.

He perked up a bit, furrowed his brow. Rosie's Point was just around the corner from Stubbies. It was a barren stretch of land stuck between a rundown farm and a tiny village, a peak of muddied ground that overlooked a steep dip into a marshy moor. It used to be blocked off with a roadside barrier to keep the kids away, but the same kids ripped the barrier to pieces, made makeshift sleds out of the resulting debris, and used them to slide down the bumpy, grassy terrain, all the way to the woodland at the bottom intersected by a quiet stream—long ago filled with the modern refuse of shopping carts, bikes, and other detritus—before climbing up and starting again. A number of years ago, a twelve-year-old girl named Rosie Fairbanks had been playing on the land when her makeshift sled hit a tuft at the bottom and propelled her into a tree trunk, breaking her neck. It didn't really have a name before that, but everyone knew its name afterward. The barriers were removed; the kids stopped playing.

"You were at Rosie's Point?"

She nodded firmly, knowing she had his interest and that her value to him had just increased. "I take my dogs out there."

He hadn't seen a dog, hadn't heard one bark when he knocked on the door. If she did have dogs, then they were the quietest dogs he'd ever encountered.

"That's a long walk from here," he said suspiciously.

"They need the exercise. It does them good."

He wasn't convinced. On foot, Rosie's Point was at least a forty-five-minute trek. She was crazy, but he doubted she would go that far out of her way. There were plenty of parks and fields nearby, so she didn't need to travel to Rosie's Point to give the dogs some exercise. *If* she had any dogs.

"Okay," he nodded. It was a coincidence, nothing more. If he had another witness who had seen the bandits near Stubbies, he would have had something to go off, but one anonymous tip, one dodgy bar owner, and one crazy cat lady with some nonexistent dogs wasn't enough, not when the whole country was claiming to know the fugitives. "Thanks for that. I'll get in touch if I need anything else."

"That's it?" she looked disappointed and took a few steps out of her door as he made to move away. For a moment, he worried she was going to follow him and stink up his car.

"Sure. Thanks for all your help." He moved quickly, didn't want to wait around for more questions. She had done what he needed her to do—she'd bought him some time, in which he'd been able to have some terrible food and suffer some terrible smells. Now he had to return to work, to his terrible boss.

11

The path that Dorothy suggested they take took them around the back of town, through a wash of green that decorated the bountiful landscape. It was like a different country, a land far removed, rather than a little town on the outskirts of Yorkshire.

They viewed the town from the back, taking a path that overlooked the backs of a line of houses. They were separated from the backyards by a tall wooden fence, through the slits of which they could see the peaceful, well-maintained gardens.

A young boy watched them from the second-floor window of one of the houses. He was standing by the window as though waiting for them to pass. He stared at them, didn't flicker when they smiled, didn't falter when Pandora gave him a wave.

"Why is everyone here so creepy?" she asked Dexter as they passed, keeping her voice low.

Dexter shrugged. "We're outsiders, I guess. This is the sort of place where everybody knows everybody else's business. They don't welcome strangers."

"You'd think they'd need us," Pandora noted. "We could probably dilute their gene pool a bit, phase out a bit of that inbreeding."

Dexter grinned and then gestured for her to be silent,

nodding toward the fence. They were out of sight from the little boy in the window but, a few houses down, through the slits in the fence, they saw the face of a young woman watching them, her rosy skin and her blonde hair visible as she poked her face close to the wood.

"Hello there!" Dexter said loudly, letting her know she'd been seen.

They expected her to back away shyly, to apologize or make up an excuse, but she didn't move. Pandora gave her a smile as well, flashed another little wave, but still the woman didn't budge.

"Creepy," Pandora hissed under her breath, lowering her eyes to the ground self-consciously as they passed.

"We're new," Dexter said when they'd left the muddy path that stretched the length of the fence. They crossed onto a pre-trodden path of grass, a shortcut to a river that ran silently ahead of them; its thin, weaving banks sat deep in the lush green landscape, snaking off into the distance. "Give them time."

"I will," Pandora said brightly. "I like it here, don't get me wrong. It's creepy, but it's peaceful, and Dorothy more than makes up for all the weirdoes."

"I used to live not too far from a village like this," Dexter told her. "In fact, the village was where we went for some excitement."

"Sad, sad man."

"Yep."

"What did you do for fun?"

He shrugged. "We used to spend our pocket money at the local shop, on sweets mostly. Hide and seek. Maybe ride our bikes—"

"Penny farthings?"

"We had proper bikes."

"And what about at night?" she pushed, a slyness in her smile. "When all the chores were done, did you all gather around the radio, play some cards?"

75

"*Actually,* we did play a lot of cards."

She laughed. "You were a kid in dire need of a Gameboy."

They stood by the river, watched the clean water rock gently by.

"Should we go to this trivia thing tonight?" Pandora wondered, suddenly solemn as she stared at her reflection in the water.

"I don't see why not."

"Lot of people there, lot of chances to get noticed."

"I don't think anyone here will notice us."

She turned to him, bemused. "What makes you say that?"

"Have you noticed any newspapers, any televisions?"

She gave it some thought. She had only been inside the bed and breakfast but had seen nothing of the sort. They had stayed in some cheap, rundown places over the last few weeks and even *they* had televisions in the room. It was implausible that an establishment as big as Dorothy's wouldn't have one.

She shook her head.

"We can lay low no problem." He put his arm around her and they both turned toward the silently moving water, to the stretch of green grass that seemed to go on forever on the other side of the bank. "I think we're safe here."

* * *

"Hello there!"

Pandora nearly jumped out of her skin. She'd been sitting on the bank of the river, staring at her own reflection, lost in her thoughts, when the voice from behind her nearly sent her sprawling into the clear waters.

She turned, startled, to see a man walking toward her, a wide smile on his friendly face, a fishing rod and a tackle box in his hands.

Pandora opened her mouth to reply but her words fell short,

dissipated into a mumbling drizzle. She clawed at the ground to get to her feet as he approached.

He was wearing a fisherman's hat, a series of corks bobbled from strings around the brim. A pair of sunglasses perched on the elongated bridge of his nose. He wore a casual blue and white striped sleeveless shirt, his darkened arms exposed to the sun.

He put the box down on the bank, swapped his rod from his right hand to his left, and then offered the free hand to Pandora. "Nice day, isn't it?"

She shook. His grip was relaxed, softened. His palms were coarse, riddled with callouses.

"Yes," she nodded, still taken aback. She wasn't expecting anyone to be nice in this town except for Dorothy, let alone approach her with a broad and happy greeting.

Dexter had needed to use the toilet. She said he should do it behind a tree, that was the benefit of having a penis after all; he said that although that may be the case, he still needed to take a shit like any woman would. He had told her to wait for him, said he would hurry back.

"Out here by yourself?" he asked, looking out toward the river.

She nodded, followed his eyes. "You fishing?"

She hated small talk, was never really any good at it. It was pointless and she preferred to avoid it, but she felt a social need in this case. Besides Dorothy, he was the first resident of Fairwood to talk to her; the least she could do was reciprocate.

"Yeah." He paused. "Well, kinda." He gave her a cheeky smile, flashed something sinister in his eyes. He moved toward her, close enough for her to smell a mixture of coffee and alcohol on his breath; to catch the warmth of his body heat and the slight odor of scented shower gel and shampoo.

She took a step backward.

"But not really," he said.

She looked beyond his shoulder, toward the clearing, to the ground where Dexter had disappeared to. "Oh?" she spat distantly, an anxious fear creeping into her tone.

He nodded, a lustful slyness in his eyes. She could feel him almost pressing against her. He leant forward. She readied herself to attack; she didn't want to, but she was confident she could incapacitate him if need be.

She felt his breath on the side of her face as he leaned in. "*Don't tell the wife*," he whispered. "But I'm really here just to get away from her."

His smile turned into something else, something warmer. He pulled away, moved to the box he'd rested on the floor. With her heart beating like crazy and her fists clenched by her side, she watched him remove a few cans of beer from the cooler before closing the lid and sitting on it.

"Truth is, there's no fish in this river." He cracked open the can and sighed pleasurably. "But she doesn't know that." He smiled. Pandora smiled back, unclenched her fists, and moved toward him.

"Want one?" he asked, giving her a can.

She accepted it. She didn't want it, but by taking it she felt she was apologizing for preparing to castrate him when he was just being friendly.

He shifted along on the box, gesturing for her to sit. She moved a hand to tell him it was okay, but he didn't see. When he looked up at her, a smile on his face and a space next to him, she felt obliged to sit.

He took a sip from his beer, his lips sucking noisily on the edge of the can. "So, where's this husband of yours?" he asked.

She looked across at him, raised an eyebrow.

"Ah," he waved a dismissive hand. "Don't look so surprised. Fairwood is a small town, word gets around."

"He's popped back to use the toilet," she said.

"There's plenty of trees around, hell, even the river. Nothing beats pissing in the river, if you'll excuse my French."

"I think it's a . . ." she paused, trying her best not to speak French. "A number two."

"Ah," he gave a knowing nod, drank some of his beer and then shrugged, "well if it's good enough for the animals . . ."

She chuckled. She liked him. There was something so pleasantly dismissive about him, like a cynical and grumpy old man without true cynicism or grumpiness.

"So, why so eager to get away from your wife?" she wondered.

He gave her a wry smile, stifled a burp with the back of his hand, and waved his wrist in an apologetic gesture. "She's a good woman, don't get me wrong, but she talks. A lot." He nodded to himself, raised his eyebrows in contemplation. "I love her, but love doesn't make it easier to listen to her nagging all day."

"How long have you been together?"

"A long bloody time." He laughed, gave the river a meek smile. "But she's a special girl and we have something good. Soulmates, I suppose you could say. Together forever, an' all that soppy business."

"That's sweet."

He took a thirsty gulp of his drink and then looked at her. "What about you?" he wondered. "You been with your fella long?"

"A few years," she said, unwilling to go into details.

Their eyes locked, they exchanged a smile, and then they both turned to look toward the river. To the glistening waters, the green fields, like banks of carpeted earth that stretched as far as they could see.

She took a small sip of her beer, sighed deeply. "Do you live far from here?"

"Not far enough."

She flashed an amused smile. "You think it's wise coming here? What if she decides to check up on you?"

He made a dismissive sound, shook his head. "She won't."

"You sound so sure."

"I know her. She'll be happy with the peace."

"Would it not be better to take a trip somewhere else?"

"Somewhere else?" he asked, looking slightly baffled.

Pandora nodded, held his gaze. "Away from Fairwood," she clarified.

He furrowed his brow, gave her a momentary stare of confusion, and then shook it off. "So, how are you guys settling into this fine town of ours?"

She frowned, pondering on the change of subject. "Okay, I suppose," she said eventually. "But we'll probably be leaving soon anyway."

He gave a little chuckle into his beer, popped a few of the foam bubbles from the rim. "Leave?" he shook his head. "You can't leave."

She turned to him, a smile on her face, expecting to see it returned. She watched him take a long drink, expected him to clarify, and when he didn't she asked, "What do you mean?"

He turned his head to stare at her. The smile had gone from his face. He looked serious, bland. He didn't answer, didn't seem to want to attempt an answer.

She stood, feeling uneasy again. She straightened herself, feigned an exaggerated yawn and a stretch, took a few steps away from him. "I better be going now," she said. "See what's taking him so long."

He nodded, lifted his can to her in a salute, the smile suddenly back on his face. "You have a good day now."

She smiled back, held up her own can, and pointed to it in a gesture that thanked him for the drink, then she left. She dumped the can, barely touched, into a bin on her way. She fired a look over her shoulder before she disappeared, watched him curiously as he put his empty can down, picked up another, and continued to drink and stare. She shook her head, and hurried away.

She heard him calling behind her as she moved, his muffled words causing her to quicken her footsteps. She didn't turn to look.

* * *

Pandora stopped, suddenly feeling very cold, very scared.

The man by the riverside had called after her, but only when she was out of sight of him and the calming river did she finally realize what he had been saying to her.

"You're going the wrong way, love."

She had reached a wooded area and had taken several steps before the panic took hold. She wanted to go back, even if it meant returning to the river and the strange but kindly man by its bank, but the forest was thick, dark, enveloping—even in the bright light of day.

She could no longer remember which way was back and which way was forward.

So she stood, still—her mind racing, her body shaking.

A distant, shrill sound broke through the deathly silence of the day. Her first thought was that it was a bird's song, but then she heard someone clear their throat and realized it was a whistle.

She moved toward the sound, careful not to draw attention to herself, not knowing where she was and even if she was still in Fairwood.

The whistling grew louder with every step and the forest that had been so suddenly thick, dark, and impenetrable, began to clear. She could see the light of day streaming through the trees ahead of her, could hear the happiness and joy in the whistle, which seemed to be following the beat of a pop song she wasn't familiar with.

The panic began to subside in her, and she even felt a little angry at herself for getting so worked up so quickly.

She told herself that she was a criminal, a fugitive. She wasn't the sort of person who got scared just because she didn't know where she was. With or without Dexter, she was a strong person who didn't—

She stopped short at the end of the clearing, her thoughts fading away, a feeling of disbelief now overriding everything else.

The whistling man stopped when he saw her and waved, "Hello again!"

Pandora found herself standing next to the river, looking directly at the spot where she had been only minutes before. The whistling man was the same man she had been speaking to, sitting on the same cooler and holding the same can of beer.

"Thought you'd join me for a drink after all?" he said, grinning.

Pandora looked behind her—the woodland she had emerged from seemed to be nothing more than a few trees, certainly nothing like the expanse she had become lost in. She looked over the river, and then to the man, who seemed unmoved by it all.

She began to ask how she got to where she was, if he had moved somewhere else to mess with her. But he spoke before she could.

"Don't worry, love," he said. "It's easy to get turned around in Fairwood. This little town of ours can be confusing as hell. You need to take a left on the path there. It'll take you back into town." He paused to sip his beer and then added, "Unless you want to rejoin me for a drink?" He patted the beer cooler. "There's still room for one more."

She looked down the path, the same one she had taken with Dexter to get here, the same one he had taken to go back. She then looked to the path that she had mistakenly taken. It spiraled out of sight and she could just see the beginning of the woodland she had entered from where she stood.

"I don't get it," she said, half to herself.

The fisherman laughed. "If you ask me, that should be our town motto."

He broke into another whistle, a sound that followed her as she left, taking a path she hoped would lead her back to the B&B.

* * *

Dexter looked for Dorothy when he returned to the bed and breakfast; he didn't want to drift in unannounced. It was technically a business, and he was a customer, but the building was so homely—it was her home, after all—he felt he needed to at least let her know he was passing through.

He couldn't find her in the foyer, the dining room, or the living room and didn't want to venture into the kitchen. He couldn't wait any longer, had to complete his morning ritual in the upstairs bathroom.

The bathroom was a little less extravagant than the rest of the house; it felt cold, untouched. The fixtures were a sickly yellow color. A ring of rust wrapped around the base of the sink like a halo of scar tissue. A drab painting of a house hung above the bath; a frosted mirror, its painted edges flaked and chipped, hung from a frayed piece of string above the sink.

He liked to read when he sat, always had. He wasn't a big reader at the best of times, hadn't read any proper books in years, but couldn't resist the urge when he was sitting on the toilet. He spied a number of toiletries on a shelf at the back of the bath, stretched toward them, keeping his buttocks on the cold plastic seat. He paused when he heard a noise from outside.

Someone opened and closed the front door. The sound of creaking hinges and approaching footsteps kicking against the welcome mat was unmistakable. The shuffling feet kicked themselves dry against the coarse mat and then began to climb the stairs.

Dexter sat upright, watching the closed door, beyond which the hallway twisted a few feet and then turned into the top of the stairs. The footsteps were labored and heavy. He guessed they were male, a guess that was confirmed when he heard the climber clear his throat; a harsh, dry, and crackling sound, like corn popping in a microwave.

He reached the top of the stairs and paused. Dexter felt his eyes staring at the closed bathroom door, questioning who was inside. He moved forward, one big step onto a creaking floorboard that groaned like an otherworldly spirit as his heavy foot tested the aging beams.

He paused again. Dexter heard his second foot join his first, heard them both shuffle, heard him clear his throat again.

"Where are they?" the man asked.

His voice was as harsh and raspy as his throat-clearing. He sounded like a man who didn't mind the odd cigar or glass of whiskey, a man whose throat had suffered under the indulgences of countless breaths of toxic smoke and high strength alcohol.

"Taking a walk." He was surprised to hear Dorothy's voice in reply. She didn't sound as pleasant and chirpy as he knew her to be. Her tone had taken on a heavy, nasally edge, but it was definitely her. He heard her shift across the corridor, from the back of the hallway—where his and Pandora's room was—to where the man was standing, just outside the bathroom door.

"Do they suspect anything?"

"No."

Dexter knew they were talking about him, and he was intrigued to find out what they were talking about, but he couldn't control his bowel movements. He had been holding it in when he heard the man climb the stairs, and now it was desperate to escape. He clenched his sphincter tight, lifted his cheeks off the cold rim of the seat.

"You sure?"

"Positive."

He muttered something, his voice passing through the door as a bass-filled drawl.

"They going to the pub tonight?" the man asked, his tone serious.

"I told them, they should—"

Dexter couldn't hold it in anymore. It escaped of its own volition. The plopping sound as it splashed into the toilet was enough to halt Dorothy in her tracks. Dexter cursed under his breath.

He heard the man shuffle away, the floorboards released their long groan as they crept back into place. He disappeared into another room; Dorothy seemed to remain standing.

Dexter finished up, took his time washing his hands, studying his reflection and wondering what the elderly couple were talking about. Why would they care where they were going? It was possible that they knew who they were and were coveting the ransom money, but if so, they would have turned them in already. They had them in their house; they were asleep in their bed all through the night—the perfect opportunity to hand them over to the police.

He opened the door briskly and stepped out with a smile on his face, pretending nothing had happened just in case one of them was waiting for him. They were. Dorothy was standing at the top of the stairs, her hands on one of the paintings that hung from the wall, readjusting the perfectly level frame.

"Oh, hello dear," she said, pretending to have just noticed him. "We were just talking about you."

Dexter looked around, only he and Dorothy stood in the hallway. "We?"

"Oh, my husband and I, I mean. He just went for a lie down."

She clasped her hands together, brought them in front of her, the stance of the sweet and innocent. The friendly grandmother who has nothing to hide.

"Okay," Dexter said warmly, quickly dismissing any thoughts he had about questioning her. If she was up to something then he would find out in time and deal with it when it arose. He didn't want to ruin what they had in this quiet, inoffensive, and backward slice of the country by throwing around accusations. "Nothing too bad I hope?"

"We were just wondering if you fancied coming to the quiz tonight, meet the locals. Everyone will be there."

Dexter held her stare; he saw something that he couldn't put his finger on. Before he could give it further thought, before he could reply, he saw Pandora coming up the stairs, a perturbed look hidden behind her beautiful smile.

Dorothy followed Dexter's eyes.

"Oh, hello dear."

Pandora smiled a meek greeting and slid past her on the stairs, moved beside Dexter.

"We were just discussing tonight," Dorothy proclaimed.

Pandora turned to Dexter. "Tonight?"

"The quiz," Dorothy said, eager to control the conversation. "You'll be there, I hope? The locals would love to meet you, I'm sure."

"Oh." Dexter was ready to refuse, blame the need for an early night, but between trying to look social and friendly for Dorothy and trying to warn Pandora against accepting the invite, he got caught up.

"Sure," Pandora said without conviction, much to Dexter's disappointment. "We'd love to."

12

Detective Superintendent Clarissa Morris had her prey in her sights. She stared him down, weakening him with her icy expression before she went in for the kill. She screamed at him, her voice rocking the office into silence. Conversations hushed; phone calls halted; fingertips paused above mice and keyboards.

The young sergeant didn't know what hit him. He quivered and squirmed in front of her, his chin pushed as low as it would go, the top of his head facing her anger.

She barged past him, throwing her arms as she stropped across the room like some villainous B-rated movie beast. She drew the blinds, stopping everyone from witnessing whatever slaughter she had in mind. They still heard, though, even when the phone calls and the conversations restarted in tones louder than before.

"Jesus, wouldn't want to be him," Sergeant Adams said, sucking in a breath through clenched teeth.

Detective Cawley nodded, still gazing at the blinds, through which he could see the dancing shadows of interoffice bullying play out for his amusement. The sergeant was new, had just transferred in two weeks ago. This was his first run-in with the boss, the evil superintendent formed entirely of bone, sinew, and malice. He underestimated her, allowed his youthful confidence to get in the way of logic, ignoring the way his balls crept back into his stomach whenever he saw her or listened to her; disregarding the way she made his skin crawl and the hair on the back of his neck stand up, preferring instead to dismiss her as a harmless, uptight, little Hitler. He was certainly learning his lesson—the question was whether it would serve him any good as there was a strong chance of resignation after Clarissa Morris finished unloading on him.

"What exactly did he do?" Cawley asked the sergeant next to him, slurping loudly from a cup of vending machine coffee that smelled and tasted like the grime scraped from the heels of a sewage worker.

"He ballsed up on some job or another," he replied dismissively, wiping the sloppy coffee from his thick, sugary lips and taking a bite from a sweet pastry. "Then he had the balls, or rather the stupidity, to talk back to her when she called him in."

Cawley made a face. Clarissa despised all of humankind, but she hated cocky little upstarts even more than that.

"Yep," the sergeant said slovenly. "She's in a bad mood. Best to stay out of her way."

"Speaking of which," another sergeant piped up from the next desk, a grin on her pudgy, dimpled face. "She's been looking for you, wants to have a word."

Cawley sunk, grimaced. "You're shitting me?"

The female sergeant shook her head, the grin still on her face. The office was like a large family household, a pattering of mischievous kids happy to watch their siblings squirm under the enforcement of the dominating matriarch. Others tuned into the conversation at the sign of Cawley's discomfort, halting their activity to listen in with crude and twisted grins.

Cawley shook his head, the idea of speaking to Clarissa in her current state was repugnant to him. "I've gotta go," he said, turning. "Tell her something came up." He could have told them not to say anything at all, to say that he hadn't shown up, but he couldn't trust them all to keep quiet—one of them would throw him under the frothy, thin-legged bus that was Clarissa Morris. The smiled dripped from the sergeant's face. "What do you want me to say?" she mumbled fruitlessly as Cawley made a hasty exit.

He went straight to the pub, knocked back a flat and un-refreshing pint of beer while listening to the prattling of a drunken idiot who wouldn't take the hint no matter how many times Max refused to reply or shifted to another stool. He had plenty of dealings with alcoholics to know that drunks don't necessarily think the world cares about their problems; they just don't care that nobody cares and don't possess the social aptitude to shut up when no one displays any interest.

He was technically on duty and wasn't supposed to drink, but there was no way he was going back to the office. He didn't know what he would tell the demon with the half-skirt and half-smile when he did return. Abigail, his former partner, had been drunk on duty a few times, especially in the last few years when Cawley noticed the emptiness behind her eyes; the dread whenever they were called out to a homicide; the misery when-ever they were filing away reports of violence and abuse like clerks at the post office.

On the inside, Abi was strong, probably stronger than he was, but she had one vice, and that vice made her weak. Max hadn't had much luck with women. He never had a good relationship with his mother, he'd only had a few short-term girlfriends before his wife, and his boss was only happy when everyone else was miserable. Abi had always been different; she had always been special to him. He was the wrong sex for her, and he had no illusions to the contrary, but she was a good friend, as good of a friend as he could have hoped for. That made her resignation, her abandonment, harder for him to take. First his wife, then his partner.

Max bought a bottle of bourbon on his way home, drank some of it straight from the bottle before he even climbed into his car. He hated drunk drivers, had seen the catastrophe that it could cause, had witnessed the horrors that one drink too many could bring for unsuspecting motorists who hadn't touched a drop, for children who were years away from even contemplating doing so and would now never be able to. He had also berated Abigail the times she had tried to drive after she'd had a few. But he ignored his own advice this time, pushed it to the back of his mind where the bitter, twisted, abyss of his conscience used to reside before it decided to expand and conquer.

He returned to his home, devoid of life and of possessions, but filled with junk, with dust and dirt. It brought a smile to his face when he saw it, a slow shake of his head. "All the shit you said about Bat-Shit Barnes," he said to himself. "And you're just as bad."

Sandra had left him some bare bone possessions in the kitchen—a fridge, a microwave, an oven. But she had taken his dishwasher and his tumble dryer, both of which he had purchased at her bequest. In the living room, she had taken the Playstation, bought as a birthday present because she obsessed over a single game. She had taken the artwork on the walls, which she had insisted they buy because the artist was local and "going places." She even took the home theater system, which he had spent his savings on after she lost her job and complained that she had nothing to do around the house all day.

All of that had been a lie. At the height of their problems, Sandra had left her laptop open and Max had logged into her emails thinking they were his. He discovered that the local artist was indeed going places, he was going to Cawley's house every time he was at work to fuck his wife. The home theater system, Cawley reasoned, had actually been a gift to both of them, background music for his wife and her lover as she resorted to the old-fashioned way of trying to get pregnant.

Cawley sat on the sofa and drank. He had no TV to watch, no music to listen to, and as the day darkened outside, he couldn't even muster the energy to close the curtains and turn on the light. So he sat, he drank, and he stared at one of the few items that she had left: a picture of he and Sandra.

He had been too humiliated to tell her about the affair, too embarrassed to even approach the subject. He had taken two weeks off work, knowing that if he was in his home then those cheating bastards wouldn't be. He learned about key loggers and tracking software and used it to hack her accounts and monitor her activity. For two weeks, he watched as they grew increasingly desperate, listened as she tried to make excuses to get him out of the house, and grew sick to his stomach as they sent erotic pictures to each other. One night he drank too much and decided to tell her, but when he stormed into the bedroom to find her asleep, looking peaceful, innocent, and as sweet as she did the day they met; he couldn't do it.

He used his anger to send emails in Sandra's name, telling her bit-on-the-side that it was over, she didn't love him, and his art was shit. He retaliated just as Cawley had hoped and, after he deleted all evidence of his involvement, that retaliation, and the veracity at which it occurred, was the only evidence left.

Cawley had found himself in limbo. He didn't want to tell her what he knew, even as her anger grew, and she began to take things out on him. He didn't want to end the relationship either, but at the same time he didn't really want it to continue. He slept in the spare room and she had tried to put the moves on him a few times, but every time he saw her naked, he thought of the pictures she had sent to her boyfriend, and every time he felt her lips on his, he wondered who else they had kissed. He began to passively sabotage the relationship, never quite knowing what he was doing but feeling a sense of relief nonetheless when she eventually exploded and told him that she couldn't take it anymore.

She called him cold, she called him heartless, loveless. "I need a child, I need a family, I need sex!" Sandra had screamed at him. "And you can't give me any of those things."

He got the impression that she wanted to hurt him, to know that her words and her actions were breaking him, so she pushed, and she pushed, but she never got through and he never flinched, because she had already broken him, he was already gone.

By five, when his shift would have been ending, Max had bypassed tipsy and had gone straight to full blown drunkenness. The alcohol didn't take away the fog that enveloped his mind like a shroud of melancholy; it sedated him, subdued him, expanded on his depressive state but took away his ability to care.

The bourbon, now half-full, swished around in the bottle as he scooped it roughly from the floor. He stared at the liquid through the glass, watched it through blurry eyes as it sloshed lazily around the inside of the bottle. He hated drinking when he was younger, couldn't see the benefit in drinking to forget or socialize—especially when too much alcohol typically created the most forward, obnoxious, and disgusting human beings that society had to offer. As he aged, he realized there was more to it; it was about cutting through the monotony of life, about finding a mental state different from the norm, especially when the norm was driving you around the bend.

It was why people took drugs, something that he didn't object to. He didn't appreciate the way certain substances could destroy the lives of individuals and families, but there was no harm in trying to break from the bullshit of the day-to-day existence. If he trusted his body a little more and if they were legal, he wouldn't object to using them himself.

He poured himself another large measure, struggling to concentrate on the neck of the bottle as the dark liquid gushed out. It tasted disgusting, it was cheap and nasty, the appearance of burnt molasses with the taste of burnt rubber. He didn't care; it did the job. He would suffer for it tomorrow, but tomorrow was an eternity away.

His mobile phone had asked for his attention since he had arrived home, buzzing in his pocket like a trapped insect. He checked it, chortled softly to himself when he saw that he had twenty missed calls and a number of text messages and voicemails, and then dropped it onto the chair where it would eventually lodge itself down the back of the cushions.

He continued to drink and to stare at his empty house as the darkness enveloped him.

* * *

The sound of the doorbell woke him. He had drifted into a dreamless void of sleep, a drooling, empty state of rest. His body jolted when he woke, his feet kicked out, knocked over the glass of bourbon on the floor.

He coughed, cleared his throat of the sticky mucus that had set up residence in his mouth like some slimy plague. He smacked his lips opened and closed; it tasted like he'd spent the last few hours licking his own asshole. He was still drunk, could feel the fading bliss of alcohol coating his nerves, but the buzz was fading and a headache was creeping in. He also felt cold, hungry, and—

The doorbell sounded again. He grumbled, climbed steadily to his feet, wiped his mouth with the back of his sleeve, and checked the clock. It was nearly nine. He guessed that he'd been asleep for a few hours, but he couldn't remember drifting off. He hadn't been watching television, hadn't looked at the clock, hadn't been doing anything that may have given him a notion of time. He'd just sat, drank and then, apparently, slept.

He stuck his head through the curtains and groaned when he saw the agitated, irritable feet of Abigail Simpson shuffling on his doorstep. He thought about ignoring her; she was probably looking for some money, some booze, or for forgiveness for her blatant stupidity in quitting her job, but there was nothing Cawley could do about that.

The doorbell sounded again, and again, a persistent, incessant ringing that threatened to tear Cawley's head open.

"Hold on!" he shouted angrily, "I'm coming."

He stuttered to the door, turning lights on and squinting through the resulting glare. He opened the door, nodded questionably at his former partner. "Abi, what the fuck do you want?"

Abigail looked desperate. She wasn't drunk, not that Cawley could tell anyway, but she looked gaunt and pale.

"I need a favor."

"Of course you do," Cawley grumbled. "Why else would you be here?" He didn't realize he'd said that aloud until he had, but he didn't care. He didn't have to hide his contempt from Simpson; she already knew how he felt.

"I have no place to go," Simpson said. "I need a place to stay, just for—"

"You have a house," Cawley interrupted. "What happened to that?"

Simpson looked around irritably, ran a hand through her hair, the dirty-blonde locks looked matted, lifeless, and clasped her hands together in front of her. "I haven't paid the rent for a few months, they kicked me out."

"Why?" Cawley wanted to know. "You were paid up before you pissed off."

Simpson sighed, lowered her weary head to her chest. "I blew it all," she said, physically deflating, her voice ushered timidly into his chest.

"That's a lot of fucking booze," Cawley noted.

"Not on that. Listen, can I at least come in, just for a bit?"

They stared at each other, waiting to see who would break

first. Cawley stepped aside, grumbling under his breath as his former partner, and former friend, stepped inside his house.

"I would offer you a drink," Max said after gesturing for Simpson to sit down. "But I'm not sure that's wise." He realized how hypocritical he sounded, and how hypocritical he probably looked with the spilled glass on the floor and the half-empty bottle beside it.

"I'm fine, thanks, although a cup of coffee—"

Cawley sat down, pretending he hadn't heard.

"I'm fine," Simpson repeated.

"So, what's the problem? Did they increase the tax on cheap cider?"

Simpson groaned, a whispering sound that vibrated out of her closed lips. "There's no need to be like that."

"Like what?" he asked with a shrug, feigning obliviousness.

"I'm sorry for what I did, leaving you in the lurch like that, but this didn't really have anything to do with you," Simpson declared, getting heated. "It was *my* job, *my* life, *my* decision. You have no right—"

"If you're trying to beg for a place to stay, you're going about it all wrong."

Simpson left a scowl with her old friend. She coughed, cleared her throat, and then turned away, staring absently at the window, watching a reflection of the room in the glass. "I lost control. It wasn't just the drink. I was using drugs, as well, lots of them. Nothing heavy, just prescription stuff, my own at first, then, when the doctor wouldn't refill my prescriptions . . ." she trailed off, received a knowing nod from Cawley. "Then the gambling started. I wasn't really into it. It didn't give me a buzz or anything, nothing like you hear from all these gambling addicts. I got nothing from it, but it helped to pass the time, keep my mind on other things."

Simpson shifted uncomfortably on the sofa. She leaned forward, clasped her hands together, and rested them on her knees before staring at her twiddling thumbs. "I lost everything. Got into a lot of debt. Legal stuff at first, then the banks stopped giving me money. I went to a few loan sharks. . . ." She sighed heavily.

"You're a fucking copper," Cawley said, unable to hide the disgust. "Or you *were*. You've seen what those bastards do to people who don't pay, even to the ones who *do*."

"I know, I know," Simpson said with a furious nod. "But I was desperate. I needed the money to pay the bills—"

"And to gamble?"

"And that," she nodded. "Yes. They started asking for their money back, getting violent. I had nothing to give them, kept using the fact that I was a copper to keep them away from me, but they stopped caring. My rent money, what little I earned, went to them. Then," she shrugged, "I had no more to give. I kept them off my back for a while, but the bills were piling up; the rent was unpaid."

"And you thought it would be a wise to quit your job?" Cawley asked, bewildered. "Your only source of income? Where's the fucking sense in that?"

"I told you, quitting had nothing to do with this. I've wanted to quit for a while, if anything these problems delayed it."

Cawley wasn't convinced. He stared at his former partner, watched her absent eyes, then asked, "You still owe them money?"

Simpson nodded. "But it doesn't matter," she added. "It's not much, not like it was. They won't bother me for a while." She gave Cawley a pleading look. Cawley could see the signs of impending tears in the corners of her eyes. "I need your help, mate. I know what I did and I'm sorry, but I have nowhere else to go. I have no home, no family, no friends. I haven't even eaten for two days. Please, I need your help."

Cawley held her stare for an interminable time. He wanted her to think he was thinking it over, that there was a chance, a good chance, he was going to say no and kick her back onto the street. A selfish part of him, the part that had been hurt by her resignation and the abolishment of their partnership and friendship, wanted her to suffer. But the truth was he had no intention of kicking her out. She was one of the few people he trusted, the only person he considered a friend, perhaps the one person in his life that he actually cared for. He was angry, but he wasn't about to destroy one of the only good things he had going.

"You can stay," he said eventually, feeling the relief that gushed from Simpson's pitiful soul.

13

"Ilike it, don't get me wrong," Pandora said, watching the emptiness outside her window, unable to shake off the creepy feeling that the old man would sneak into view again. "But something about it doesn't feel right."

"You're not used to the quiet," Dexter assured her. "That's all it is."

"Really?" she didn't look convinced. "What about—" She stopped herself. She hadn't told him about getting lost. She trusted him, and she knew that he would believe her, he always did, but she thought that would somehow make it worse. She hadn't tried to rationalize it in her head because she didn't think she could. She was worried that if she went down that rabbit hole then the only solution would be a blackout, a relapse— a moment of madness brought on by stress, fear, paranoia. She couldn't deal with that. "—What about the people?" she finished.

Dexter gave her a gentle and dismissive shrug, his eyes on his phone. He barely knew how to use it, but he knew when it was working and when it wasn't, and now Pandora had seen that it was struggling to find a signal.

"Even the friendly ones seem a bit . . ." Pandora rolled her eyes, shrugged her shoulders. "Weird."

Dexter looked up. "I think we need to make allowances," he told her. "It doesn't matter how weird it gets, these people don't know who we are, they are hiding us, and we're safe."

Pandora met his eyes. "Has something happened to you here?" she asked.

"What do you mean?"

"I don't know. You've been a bit off since you came back here from our walk."

He shook his head, but Pandora sensed that he was hesitant. "No, everything's good." He returned his eyes to his phone and then added, "Why, did you hear something?"

"Hear? No. But—" she sighed deeply. "I met a guy by the river."

Dexter looked up. "Oh?"

"He was nice at first. Friendly. A bit like Dorothy, but then he turned."

"Turned?"

She nodded.

"How?" he wondered.

"I'm not sure exactly," she said with a twisted face. "I mean, he wasn't mean or anything, just a little *off.*"

"Off?"

"Yeah."

"Was that it? He was *off*?"

Pandora nodded.

"Hm." Dexter held her gaze, lowered his eyes to the phone again. "He probably just hasn't seen many beautiful young women before. And it's a small town, he probably isn't used to new people, especially ones that look like you. Trust me, if you had suddenly shown up in the little town I grew up in, I would have been *off* as well."

Pandora smiled. "Maybe."

"Definitely. You're a rare find, Pandora. I know you hate me saying this—"

"I do, because it's cringe."

"—But I'm going to say it anyway. You're an amazing person, and you do strange things to even the strongest men." He learned across, kissed her on the lips. "I love you."

She smiled, her fears immediately abating. "I love you too."

"There's probably nothing to worry about. We should just try to enjoy ourselves. We've been holed up in abandoned buildings and shitty B&Bs for years. All those nights that we spent eating takeout pizza in the dark, pretending we were dining in fancy restaurants; the nights we spent drinking on the beach, pretending we were on holiday. Remember what you said to me when we robbed that building society in that beautiful little village and ended up hiding in that old couple's backyard?"

"I said that this is the sort of place we should be vacationing in."

"The sort of place where we should be eating fish and chips by the seaside, playing a few arcades, going to a meal. But instead we were ankle deep in mud hiding in an old couple's rock garden." He shrugged. "It's the life we chose, now we owe it to ourselves to choose something different."

"You mean, that's it? No more?"

He reached for her hand, held it tightly. "If I gave you the option of continuing, even after everything that went wrong, or saying no more, settling down and enjoying ourselves, what would you prefer?"

"Settling down, any day."

"Then let's do it. We have more than enough money stashed away. We can wait for things to blow over, get out of town, and then start a new life somewhere else."

Pandora beamed brightly. All her worries faded away as she looked into Dexter's eyes. "Perfect," she said.

"In the meantime . . ." He looked around, gestured to his surroundings. "We can treat this as the honeymoon we never had."

He pulled her hand to his mouth, kissed her there, on the lips, on the forehead, and then pulled back. He picked up his phone, "Now, if only I could get this bloody thing to work."

He tapped a few buttons, turned the phone off and on, and then walked around the room. To the window, to the door. "I can't seem to find a signal," he said eventually.

Pandora shrugged, "Gotta be something."

"Dorothy did say there was no reception."

"Here," Pandora took the phone from his hand, sure he was just doing it wrong. She had bought it for his birthday, replacing a plastic brick so old that the keypad may as well have been in Morse code. He was reluctant to use it at first, but she had persuaded him, only to receive random calls and blank text messages from him for the next few weeks.

She fiddled with it for a while, her eyebrows arching into a frown as she concentrated. She shook it, held it up. "No signal," she said.

Dexter groaned.

She giggled. "Who do you plan on calling anyway?"

He shrugged casually. "No one. I was just going to browse the web."

She shook her head, her mouth agape. "Browse the web?" she parroted. "Where did you pick that one up?"

"What do you mean?"

"Two weeks ago, you referred to it as the 'inter web,' without the slightest grain of irony. A few months ago, you were still calling it 'the email.'"

"I'm learning."

"You're an embarrassment," she said with a grin. "It's a good thing I love you so much." She gave him a kiss on the cheek, tossed the phone onto the bed. "I'll get mine from the car. I think the charger is in the back."

* * *

101

The day was turning orange as the sun dipped and the brightness muted. Pandora walked through the open door of the bed and breakfast and greeted it with a smile, sucking in a deep and enjoyable breath. It really was far from what she was used to, far from what she thought her ideal place would be, but Fairwood was beautiful. It didn't feel right, it didn't feel normal, but Dexter was right, it was just what they needed.

She was happy to write off her fears as inexperience stemming from her mistrust of small-town life. She had spent her life in the suburbs, where gossip was fueled by curtain twitching, and where troubled young girls like Pandora could become the topic of countless conversations over coffee and hushed words over fences. Dexter had informed her that small-town life was essentially the same, only more intrusive and on a grander scale. His stories were to blame for her hatred of small towns, but she was happy to reserve judgement on its people considering he had once been one of them.

She stood in the open doorway for a while, admiring her surroundings. The street ahead was silent and bare, the houses opposite—a pair of stone-built semi's set against picturesque gardens of summer grandeur—seemed unoccupied. There was no activity through the windows, no one lounging in the garden, hoping to soak up what little sunshine remained. Down the road, beyond a sharp turn that preceded the track down to the river, she could see the brim of the sun as it lowered into a mass of trees—its fading light streaking through like a grated fireplace.

The trees to the left—a blockade that marked the end of the cul-de-sac—drank the last drops of natural light and prepared to wallow in the bath of the half dozen fluorescents on the road ahead.

Her eyes were on the distance as she walked, admiring the view as the streetlights popped on, lightly coloring the graying town with synthetic life. It wasn't until she crossed the empty road, walked the empty path, that she noticed their car wasn't where they left it.

She stood motionless for a while, concern on her face as she tried to remember where they parked. She recalled their arrival into the town, she remembered the old man sitting on the path, remembered spotting the bed and breakfast and then—

She put her hands on her hips. She was definitely standing where they'd parked the car. She shook her head, offered one last glance to the day, the beauty of which had been dimmed by worry, and then hastened back into the building.

"Did you go out today?" she asked when she returned to the room. She knew it was a stupid question; Dexter *had* gone out, he had gone out with her. He hadn't taken the car, neither of them had, but the idea that it had been stolen, in a town as quiet and innocuous as Fairwood, was absurd.

Dexter replied with a look of bemusement.

"The car isn't there," she said, waiting by the doorway.

"What do you mean *'the car isn't there'*?"

"What do you think I mean? The car isn't where we left it."

He rushed out to check for himself, dubious of the claim, only to return moments later, breathless and just as confused as she was. "It's gone. I looked up and down the street, even the next street. It's nowhere, and there's something else, something I didn't notice before." He paused to catch his breath. "There are no other cars in the town."

* * *

Dexter didn't want to leave Fairwood, not yet. He liked the fact that they could enjoy themselves without fear of being handed over to the police. He liked the quiet and the peace. And while he wouldn't admit it to Pandora, a part of him also liked the fact that Fairwood reminded him of home. Not the farm, the labor, and everything he had gone through with his family, but the good part of home, even if it remained only as an intangible feeling and to an actual memory.

But he only liked it when he knew he could escape it. Without the car, he was trapped.

Dexter and Pandora took one last look outside, just in case they had overlooked a garage or driveway at the back of the building, and then they returned, looking for Dorothy.

They found the jolly proprietor pottering about the kitchen, her bountiful face ablaze with heat and sweat. She gave them a warm smile when she saw them, a smile that quickly faded when she noticed how agitated they were.

"What's wrong, dearies?"

"I think our car's been stolen."

She looked confused for a moment. She gave a gentle shake of her head. "That's not possible. This is Fairwood."

"What's that supposed to mean?" Dexter asked, unable to hide the frustration in his voice.

"We parked across the road," Pandora cut in, the previous glimmer on her face now a hashed assortment of worry and panic. "It isn't there."

"Are you sure?" Dorothy asked.

"Of course we're sure," Dexter said abruptly. "It's not there, it's been stolen."

"Stolen, dear?" Dorothy didn't seem nearly as agitated as Dexter was. "I don't think so."

"You don't think so? Are you serious? It's been stolen. It was there, now it's gone."

She still didn't look convinced. He felt himself getting wound up, and he opted for a ploy to try to get her riled up, kick her into action. "We need to phone the police," he said, feeling Pandora's eyes burning a hole into the back of his head as he did so.

He looked around, a gesture that suggested she should tell him where the phone was. She followed his eyes, not uttering a word.

"Where is it?" he wanted to know.

"*It*, dear?"

"The phone."

She wiped her hands on her apron, leaving a dusting of flour on the blue and white material. She ran the back of her hand over her forehead. "Oh, would you look at that," she said, inspecting the sweat on her hand. "I'm sweating like a pig."

Dexter watched her, waited for a response. The kitchen was a clutter; a mess of pots simmered away on the stove; juice from diced meat sat on one chopping board, remnants of vegetable peel on another. The air was thick and humid; it stuck to Dexter's flustered skin as he studied the calmly bemused old lady.

"Well?" Dexter said eventually.

"Yes, dear?"

He groaned, felt his back teeth grind together in an instinctive act of annoyance. "The phone, where is it?"

He had no intention of using it, he wasn't dumb enough to involve the police, but the longer the merry bed-and-breakfast owner frustrated him with her indifferent incompetence, the more he felt like doing it just to piss her off.

She beamed a wide, happy smile. "We don't have one, dear."

"What?"

She continued to smile. She gave him a gentle, dismissive shrug. "No need for one really."

"But this is a business."

Again she shrugged, turning her head away momentarily to study one of the pots as it prepared to boil over. "Well, it's more of a home really. Like I already told you, we don't get many visitors here."

Dexter opened and closed his mouth, shook away the anger that threatened to envelop him. He didn't want to be annoyed with the woman—he liked her, she possessed an unshakeable glee that he found charming and touching—but in the heat of the kitchen, under the strain of losing his car, his patience was fading.

He turned on his heel and walked out of the kitchen, pulling Pandora with him into the cooling breeze of the living room.

"Where are you going?" Dorothy asked, skipping behind them, her red and smiling face gleaming at them from the kitchen doorway. "Dinner is ready soon."

Dexter paused, studied her momentarily. He realized that her smiling delight, what he took to be a happy outlook on the world, was something else entirely. She wasn't fazed by the theft of one of her customers' cars right outside her house, wasn't moved by their anger or frustration.

"I'm going to see your neighbors," Dexter told her.

"Why would you do that?"

"One of them must know what happened."

"I doubt it, dear."

"Then one of them must have a phone. I'll call the police, bring them here. Let them sort it out," he stated, hoping that the show of intimidation would flap the unflappable woman.

She shook her head, put her hands into the kangaroo pouch of her apron, and offered him a meek and almost apologetic smile. "I wouldn't count on it."

"What do you mean?"

"This is Fairwood, dear," she said, as if that was all that was needed.

"What the hell is that supposed to mean?" Dexter snapped. He felt Pandora's arm on his elbow, trying to usher him away.

Dorothy didn't seem daunted. "No one has a phone around here," she explained.

"How can that be?"

She shrugged. "We don't have need of those things."

Pandora stepped forward, piped up, "What if you need to get in touch with someone?"

"Someone?"

"Someone outside of Fairwood."

Again Dorothy looked bemused. "Why would we want to do that, dear?"

Pandora and Dexter exchanged a glance in the resulting silence, both of them stumped. There were plenty of reasons they could give, dozens they could think of, but what they couldn't contemplate was how a community, how anyone in the twenty-first century, could survive without acknowledging the world beyond their village.

"Dinner will be ready soon," Dorothy said, breaking the silence and beaming another wide smile. "Then we can all go to the quiz, right?" She looked at both of them in turn. They studied her face, her smile, her words, then they nodded. Speechless.

Satisfied, Dorothy returned to the steamy kitchen, leaving Dexter and Pandora swapping creased and bewildered expressions in the living room.

14

"So, what, we're just going to sit here and pretend it never happened?"

Dexter shrugged.

"Are you serious?" Pandora practically squealed with disbelief. She thrust her hands to her hips, loomed over her partner sitting on the edge of the bed.

"What else are we going to do?" Dexter asked, shooting her a sincere expression.

"It's not just the car, Dexter," she hissed. "Don't forget, we have our money in there. We have a fucking *gun* in there," she said, looking to the door and hushing her words.

Dexter nodded.

"It's all gone, just like that," Pandora said distantly. "Every last penny."

They hadn't stolen much; everything in the earlier heists had been blown almost instantly: new phones, new clothes, drink. They spent like they might not see the next day, because they weren't convinced they would. After a few robberies, after their faces had started to appear all over the country, they retreated into the seclusion of themselves. The final heist was the biggest one, the only one worthy of any true fortune, but after shooting and killing the guard, they had left with less than they'd planned. The accumulation of those final robberies still amounted to a lot of money—enough to set them both up for life, should they ever find a way away from their own infamy—and all of that money was stored in the trunk of their car.

Fairwood didn't seem like the home of criminals, of teenagers bent on breaking into cars to steal what they could, or of more upmarket criminals willing to steal the car itself. They couldn't be sure that any bed-and-breakfast staff wouldn't rifle through their belongings, discovering their fortune and their identities, so they'd left it all in the car. It felt like the right thing to do at the time; if not for the theft of their car, it still would.

"We'll get it back," Dexter said. "We have enough on us to get by." He pulled a wallet out of his back pocket and flashed a few notes. "And no one knows us here, that's what's important."

Pandora shook her head, ran a trembling hand through her hair. She looked to the window, her eyes peering through the graying day and the silky screen of fog that rose like a sea of cigar smoke to greet the emerging evening.

They still had each other, still had their freedom, that was what mattered most of all; she knew that and she appreciated that, but she couldn't help but feel that everything they had done, everything they had gone through—all the misery they had caused—was all for nothing if they didn't have a penny to show for it. As much as she wanted to escape this life of theirs, as much as she wanted to go clean and live a normal existence, she couldn't bear the idea that nothing they had done—the years of running and hiding, the murder—mattered.

A veil of melancholy hung over Pandora. Dexter put his arm around her, held her close.

"We'll get it back," he repeated with more confidence. "Don't worry."

He stood, stretched out his fingers to grasp and toy with

strands of her hair. He tilted her head sideways, resting it against his own. "We'll go to this trivia or quiz thing tonight, see if we can do some investigating. We'll find out who took the car, don't worry."

"You sure it was someone from Fairwood?" Pandora asked.

"Yes. They make a big deal about others coming here, so it doesn't seem rational that someone can pop in unseen and unannounced just to steal our car. Something's amiss here; something's not right, and tonight we'll find out what that is."

15

The radiance of Fairwood had dimmed. Pandora treated the sights of the stone buildings, cobbled paths, green gardens, and silent streets with a burgeoning contempt as they made their way to the pub.

They saw a few people on the way, exchanged glances with some, a smile with one, nothing with most. They were determined to find out more about the town, discover the secret to this quiet village where no one drove and no one had access to the simplest of technologies.

"Maybe we stepped into the past," Pandora said quietly. They had left the bed and breakfast a few minutes earlier, had walked arm in arm on a path that wound through the town's populated center—although *populated* didn't seem apt for such a quiet segment of nowhere. The only person to smile at them was a young boy; he had stood in an open doorway of one of the houses and flashed Pandora the widest, friendliest smile she'd seen in a long time before he scarpered back into the house with a playful air. It was nice to see that, although lacking in amenities, Fairwood still had its share of friendly, playful children.

"Maybe that's why they don't have phones or cars," Pandora continued on her wandering trek through the absurd.

"Yet they didn't say anything when we pulled up in

something that could have been an alien spacecraft as far as they were concerned."

"Hmm," Pandora mused playfully. "Good point."

The Gentle Giant pub sat at the end of a short street. It was a red brick building set into a graveled garden that was flanked with a neatly manicured layer of grass. Two oak-finished picnic benches, complete with wide-brimmed parasols, sat either side of the open double doors. They were both surprised to hear the overflow of conversation and music coming from inside the pub, the first semblance of noise pollution they'd encountered since their arrival.

They exchanged a glance, equally impressed and worried by the sound of a room full of patrons enjoying themselves.

"Are we sure this is a good idea?" Pandora said, slowing her steps as they approached a wooden gate that opened onto the graveled surroundings of the pub. "It's not too late to go back."

"And what, stay in our room until everyone forgets our faces?" Dexter shook his head, wrapped his arm around her. "Come on, Pan, since when were you the shy one?"

She laughed softly, tried to brush off her worries.

She thought she heard the commotion decrease as Dexter led her through the open gate, their feet crunching on the stark white gravel. The voices seemed to soften, the music lower, as they approached the pub. She gave Dexter a concerned glance, but he wasn't looking at her. He didn't seem as concerned, obviously didn't feel a chill creep up his spine like she did; didn't feel the sense of unease that gnawed at the back of her mind.

They crossed the threshold of the pub, entered into the darkened, lively interior, and ushered in a silence that forced Pandora to halt. Dexter stopped by her side, sensing her resistance.

The music still played—a soft rock song from the early seventies that Pandora recognized only in a bastardized form from a commercial—but the conversations ceased. Through the doorway, the room opened up, with rows of tables on either side and a large bar ahead. Some people were standing at the bar, others loitered between it, the rest occupied the half dozen tables. None of them spoke.

Pandora looked to Dexter, a desperate pleading look, a look that suggested their time had come, their game was up; they had been recognized and there was nothing they could do. The scene played out like a spaghetti western, after the arrival of the outlaws and the sudden deathly silence, the conversations and the noise returned with a simultaneous, deafening chatter.

Pandora mouthed, "What the fuck was that?" to Dexter, who gave her an innocent shrug.

She knew she was just being paranoid, but when she walked to the bar, she felt like everyone was watching her. She tried to take Dexter's lead; he didn't look deterred in the slightest and flashed the bartender—a pale, sickly looking man in his thirties—a wide smile.

"What're you drinking?" Dexter asked her.

She shrugged, inspected the drinks on offer, the shelves of spirits, wine, and tonics. "Jack," she said, nodding to the bottle of Jack Daniels.

She looked around the pub, caught a few stares, people who diverted their gazes when she caught them looking. She searched for familiar faces and saw the old man by the river sitting in the corner, thirstily drinking a pint of beer. A woman, probably his wife, sat opposite, talking at him—she didn't seem to be looking at him, wasn't concerned if he was even paying attention to her. After taking a long drink of his beer he looked up, saw Pandora looking at him. She felt her heart jump, felt the need to turn away, but her anxieties eased when he gave her a beaming smile, nodding to his nattering wife with raised eyebrows and a gesture that said, *This is the reason I need to get away.* Pandora smiled back and felt a little more at ease.

Dexter ordered the drinks, leaned an elbow on the bar as he waited for the bartender to serve him.

"That's better," he said, obviously taking note of Pandora's smile. She watched him turn to the bartender "So, when does this quiz start?"

The bartender held Dexter's stare sternly, then he softened his features with a smile, glanced at a clock on the wall behind him, and answered: "A couple of hours."

Dexter nodded, looked around the packed pub. Pandora had spotted Dorothy sitting in the corner with a few others. She thought she recognized one of them as the strange old man they'd encountered on their arrival in town. The creepy individual who had greeted them with ambiguous silence was now chatting heartily with Dorothy.

"Is this place always this full?" Dexter asked.

The bartender regarded him seriously for a moment, switching to a smile before replying. "It is tonight."

Dexter nodded, and they both waited for an explanation and then shrugged it off when one didn't come. The bartender clearly wasn't comfortable talking to customers; he was probably new or didn't like outsiders. Either way, they each offered him a pleasant smile as Dexter paid for his drinks and then they scouted for a table.

They spotted a small empty table at the far end of the pub, nestled at the back of the smoky room between two elderly couples—duplicate pairs that sat in silence, tables apart, decades of domestic indifference behind them, a night of drinking to forget their misery ahead.

Dexter gestured to Pandora and they shuffled over, through the smoky throng; the air thick with heat and body odor; the clammy touch of wayward hands and imposing shoulders. Pandora stopped when she heard Dexter's name, looked over to see the brimming face of Dorothy glaring at him, gesturing him over.

He paused, frowned. Her heart kicked at her ribcage at his sudden reaction.

"Something's wrong," he said, looking horrified.

Pandora stopped abruptly, the smile quickly fading from her face. "What, what is it?"

He nodded to Dorothy just as she shouted on him again. "She knows my name."

"And?"

"I didn't tell her," he said, looking at Pandora with the expression of someone who was preparing to drop the glasses in their hands and bolt for the door.

She grinned, gave Dorothy a little wave. "I told her," she said softly. "Come on, let's go sit with her."

"You told her our real names?" he asked as they made their way over, watching as Dorothy spoke to her friends—introducing the newcomers and making room for them.

"I don't see why not."

"I already told her fake names."

Pandora shrugged indifferently, brushing past a smiling man cradling three pints of beer, the frothy liquid precarious on the rim of the glasses as he slalomed his way through. "It was a mistake, but she didn't seem to care."

"What if they put two and two together?"

"You mean what if they don't recognize our faces from, well, *everywhere*, but recognize our first names?"

Dexter frowned.

Pandora grinned, "Come on, you paranoid git. Relax, let's have fun."

Pandora recognized the man sitting next to Dorothy, the same man she had seen from her window looking out over the backyard, the one who had been watching her. She regarded him warily but was pleased to see that his vacant expression had been switched with a pleasant smile. He nodded softly to her as her eyes crossed his, a friendly greeting.

"This is my husband," Dorothy said as Dexter and Pandora shifted in among the group. She opened her palm out, gestured to the others. "This is Matthew and Barbara," she pointed to a middle-aged couple who regarded the newcomers shyly, the man using his pint to wave a greeting; the woman grinning a toothy smile. "This is Adam, Steve, and Susan," he said, pointing to three older people who each offered more enthusiastic greetings.

"So," Dexter said after the introductions and small talk, rubbing his hands together. "Are you guys ready for the quiz?"

They all looked at each other, then turned toward Dexter and nodded almost simultaneously.

"This should be a good one," Dorothy added with cryptic delight. "It's a big one; a *special* one."

"Really?"

She nodded, offering little else. She drained the wine in her glass, stared mournfully at the residue that clung to the moist glass and then stood. "Who wants another drink?"

A chorus of affirmation rose from the group. Dexter and Pandora both held their hands over their glasses, shook their heads. "We've just started," Dexter said.

"Ah, don't worry," Dorothy declared, waving her hand dismissively "You've got a lot of catching up to do. What'll I get you?"

They drank fast, and when they finished one round, their drinks were topped up. It seemed everyone at the table was willing to buy them drinks. Dexter tried buying a few rounds of his own, but, much to his delight, they refused.

After an hour, Dexter and Pandora were well on their way to tipsy. Through their alcohol-tinted spectacles, Fairwood seemed like the perfect, idealistic town it had appeared when they first entered. Friendly locals came to the table to introduce themselves, seemingly delighted to meet the couple. Dorothy was glad to do the introductions as Dexter and Pandora acquainted themselves with the inhabitants of the town.

After a long and awkward introduction to a simple-looking man in his twenties—acne covering his greasy face, a cow-like strand of hair threatening to poke his leering eyes and a swagger that suggested an exaggerated case of rickets—Dexter asked the man what he did for a living. He received a long, confused smile in reply before the simpleton waddled away to join a group of like-minded youths by the bar.

"He's a strange one," Dorothy said, noting Dexter's baffled expression.

Pandora watched as Dexter nodded, knowing he was thankful that Dorothy had said it and he didn't have to lie his way around the fact.

"He's quiet," she pushed. "He's not very good around people."

Pandora smiled sympathetically, thinking that the strange youth probably had a dungeon or two full of people he could practice his social skills on.

"So, what does he do?" Dexter asked Dorothy.

"*Do*, dear?"

Dexter gave her a stern stare, and Pandora wondered if she was going to force his questions down the same surreal route as she had taken earlier. "For a job," he reiterated plainly. "Does he work?"

She smiled, as did the others at the table who'd heard—everyone excluding Dorothy's husband who, for the last ten minutes, had sat at the end of the table looking forlornly out into the abyss of the smoky pub.

"No one works in Fairwood, dear," she said after a while.

"No one?"

She shook her head.

"But this can't be a cheap place to live . . ." He paused to study each of their faces in turn. "Are you all on benefits?" he wondered, obviously thinking his question absurd when it left his lips.

They laughed, thinking the same.

"How do you get by?" Pandora asked.

Dorothy shrugged, suggesting they *got by* with so much ease that she didn't give it much thought. "We exchange what we need."

"Like a barter system?"

"I suppose so."

"But what about you? You work at the B&B."

"I prefer to think of it as my home, and my customers as my guests."

Pandora nodded slowly. It was absurd, and Dorothy was clearly just an old woman who wanted to sound modest and welcoming. Although, she wished they were just guests as they no longer had any money to pay her. They hadn't settled the bill when they arrived and, now that they had lost their money, she doubted they would be able to settle when they left.

"What about the bartender, the shopkeeper—"

"They serve the community, dear. They're our friends; they're Fairwood's friends."

Dexter took a long and slow drink, caught Pandora grinning wryly at him out of the corner of his eye.

Pandora hoped he understood that she didn't want him to take it any further, didn't want him to question the show of camaraderie and community Dorothy was putting on for her friends in the presence of her guests. She watched him drain his drink, put the empty glass beside the full one that someone—whose name she hadn't retained before they gave them the drinks, greeted them, and then returned to their seat—had bought him moments before.

"So," Pandora chirped, directing attention toward herself as she scoured the pub, even more full than when they arrived. "What's so special about this quiz?"

"There's nothing really all that special about it," Dorothy said. "It's just a way for us all to get together. Plus," she said with a lowered voice. "There's a prize at the end."

"Oh," Pandora chimed with exaggerated excitement. "What sort of prize?"

Dorothy winked, touched her nose.

"Oh," Pandora put on a hurt, puppy dog expression. "It's like that, is it?"

Dorothy laughed, a loud and joyous laugh. She patted Pandora on the shoulder. "I like you dear," she said. "You're a catch." She looked at Dexter, a stern expression on her bubbly face. "You be good to this one, eh?" she warned.

Dexter held up his hands innocently.

"You're lucky to have her," she warned again.

"I am," he said, smiling at Pandora. "I know it, don't worry."

16

The quiz went on for a couple of hours. Dexter and Pandora participated as much as they could, but they were plied with so much alcohol throughout that they could barely understand the questions by the end, let alone answer them.

It was competitive, more so than they'd imagined. At the end of each round, the papers were passed around to be marked by the team on the next table while the bartender shouted the answers. There were a number of complaints and bickering over misspelled or shortened answers.

The players only went to the bar at the end of each category, when the bartender paused to serve a few rounds. Dorothy and her friends bought drinks for Dexter and Pandora throughout the night, topping them up before they'd even finished. At one point, they both had two full drinks bought for them while they were still nursing a third. The drink helped to settle their nerves, and they felt they were being accepted into the community; everyone in the pub was conversing with them. They greeted them with friendly smiles or small talk when they went to the bar or toilet, and they smiled and acknowledged them while they were sitting with Dorothy and her friends.

They were being welcomed, and the more they drank, the

more welcomed they felt. They were both at ease, comfortable, and enjoying themselves.

By the end of the quiz, when the papers were collected and the scores were tallied, Dexter and Pandora were beyond tipsy. They were slurring their words; she nearly tripped over the back of the chair on her way to the toilet; he lost half of his drink down his top when he missed his mouth. The others seemed to be drinking and reveling too, though, so they didn't mind their drunkenness.

The music returned after the quiz, the voice of the bartender replaced by the heavy tones of classic rock.

The conversation was less joyous, less friendly than it had been before. Tension hung heavily over the group and spread its way around the room, seeping through the sedated pulse of intoxication that coursed through their bodies.

Dorothy's husband, Eric, bought them more drinks, topping them up just as they drained their glasses.

"You're slacking," Dexter nodded with a joking slur. He received a half-assed smile before Eric scuttled out of his seat and headed to the bar. Dexter watched him converse with the bartender briefly and then turn his attention to a suddenly despondent Dorothy.

"The depressing effects don't usually take effect until much later on in the night," he noted.

She raised her head, gave him a confused half-smile. He gestured toward her glass; she had been drinking gin and tonic but had barely sipped a drop from the one that had been in front of her for the last hour.

She completed the smile and then looked away.

"Eddie and Marie won," Eric said when he returned to the table, putting the drinks down with a disinterested thump.

Dorothy didn't raise her head. She sighed heavily. "It should have been us," she said bitterly.

Pandora grinned. "Maybe next time, Dotty," she slurred.

Dorothy turned to face her; the smile was gone from her ruby face. She didn't say anything, just stared then turned away. "Come on," she said to her friends. "Let's go."

"You're leaving?" Dexter asked, preparing to stand. "So soon?"

Dorothy and her friends barely even regarded Dexter or Pandora. They stood, put on their jackets, collected their belongings and walked to the bar, talking to the bartender. They all turned back to look at the drunken couple briefly; Dexter and Pandora smiled at them, but it wasn't returned.

"You think we offended them?" Dexter slurred.

Pandora giggled. "Do we care?"

Dexter shook his head, laughed. They were far too drunk to care, far too drunk to stop themselves from falling into a fit of uncontrollable and pointless laughter.

They didn't hear the music stop, but when they opened their eyes, awoke to the sudden dimming of the light around them, they stopped laughing immediately. Everyone in the bar was standing over them. No one was smiling anymore; no one was ready to offer any greetings or small talk.

"What's the matter?" Dexter asked, halting his laugh with a stifled hiccup.

The bartender, standing at the center of the mass, answered: "They've come to collect their prize."

Disappointed faces stared on; two eager faces flickered. Dexter swallowed thickly, looked toward Pandora, who was returning the stare of one of the flickering, lustful faces. She looked worried, seemed suddenly sober.

"What's the prize?" he asked.

The lusting man turned his eyes from Dexter to Pandora and then back again. "You," he said with a grin.

He grabbed her roughly, first by the arm—his thick fingers sinking into the soft flesh above her elbow—until she resisted, at which point he grasped a clump of her hair and tugged until she relented.

Dexter tried to intervene, but his reactions were slowed by the alcohol and the others stopped him before he could pry Pandora's hair away from the eager hand. They piled on him, he felt their grasping hands on his body, forcing him back, keeping him pressured. He struggled to breathe in the gathering throng of bodies that piled on top of him, struggled to resist as they hauled him upward and began to drag him across the floor, his legs kicking out behind him.

He heard Pandora screaming, heard her orally assaulting her tormentor and then trying to reason with him, but he couldn't see her. He thought he caught a flash of her golden hair at one point, seen through the thick wall of pulsating, grasping bodies, but it could have been anything.

He clawed at his attackers, at the wall of flesh, at himself, at the hard floor beneath him. He was like a child throwing a tantrum, forcing every muscle into any action he could muster. He picked up something from the floor; it was small and hard with a little pin attached. He attempted to stab someone with it before setting himself to hurl it at them. He stopped when he brought it in front of his face, when he saw what it was. It was Pandora's brooch, the little bronze butterfly given to her by her grandmother, a piece of jewelry that was second nature to whatever outfit she wore, even though it didn't go with anything.

He lost his fight at that point; he was too tired, too drunk. He gripped the butterfly tight in his hand and prayed that she would be okay. The noise became almost unbearable, heard over the sound of his own pounding anger, his own rushed breath and Pandora's tormented cries. They were all yelling, spitting violent obscenities and chants, eager for their pound of flesh. He felt more hands poke through the bodies, heard screams of blood lust when they grasped at his flesh, tugging and picking at his clothes and skin. He was powerless to stop them, too inebriated and outnumbered.

* * *

Pandora was dragged ahead of Dexter as the one with the lustful eyes joined in. She swung, she fought—they grabbed at her, pulling her hair, her clothes.

She had more fight in her than Dexter, there were fewer men on her and she had things to fear that he didn't. They hadn't forced themselves on her sexually, but she had to assume that that was their intention, and she knew she had to keep fighting, to keep swinging, to stop them.

She caught one of them clean on the jaw and felt him loosen his grip. She kicked out again, catching another, reducing the number of hands that grasped at her clothes, her hair, her flesh.

She struggled loose, free of their grasp—lingering fingers on the edges of her jacket. She turned, saw the rabble of people surrounding her partner, of which she saw nothing; looked toward the exit, saw an armful of people waiting there for her, watching her next move. She turned back to her attacker, back to the exit, back to Dexter; then she felt the full force of a fist between her shoulder blades. It knocked the air and the fight out of her, threw her upper body forward; shocked her system into a dizzying coughing fit. She lunged toward the floor, stopped short of hitting it, then the fist clipped her on the back of the head and she couldn't stop herself from falling.

17

Cawley woke with the illusion of freshness, of feeling alive, devoid of the retributions from a night of drinking. That feeling subsided after he took his first few breaths and his hangover caught up with him.

The previous night, following Simpson's arrival, he had stayed awake for another hour or two in the hope he could refresh himself from his early drinking and avoid a hangover. It clearly hadn't worked. His head throbbed and pulsed, and he still felt tired despite being asleep for more than half of the last twenty-four hours. His stomach kicked and rocked, spitting a foul concoction of gastric breaths into his rancid mouth.

He lifted himself up on his elbows, wiped a thick stream of sleep from his eye, picked a dried strand of saliva from his chin. He looked across the living room. Abigail was curled up on the chair, her head tilted awkwardly to the side, her hair cascading over her face, her eyes closed; her breaths slow and steady. She was sleeping, that was a plus. Cawley had doubted whether his troubled former partner would sleep at all—she looked like she hadn't closed a fitful eye in weeks—but she was going to have an awful agony in her stiffened neck when she woke.

He had given Abigail a pillow and a spare duvet, gave her the choice between sleeping on the floor or the chair. They had a guest bedroom but that, like the bedroom Cawley once shared with his wife, had been ransacked. Cawley had nodded off on the couch, his last words to his former partner being the directions to the toilet: "The only room up there that the bitch hasn't stripped bare."

Cawley squinted at the clock, straining his eyes through the line of light that blistered through a gap in the curtains and stabbed at his brain. It was just after eight. He was due at work in less than an hour.

He groaned, cursed under his breath, and rubbed his tired eyes. He didn't feel like working at all, didn't want to face the office or the evil that resided within. He scrambled to his feet, took his mobile phone from the coffee table and carried it into the kitchen, dialing the number to the office.

A pleasant, early morning voice—a female fit for children's television—answered with a peppiness that fired bile from his stomach into his throat.

"Detective Cawley," he told her in an almost incoherent grumble. "I won't be coming into the office today. Something's come up."

"May I ask what?" she wondered.

He peeked into the living room. Abigail was still sound asleep.

My former partner, my former friend, is asleep on my sofa and has nowhere else to go; my wife is a malicious bitch who is trying to strip me of everything I own just because she once slept in it, sat on it, touched it, looked at it, or fucked a local tramp on it; and my boss is the devil incarnate and will rip me a new asshole when she finds out what I did. That's what he wanted to tell her, that's what pressed against his tired, aching brain, desperate to find a release.

What he actually said was, "Personal problems."

She didn't seem satisfied. After all, what middle-aged detective *didn't* have personal problems. She'd heard it all before and had probably heard it dismissed as a worthless excuse from her superiors, but she didn't make the decisions, *they* did, and by the time she relayed the information to them, Cawley would be asleep, comatose, or nursing a cup of coffee and waiting for some painkillers to kick in. He could deal with the retributions when he returned to work, whenever that was.

He hung up, turned the phone off, and dropped it into his pocket. He splashed some water on his face and took a swig of milk from the fridge before heading back to the couch, back to his slumber.

Simpson opened her eyes when Cawley returned, alerted by his presence. When she saw him she lifted her head, quickly jolting back in pain when the strained muscle in her neck revolted.

"Sleep well?" Cawley asked sarcastically as Simpson moaned and rubbed the offending muscle, her neck cricked to one side.

She mumbled a reply.

"What time did you drift off?" Cawley wondered.

Simpson looked at the clock. "Just after you, I think."

Cawley suspected that wasn't true. He had been drunk, but he was still alive and walking, which meant he didn't drink a full bottle of bourbon by himself. He was a lightweight. He knew his limits, and a full bottle was well beyond those. The empty bottle of bourbon by the chair meant that Simpson had knocked it back after he had fallen asleep, but Cawley saw the guilt in her eyes, he saw the way she looked at the empty bottle. He wasn't going to rub it in.

He picked up the bottle and took it to the kitchen, not mentioning the disappearing contents. He flipped on the kettle, dropped the bottle in the bin. "Tea, coffee?" he shouted over the sound of a boiling kettle.

"Coffee. Strong. Black."

Cawley made the drinks, the notion of returning to sleep now gone. He swallowed a couple of painkillers with the scalding liquid of a sweet and milky cup of tea and then stared at Simpson, who sucked in the heat from her steaming cup of coffee.

"So, any plans on going back to work?" he asked.

Simpson gave him a bemused look, not sure if he was joking or setting up another round of insults. She shook her head, took a sip from the hot liquid, and cringed. Too hot, Cawley assumed.

"You going to try something else?" Cawley wondered. "Learn a trade maybe, or—"

"Don't do this," Simpson interjected.

"Do what?" Cawley asked, playing innocent.

"You know what. *This*," she gestured with a raise of her eyebrows. "Don't make it all about the job. Let's not talk about that."

"We were partners for—"

"That doesn't matter," Simpson cut in again. "It's over now, no matter what you say. I know I upset you—"

"*Upset* me?"

"*Annoyed* you then."

"That's more like it."

Simpson nodded. "But I've left now," she continued, "and I'm not going back."

Cawley nodded slowly, looked down at his cup, then at the floor; his hands; the television; back at Simpson. "So what else do we talk about?" he wanted to know. "Television, the news . . . do you like football?"

Simpson glared at him momentarily, and then shook her head. "Where's your toilet?" she asked.

Cawley pointed a finger toward the stairs. "Like I said, the only room up there that Sandra hasn't stripped."

Simpson nodded, stood, held the pained muscle in her neck and strained her rigid body. "How are things with you and the wife?"

"*Ex*-wife."

Simpson nodded.

"She's an evil witch," Cawley said simply, sinking back into the couch.

"You two used to be so sweet together."

"Did we?"

"Not really." Simpson laughed. "You don't have much luck with women, do you mate?"

"Maybe if they didn't insist on screwing me over."

"That's life, Max. If you're not the one breaking hearts, then you're the one having your heart broken. That's why I keep my relationships short, sweet, and mostly sexual."

"Maybe that's why your life is empty and you're a drug addict?"

Simpson gave it some thought. "You're probably right. Maybe we're all doomed. Tell you what, if we're both sad and lonely in ten years, let's get married. Do all that conventional white wedding bullshit that you straight people like so much. I'll even wear a dress."

Max laughed, nearly choking as a dry wad of saliva wedged itself in his throat. "So we can be miserable together instead of on our own?" he croaked.

Simpson nodded. "Isn't that what marriage is all about?" She winked, stretched. "Anyway, I need a piss. Let's just hope that wife of yours didn't nick the toilet when we were asleep."

18

Cawley grinned when he heard the jangling sound of a key rattling in his front door. Simpson looked across at him curiously as Max flung himself from the couch with the glee of a child preparing to answer the door to his friend. He rubbed his hands together, gave Simpson a wide-eyed glance, and then headed for the door, which opened just as he approached.

"Hello, dear," he said placidly.

Sandra nearly jumped out of her skin. She held a hand to her chest, took a step backward. *"Ohmygod,"* she gasped in one breath.

"Surprise you, did I?" Cawley asked, unable to hide the enjoyment on his face. He stepped forward, peeked over her shoulder, toward the empty driveway and street beyond. "Is your beloved brother not with you today? Shame, I rather enjoy his company."

"What are you doing here?" Sandra asked sharply, the shyness of the previous meeting gone now that there was no one there to take pity on her.

"Me?" Cawley feigned confusion. "What am I doing here, in my own house?" He shook his head slowly, keeping his gaze locked in hers the whole time. *"How dare I?"*

"You should be at work," Sandra hissed, pointing an accusing finger at him.

Cawley pointed right back at her. "*You* should get the fuck away from my house."

"*Our* hou—"

"Don't start your shit," he cut in. "The house is in my name."

Sandra seemed taken aback. She looked around, flicked her eyes from the floor, to the door, and then to Cawley again. "I came for my stuff."

"*Your* stuff?"

She nodded firmly.

He shrugged. "I have a loaf of bread left in the kitchen. Do you want that?"

She frowned at him, twisted her mouth into a grimace. "Don't you get snarky with me."

"I'll do what the fuck I like," Cawley said, retaining his calm, enjoying himself. "This is my house." He slapped the keys out of her hand and held them before her like a dangled carrot. "And *my* keys. Now, I suggest you get the fuck out before I arrest you for breaking and entering."

She opened her mouth to reply but words failed her. She set her face into attack mode—the expression of a rabid dog—prepared to stare him down while she thought of a response. Cawley slammed the door in her face before she uttered a word.

"Buh-bye now!" he yelled through the glass.

He heard her grumble, groan. Could almost sense the sound of her grinding teeth. He grinned to himself, knowing that his ex-wife would now take her anger out on her brother or her father, or better yet, on her new boyfriend who wouldn't know what hit him when his girlfriend turned into a savage, heartless bitch.

He rubbed his hands together, stretched, and gave a satisfying yawn as he watched Sandra's silhouette turn and waddle away.

The perfect start to a less than perfect day.

19

He remembered the cold, the chill that crept through his bones and split his nerves with its freezing touch. He remembered the darkness: so deep, so strong, so empty. He remembered the smell: mold and damp, a cloying stench that threatened to clog his nostrils with its insidious must. He didn't remember much after that.

When Dexter next pried open his eyes, peeling apart a sticky seam of sleep that had sealed his matted eyelashes to his eyelids, he was in a dark room that reverberated with the hollow echoes of his pained breaths. He could see his own breath in front of his face, expelled from his dry and bloodied mouth in a thin, misty vapor.

He wiped the back of his hand over his forehead, scanned his hand and wrist for signs of blood. There were none, yet his head throbbed with an unbearable agony. He poked and prodded around the base of his skull, gritted his teeth, and hissed a breath of belligerence when his probing found the source of his pain. At some point someone had hit him, beaten him into submission, and then thrown him into the room. The pain in his head—partly caused by his alcohol consumption, mostly attributed to his wound—and the dried blood on his fingertips were testament to that, but he couldn't remember any of it.

He remembered being inside the room. He hadn't been able to see at the time, hadn't registered anything of its surroundings, but he had picked up on the smell and the sense of isolation. There were no windows, no portal to the outside, so he couldn't tell if it was night or day, if it had been minutes or hours since his abduction. He was no longer under the sedative effects of the alcohol, so he assumed that at least half a day had passed.

He was alone in the room. A rusted stanchion rose out of the cold concrete in front of him, impaling the dusty ceiling above. He couldn't move. His left leg had been shackled to the stanchion with a thick chain attached to a tight clasp that dug into his ankle and scarred a welt of red flesh.

He drank in more of the room, blinking away a blur that had cornered his vision upon waking. He was in a basement, no bigger than a dozen square feet. It didn't look used, was barely maintained. Dust littered the walls and ceilings in dirty gray veils. A thick pipe protruding from the wall was so dense with rust that it looked like it had been wrapped in a sheet of corrugated iron. There was a sink in the far corner, but the ceramic bowl had chipped and split. Even from his seated position, on the other side of the room, Dexter could see that the mangled, grimy basin would barely be able to sustain the water that he doubted still dripped from the rusted tap above. At the top right of the room, he saw the beginnings of a staircase, the rest of which was blocked by a partition wall that had been veiled with the same sheets of gunmetal decrepitude as the others.

He tried to think back to the abduction. He remembered the grinning faces and the grasping hands. He remembered Pandora's cries and how much he wanted to—tried to—get to her. He was alone, cold, and in pain; he was hungover, injured, anxious, and vulnerable, yet he knew that wherever Pandora was, wherever they had taken her, she was suffering a lot more than he was. That made him feel a hell of a lot worse.

* * *

The grinning man smelled like her grandfather used to smell. It was a stench of strong whiskey, old clothes, and a dated, overpowering cologne that she imagined was sold in rickety old shops alongside unfiltered cigarettes and cure-all tinctures. As much as he smelled like her grandfather, he didn't look like him. Her grandfather didn't have narrow eyes that looked like he was constantly trying to squint away an offending light; didn't have this crude smile, the way one corner of his lip curled upward.

Her grandfather had a raspy voice, the result of a lifetime of smoking and heavy drinking. As a child, she'd always thought it gave him a distinguished quality, adding a smoky intelligence to his voice that his mind didn't possess. He was a good man, a kind man, but not a smart man. This man, the one who had groped her, leered at her—the same one who had abducted her and dragged her here—spoke with a slimy, greasy texture. She hadn't been able to see him most of the time, but she imagined him grinning lustfully when she heard him speak, imagined him licking his lips or reaching for his crotch.

She couldn't remember much of the night. She remembered being struck from behind, but after that it was a chaotic blur. She had been half-dragged half-carried out of the pub. She had a partial memory of staring at the stars with her arms and legs stretched out and held at either end, her backside bouncing and grazing the cold concrete beneath her. She remembered being inside a house. It was warm, homely, safe. She felt safe momentarily, as if waking up from a horrid nightmare, but then she'd seen his face again and the nightmare continued.

Since then she had either been asleep or unconscious because now it was morning. She was lying on a bed, she could feel the soft mattress and padded duvet underneath her, pressing gently against the wounds caused by the grazing concrete.

She had been blindfolded, but she could see the thick orange of day bleeding in through the black material.

He stood over her for an indeterminable time. At first, she hadn't known he was there. She had been listening to the silence, trying to figure out what had happened, but then she moved and he commented, greeting her with a sickly, "Good morning." She jumped at the sound, startled to hear his breath—his greasy, slimy breath—so close to her ear.

She didn't know what he wanted to do, didn't know what he had planned for her. There were two of them, him and his wife, they'd both dragged her there, she was sure of that, but she doubted that the wife would play any part. She was *his* prize . . . his *toy*.

20

Cawley needed to get out of his house. The bare building was depressing him. It wasn't well looked after anymore. Not only had Sandra done most of the cleaning, but what little Cawley had done he no longer had the time, or the patience, for.

During the first few weeks, he had made sure he found time to clean. He felt like he was getting one over on Sandra by washing the dishes, vacuuming, and dusting, but then he'd lost his enthusiasm. The dishes piled up for days on end, the dirt and dried food became so much a part of the pans and plates that many had to be thrown away, no amount of scrubbing or washing could save them. His house was so thick with dust that the few pieces of remaining furniture appeared to be topped with carpet fragments. Any spills onto the floor were simply covered with a tea-towel or a napkin, as if the limited absorbent qualities of the materials would make the stain disappear. The house was not only sparsely furnished; it was cold, damp, and dark: an inhospitable squalor.

He went to the park. The sun was shining and there wasn't a cloud in the sky. The children were still at school and most people were at work, so he had the day to himself, save for a handful of dog walkers, joggers, and bleary-eyed alcoholics, of which Abigail Simpson was one. His former partner had decided to join him; she hadn't asked, hadn't offered to keep him company or even inquired if Cawley minded her presence, she just followed him out the door.

"Lovely day, isn't it?" Simpson asked as they entered the park. A cold, unseasonal breeze washed over them, disappearing as quickly as it appeared. Cawley scolded his friend, blaming her for it. She was cursed.

"Sure," Cawley answered without conviction.

"It must be sixty-five, seventy degrees out," Simpson noted, shielding her eyes to peer into the sky.

Cawley looked up as well, expecting the skies to cloud over. When they didn't, he returned his gaze to his friend. "You look very perky today," he said in an accusing tone.

Simpson looked at him with wounded timidity. "Is that such a bad thing?"

Cawley shook his head. "Not bad. Just suspicious."

Simpson shook her head disapprovingly. She sat down on a bench overlooking a slightly overgrown field, strewn with spots of scattered flowers and weeds. Three youngsters still in their school uniforms—ties loosened around their necks, shirts hanging out—kicked a football about. They regarded Simpson and Cawley carefully at first, then continued playing.

"I never skipped a single day of school, you know that?" Simpson said absently.

Cawley stayed standing, pondering flashing his badge to the truant teens to scare the shit out of them. He looked down at Simpson, creased his brow. He contemplated making a cruel observation, noting the oddity of a woman who never played truant once in her schooldays yet didn't think twice about missing dozens of days at work before eventually leaving altogether. He stopped himself when he realized he had also skipped work today and didn't have a valid reason. He skipped work because he hated his job, hated his life. Wasn't that why Simpson had skipped all those days in the past? Wasn't that why she eventually quit?

Cawley swallowed thickly, wary of the realization. "Me neither," he said eventually. "I was a goody-two shoes at school. A teacher's pet."

Simpson looked astonished. "You?"

Cawley laughed softly. "Yep."

"Bullshit."

"It's true. I was always the first kid to raise his hand, the first to offer to read aloud."

"*Fuck me*," Simpson said, stifling a laugh. "So what happened?"

Cawley shrugged. "Life." He sat down next to his friend, looked at the youngsters playing football then at a young woman power-walking on the path behind. He sighed, a long and tiresome sigh that served to pad the silence.

"So, what's with the positivity then?" Cawley asked eventually, noting that Simpson was still grinning as she studied her sun-drenched surroundings.

"I'm not allowed to be positive?"

"Oh, you're *allowed*, I've just never seen it in you before."

"Never?"

Cawley tilted his head introspectively from side to side, "In the beginning maybe."

Simpson nodded, turned towards her friend, a smile still on her face. "You know, I never saw *you* in the beginning. I wasn't around in those days. I would have loved to see you."

"You didn't miss much."

Simpson disagreed with a shake of her head. "They said you were super fit, super confident, the life of the party."

Cawley nodded approvingly.

"They said that you loved the job and everyone loved *you*."

Again Cawley nodded.

Simpson paused and seemed to study Cawley's face momentarily. "So, what the hell happened?"

Cawley glared at his friend.

"You know what I mean."

Cawley shrugged, turned away again. He didn't want to go over it with Simpson. They weren't too dissimilar, but he didn't want her to know that.

When he didn't answer, Simpson changed the subject, trying his best to avoid the silence. "How are things with work? Has it fallen apart in the two days I've been gone?"

Cawley sighed. "Same old, same old."

"Clarissa?"

"Still a bitch."

"How are things with Bleak and Bright?"

"Going nowhere. Probably not even in the country anymore."

"You sure?"

Cawley shrugged. "They were celebrities, stars. But the public are turning against them now."

"You not heard the latest on Twitter?"

Cawley stared blankly at his former partner and Simpson sighed. "Look who I'm asking," she said. "You only discovered mobile phones three weeks ago."

"I know what Twitter is," Cawley said. "I just don't use it."

"Yeah, sure," Simpson grinned. "Anyway, most of their fans are still on their side. They're either saying it's a conspiracy to turn them against the bandits, or they're resorting to destroying the reputation of the guy they killed, saying he was a psychopath who deserved it."

"He had a child. That's sick."

"Welcome to the internet. The good news is that the young girl's suicide has turned many against them, but most are still on their side. Hashtag 'Support Bleak and Bright' and all that bollocks."

Cawley shook his head. "What is the world coming to?" He sighed. "Anyway, as I said, they will probably be long gone by now."

Simpson turned on the seat, wrapping her arm around the back, lifting her leg under her, her full attention on Cawley. "You see, I don't think so," she said, offering her own theory. "I was thinking about it last night. If I was them, if my face was everywhere, I'd *never* try to leave the country."

"It's the sensible thing to do."

"Exactly, so it's what everyone will be expecting. Everyone's on full alert, all airports and train stations are being monitored. Hell, they've already arrested half a dozen people just because they sorta looked like them. What chance would the real bandits stand of going unnoticed?"

"So, what, you think they're still in the country?"

Simpson nodded. "Maybe even in the local area."

Cawley gave a slow nod of his head. "The thought had occurred to me."

"But?" Simpson said.

"But I have nothing to go on. If they still were hanging around, waiting for the dust to settle, then it would be a matter of time before they had to resurface. They would need to eat, drink . . ." He shrugged. "There's been nothing yet. Nothing concrete anyway."

"There must be something to go on."

Cawley paused to study his friend's face. He wasn't supposed to discuss the case with anyone, but he doubted it mattered. Simpson was still a detective at heart, she knew what she was talking about, knew enough about the job to offer some insight. Cawley also felt good talking to her about it.

"Nothing," he submitted. "I've been running after crazies. There's a shit-ton of them phoning up saying they've seen the bandits. You know what it's like, they all want their fifteen minutes, they all want to fuck us over. Then you get the ones who try their best to help, drag us halfway across the county just to tell us they saw someone who *may* have looked like one of the criminals, only he was older, shorter, and possibly a dog." He shook his head, a smile creeping onto his face. "We even had Bat-shit Barnes on the phone."

Simpson looked amused; a mental image of her, and all of her previous exploits, was all it took. "What'd she say?" she wondered. "Have the spirits been talking to her again? Or was it the toaster this time?"

Cawley laughed soundlessly. "She said she saw them up at Rosie's Point. Said she walks her dogs up there."

Simpson didn't laugh. "And?"

Cawley looked perplexed. "That's it," he explained. "I left after that. I couldn't take the smell, or the bullshit, any longer. God knows what cock-and-bull nonsense she would have come up with. Probably that she saw them paragliding on unicycles, or—"

"So you think she was lying?" Simpson asked, looking confused.

"Of course she was, she's insane. Why would she expect me to believe that she walks for nearly an hour, bypassing count-less fields on the way, just to give her nonexistent dogs some extra grass to piss on?"

"She *does* go to Rosie's Point."

"What?"

Simpson nodded sternly, locking Cawley's gaze in hers. "I had a friend who lived near there. I used to see her out there all the time walking her dogs."

Cawley looked stumped, his mouth agape. "You're shitting me?"

Simpson slowly shook her head. "I think you better go and see Barnes again."

21

Dexter picked at the welt around his ankle. The red skin wrapped around the edges of the shackle like a macabre frame, the skin underneath pressed tight against the bone. The sharp pain and the mundane activity took his mind off other things, things he couldn't bear to think about.

A noise interrupted him. A hollow echo of distant, approaching feet. He'd heard a number of heavy footfalls over what he assumed to be the last few hours. The noises came from above, some soft, some heavy. These were different, though, louder, closer.

He heard a floorboard creak, heard a hissed breath of frustration. He looked toward the bottom of the staircase, the source of the noise. Another footfall; another creak on old wood; another displacement of antique dust. A cough: soft, polite, gentle.

His heart pounded in his chest, a forceful mixture of trepidation and anger.

The legs came into view first: naked, chubby calves; short, thick thighs. A pair of sandals through which poked ten dumpy digits that curled in on themselves, the nails coated with faint traces of cracked, red varnish.

They halted on the second to last step and shifted their feet awkwardly, the shape of their short sandals marking an imprint in the dust. They hesitated; he could hear them taking heavy breaths. Then they turned around, headed back up the stairs. He stared at the bottom stairs as he listened to the woman creak her way back to the top and gently swing the door closed behind her.

His heart settled in his chest. He returned his hands to his ankle, his fingertips shaking violently as he plucked and rubbed the flesh. Eventually he gave up, throwing his hand violently in a gesture of disgust and despair. He leaned back, rested on the cold, unforgiving concrete floor, and stared upward.

The dust on the ceiling unsettled as soft footfalls on the floor above worked their way across the room, paused at the far end and then walked back to the center where they settled with one heavy thump.

Dexter closed his eyes and tried not to think about Pandora, but he couldn't stop the images of her from flooding his mind.

*　*　*

She needed to use the toilet. Her bladder was full, and she had been struggling to hold it in for so long that her entire body ached from the effort. She was waiting for the moment when the sweaty perverted man tried to rape her; she was saving it for him, if not to discourage him then just to piss him off and win herself a small victory. But she couldn't hold it any longer.

She didn't want to wet herself when he wasn't there. She didn't want to lie in a pool of her own quickly drying urine, didn't want to have to suffer the stench and the discomfort of the liquid waste from a night of drinking soaking into her clothes and into the bed.

She thought she was alone as she writhed and twisted uncomfortably on the bed. She had heard the man leave a while ago, had listened to his footfalls fading as they distanced themselves from where she lay. She thought she had been asleep since then, she remembered seeing Dexter, remembered being somewhere else. She had been dreaming, something unpleasant, something violent and chaotic—she remembered screams and shouts and sweat and blood—but nothing to do with the people currently holding her hostage. She had to have fallen asleep at some point, and if she was asleep then she wouldn't have been able to hear him returning to the room to leer at her again.

She felt the presence of someone else in the room long before they approached her. She thought it was him again and cringed at the image of his face ogling her as she twisted in discomfort. Then she heard a female voice, soft and reassuring.

"Are you okay?" it asked.

She hadn't really seen the woman. She briefly remembered her from the pub, had a few glimpses of her in her tormented memory, but those glimpses had been overrun by the images of her sadistic husband.

"I'm going to take away your gag," the voice explained in a pleasant tone. "Don't scream."

Pandora stopped writhing, letting the elderly abductor know that she would cooperate. She felt her small, fragile hands on her face, felt the wrinkled tip of her fingers as they brushed her mouth and peeled the gag from between her lips.

Pandora breathed in deeply, as if sucking in oxygen for the first time in a long time. She gasped, rasped, and then licked her dry and cracked lips, running her slightly moist tongue over the cuts and welts.

She felt the old woman back away. She smelled like soap, unscented and sterile. Her breath lingered near Pandora, she caught the stink of morning coffee and milk; sweet, soured, and musty.

"What's wrong?" the old woman asked.

"I need the toilet," Pandora said, surprised at her voice, which no longer sounded like her own.

There was a pause as the woman weighed this up. "One or two?" she asked eventually.

"One," Pandora said, suddenly dreading the thought of ever plumping for the second option.

"I'll get you a pot."

Pandora shook her head violently, her closed eyes pleading with the woman through the blackened veil of the blindfold. "Please," she said. "Let me have some dignity."

There was another pause, then the woman relented. "Okay," she said softly. "But don't try anything."

"I won't. I promise."

Pandora flinched when her wizened hands rested upon the bare flesh of her stomach. Until then she didn't realize that her skin was exposed, that her blouse had been torn so heavily that the majority of her torso showed. The old woman moved her hands slowly toward Pandora's arm.

"I'm going to help you up," she said, taking her hand and tugging gently.

"I need to see where I'm going," Pandora pleaded. "Please. Take my blindfold off."

"I can't do that."

"Why?"

She was silent.

"Please. I won't look at you."

"That's not my problem."

"Then what is?"

Another pause. Her hands were still on Pandora's elbow, seemed to be pushing more into her flesh by the second. Pandora thought she had the old woman where she wanted her, thought she could appeal to her human side just as she could appeal to her female side, but her next words quickly diminished any hope.

"Do you want to take a piss or not?" she spat bitterly.

Pandora choked on her words. Felt the pressure of her fingertips digging dangerously into her arm. "Okay."

She dragged her upright, the caring tone in her voice now completely gone. She helped her to her feet. Pandora felt woozy, struggled to remain standing. She moved toward the old woman for balance and support but the woman moved away, keeping Pandora at arm's length while her hand clenched her elbow tightly.

She managed to remain standing and staggered behind the woman as she led her to a nearby bathroom, probably an en suite.

"I can do this myself," Pandora said hopefully, as she felt the touch of tiled floor beneath her feet and the ceramic of the toilet with her outstretched hand.

"No, you can't," the old woman insisted. "Take your pants off."

"Please, let me do it myself."

"Take your pants off," she repeated, sternly.

She had briefly hoped to use the opportunity to attempt escape, to take advantage of the woman's fragile nature and compassionate tendencies, but this no longer seemed like the same woman and the shock and fear had thrown Pandora on a different course. With a trembling hand, she removed her knickers, suddenly realizing that her skirt had been torn free as she felt the thin underwear slide freely down her naked legs.

She felt the woman's arm brush past her, felt her lift up the toilet seat, and felt the pressure applied to her arm as the old woman tried to usher her downward.

"Sit."

Pandora remained standing. She was scared and felt ashamed. But that shame and fear combined to create an angst that she knew she needed to use as soon as she felt it rising. She lashed out, quickly throwing a fist at where she assumed the woman was.

She felt her hand connect with flesh and bone; felt the punch follow through as the target toppled; heard the screams of surprise and anguish as the connection was made. She quickly kicked off her underwear, freeing herself from the threaded shackles, before launching a few kicks in the direction of the fallen woman. She connected with the hard ceramic of the toilet bowl, felt her toes crunch and twist under the impact. She ignored the pain and continued to kick until she landed a few heavy thumps into the mound of flesh that lay on the bathroom floor.

She was breathless and in pain and she still needed to use the toilet, but she had won; she had beaten her kidnapper. The blindfold was tied tightly behind her head, and she tried prying it free but couldn't. She toyed with the knot, snatching and pulling at it until it came free and the rag slipped from her eyes.

A surge of adrenaline cut through her like a drug. She could see the crumpled woman lying on the floor at her feet, a twisted scowl on her bruising face as she looked up at Pandora and struggled to regain her breath and composure. She glared at the woman, spat at her and then turned toward the doorway, ready to run away, to escape the clutches of the perverted pair, to find Dexter and to get out of Fairwood.

The husband was standing in the doorway. His arms folded across his chest, an appreciative sneer on his face. She knew, from one look into his sadistic eyes, that he had been watching the whole time. He had been giving his wife directions; he wanted to see Pandora suffer, wanted to see her humiliated.

He lowered his arms, balled his fists, and moved quickly toward her. She tried to fight, tried to struggle, but he was stronger than her and, when his wife managed to drag herself from the floor to help him, she was outnumbered.

She wet herself in the struggle, giving him the humiliation that he sought. They both laughed, snickered like school children, as they dragged her back to the bed and tied her up without drying her dripping legs or returning her underwear.

22

This time the dogs yapped when he knocked on the door. The sound pleased Cawley, reassured him that he was on the right track. Although, judging from his previous experience with Bat-shit Barnes and her catalog of crazy, he wouldn't be surprised to open the door to find her on her all fours yapping away like a rabid primate.

He shifted his feet impatiently as he waited. He had left Simpson at his house. He asked her if she wanted to come along, promised her it would be a case she could sink her teeth into, one that would recollect the big, exciting cases they had in the past—the drug busts, the fugitives, exciting cases that were now wedged too sparsely between all the misery and the paperwork—but Simpson refused, seemed to prefer the solitude of Cawley's house.

Barnes left the door on the chain as she opened it, dipping her prominent Neanderthal brow to shield her gray eyes from the afternoon sun.

"You again," she said, more a statement than a question. "What do you want?"

"I'm here about the bandits. I need your help."

She frowned, closed the door and unhooked the chain. She opened it fully, stood in the doorway and looked him up and down suspiciously. "I already told you—"

"But now I'm listening." The words had been formed and spoken before he had a chance to stop himself. He deflated, cursed under his breath. She looked annoyed.

"How dare you?"

"I'm sorry, that's not what I meant."

"Then what did you mean?"

He held her inquisitive stare momentarily, then shook his head.

"I try to help you and this is the thanks I get?" She shook her head. "You should be ashamed of yourself."

He was. He was ashamed of his house, his job, his life. He thought about telling her that in a moment of exasperation, but the sound of his phone ringing in his pocket stopped him. Part of him was happy for the distraction, happy to answer it without even glancing at the screen, that part of him had, briefly, completely forgotten that the last thing he wanted to do was answer his phone.

He deflated further when he heard the sarcastic voice of his boss on the line.

"You sound a lot better."

He mouthed an expletive, held up a hand to Barnes to ask her to remain patient, which she did with her arms folded across her chest.

"I had some herbal tea, some honey, did me the world of good," he said plainly.

"Are you taking the piss, Cawley?" she spat aggressively.

He was. He didn't know why he was but he definitely was, and he wasn't stopping either.

"I wouldn't dream of it."

"Where are you?" she demanded to know. "Why aren't you here? What makes you think you can—"

"One question at a time please."

He shifted the phone away from his ear to avoid the barrage of obscenities that she screamed at him.

"Are you finished?" he asked politely when the sound of her screams had faded to a string of mumbled curses.

He heard her grumble affirmatively and then prepare another line of aggressive questioning, at which point he hung up, muted the phone, and dropped it back into his pocket. He knew he would regret it later, but he didn't care. He didn't want to deal with psychopaths anymore. He smiled at Mrs. Barnes, content to deal with the degree of crazy that didn't wander into the realms of ball-squeezing manipulation.

"Who's that?"

"That was my boss."

"Was?"

He nodded, gave a succinct and dismissive shrug. He doubted he would still have his job after that phone call, but the crazy witness currently propping up her own doorway with a food-encrusted scowl of mistrust—stinking of body odor and animal ammonia and wearing clothes fit for a fire-sale at a charity shop—didn't need to know that. Cawley still wanted to catch the bandits, not because of his job, not because of the fame that would result from their incarceration, and not even just because of the career-saving respect, but because that fame would piss off Sandra and Clarissa, who both thought of him as a washed-up nobody.

"I need your help," he said earnestly. "I know what I said, and I'm sorry; I should have listened to you first time around." He smiled as warmly as he could. "But I really do need your help."

She gave him a long and cold smile that seemed to thaw by the second. Eventually she nodded, stepped aside, and gestured for him to enter. He thanked her and held his breath before doing so.

23

Dexter dreamed he was dying. He dreamed he was being beaten into the abyss while Pandora watched, her face devoid of emotion. He knew he was dying, he knew he was breathing his last breaths, yet he cared more about Pandora's situation than his own. He didn't know what was wrong with her but he remembered her screaming, he remembered feeling helpless, angry, and agonized in one collective, emotional mass.

He was happy when he woke, happy to get away from the dream. That happiness didn't last long. He didn't know how long he had been asleep and he doubted if the sleep had been natural; he hadn't been in the mood for a siesta and was most likely suffering from slips of consciousness brought on by a lack of sustenance, lack of sleep, and the beating he had taken the night before.

He smelled food when he opened his eyes and saw a sandwich on a plate in front of him, just out of his limited reach. The bread looked stale, had a few flecks of suspect mold around the corners, and the contents—lettuce, tomato, cheese—looked well past its prime, but he was hungry. The sight of the sandwich attracted his full attention. He didn't notice the man sitting on the other side of it, his thick thighs straddling the back of a hardback chair.

"Hungry?" he asked.

Dexter growled at him, an instinctive reaction that surprised him.

"I'll take that as a yes." He pushed the plate forward with the toe of his boot. It crept along the concrete floor with a grinding sound that cut through the empty room with a deafening squall.

Dexter hobbled forward, scooting along the floor. He cautiously reached for the plate but the shackles wouldn't extend that far. He sat back down, scowled at the man in the chair.

He recognized him from the pub. The one who came over after the quiz, the one that had taken Pandora away. He had sinister eyes and a creepy and arrogant smile. He had a way of looking at you that suggested he was not only better than you but he owned you.

"What do you want with us?" Dexter asked.

The man gave him a casual shrug and a wayward glance into his own thoughts. "I want you to suffer," he said eventually.

"Why?"

He shrugged again, offered a gentle and almost innocent chuckle, as though the situation humored him.

"Is this about the money?" Dexter asked. "I don't have it right now, but I can take you to it," he lied. He had no idea where his car, or the money, was. For all he knew, this was the man who had taken his money.

"I don't want your money."

"There's a reward as well—"

"I don't want your fucking money," he repeated.

Dexter paused, looked him up and down quizzically. "Then what is this? Is this a game to you, to the town?"

"A game?" he seemed to weigh this up, then he shrugged and answered cryptically, "I think it's a little more than that."

"You *think*?"

He nodded.

"Where's Pandora?"

"I can't tell you that."

"If you hurt her, I'll—"

"You'll what? You'll shoot me, like you did that poor guy in the bank?"

The memory flared a furious spark in Dexter's mind. He hated himself for being a murderer, hated the creepy kidnapper for reminding him of it. "Fuck you," he snarled succinctly.

The man laughed boorishly. He stood, arched and straightened his back with a sigh.

"You're sick," Dexter said calmly.

The man regarded him out of his periphery. He shook his head, turned and left. "Eat," he said over his shoulder. "You need to keep your energy up."

"I can't reach," Dexter said as the man retreated around the partitioned wall and ascended the stairs.

He didn't answer, didn't turn around. Dexter was sure he heard him chuckle softly under his breath.

* * *

He stared at the sandwich. He was hungry, he wanted it, even though it looked as appealing and as nutritious as the plate on which it sat. The thought of food helped to take his mind off other things, but it also stirred his gastric juices, which threatened to burn through his stomach.

He knew the man had left it there to toy with him. He was a sadist and clearly got his kicks from fucking with him. How else he got his kicks, and with whom he got them, Dexter didn't want to ponder.

He smacked his chapped lips together, ran a heavy hand over them.

He heard the door at the top of the stairs open, heard the sound of slow footsteps descending. He saw the female legs again, the chubby thighs and the dusty sandals. This time they didn't stop on the second step, didn't turn around, change their mind, and leave the cold basement.

The woman was smiling; her chubby face seemed to be brimming with delight. She was carrying a plate, held out in front of her like an offering to a revered god.

"I brought you some food," she said warmly, flashing a look of pride as she showed him a freshly made baguette, bursting with a range of meat and vegetables. She couldn't have looked more motherly, with a warm smile on her ruby-cheeked face and an apron around her waist; she was the beauty to her husband's beast, the Jekyll to his Hyde. Dexter almost felt sorry for her.

She took the stale sandwich away, put it on top of the chair that her husband had sat on. She slowly handed the plate to Dexter, like a cautious child handing a piece of broken bread to the mouth of a timid animal, waiting for it to snap.

"What is this?" Dexter couldn't stop himself from asking.

"*This*, dear?"

He cringed at the word *dear*. Images of Dorothy forced themselves into his head. The high-spirited, homely woman who had led them into the arms of their kidnappers. She may not have been the one who abducted them, may not have been the only one who plotted to do so, but something told Dexter that she played a big part in it.

"You're feeding me?" he asked.

"I just want to make sure you're healthy. You need to keep your strength up."

"Why?" he wondered. "What do you plan on doing with me?" He thought of evil witches in gingerbread houses, of curious children and large ovens.

She looked offended. "I just want to make sure you're okay. You look a bit pale. You haven't eaten all day."

He nodded unsurely and reached forward, gently taking

the plate from her hand. She beamed a proud smile, straightened up, cupped her hands and placed them in front of her, staring expectantly as he prepared to take his first bite.

He was hungry, desperately so. The alcohol, the beating, and the worry had stripped his stomach, and he was desperate to fill it. He could smell the peppered meat, the mayonnaise, and the rich cheese all compacted into the warm and fresh bread. He took a big bite, then another, before long he had eaten through a quarter of the sandwich, barely pausing to breathe or chew.

She watched him the whole time, a smile of enjoyment on her face as he tucked in. He gave her a courtesy glance of appreciation at one point, even mumbled his muffled gratitude.

His dire hunger made the sandwich taste better than anything he had tasted in a long time. He tore through the warm bread, the rich cheese and mayonnaise, the roasted vegetables and the preserved meats with the savagery of someone eating his final meal. He stopped halfway through; he tasted something strange, something that didn't fit. Something pungent, almost chemical. He slowly chewed as he worked it around his mouth; the taste was faint but definitely there.

He took another bite, a big, hearty one. This time the taste was stronger and was accompanied by a bitter and burning smell. He recoiled, pulled back mid-bite. What he initially thought was a string of melted cheese sucked out of the sandwich and hung from his mouth. It was off-white, flecked with numerous colors, and spotted with various blotches from the sauces.

He lifted it from his chin, stared at it. He pulled it out of his mouth, straightened it out. The stench and the taste were overpowering now and it certainly wasn't cheese. He looked up at the grinning woman, saw a look of something less homely in her smile.

"What is it?" he asked as he studied the food-encrusted object.

"Underwear," she said simply.

He saw it then. It was a pair of knickers, small and thin with a frilly lace around the edges. Between the blotches of red sauce, he saw a large stain, caused by a liquid that had soaked the underwear and had left its mark with a jaundiced blotch.

"Your girlfriend's to be exact," she said.

He looked at her, his eyes wide with horror.

"She pissed herself this morning." She paused, a grin exploding into hysterics on her face. "Did you enjoy?"

The homely, motherly expression had completely gone from her face; she looked evil, devious. He was angry but too shocked to express it. The old woman was in hysterics, as she backed away and disappeared up the stairs, leaving Dexter alone with his tainted sandwich and an awful taste in his mouth.

24

Detective Inspector Cawley got all the information he could have hoped to get from Bat-shit Barnes, and this time he believed her. She said that she had seen the bandits at Rosie's Point. They had parked near the edge. She had been admiring the view; he had been staring intently at a map in his lap.

She said she didn't know who they were, something that would have typically roused suspicion in Cawley considering the bandits had been national news for weeks, but after he'd been inside her house, after he'd witnessed a distinct lack of televisions, computers, or any access to the outside world other than the front door, which let the stink out and the air in, he believed her.

She watched them drive away in the direction of Stubbies and after spending half an hour or so with the dogs, she walked to the bar with her dogs in tow. She had been in the pub before, often dropped by for a quick drink, and she knew the bartender. He was usually friendly with her and her dogs, she suggested that he even flirted with her a few times (this Cawley *did* find hard to believe), but this time he had stopped her at the door, wouldn't even let her inside.

She noticed that the glass in the door had been broken, she

saw blood and signs of struggle all over the entrance, but she couldn't see inside, couldn't see anyone else nearby. He ushered her away before she could question him. He even watched her leave, making sure she didn't turn around and try to enter the pub again.

"The parking lot?" Cawley had enquired.

"Empty."

"Anyone else there, any potential witnesses?"

"Witnesses? You don't believe me again?"

"Witnesses who saw the fight, not you."

"Oh. No. I just saw him."

It was late by the time Cawley left Barnes to her dogs—three scruffy things that she kept in the kitchen—and her madness. He planned on going straight to Stubbies and harassing the bartender to tell him the truth, but a phone call stopped him.

He had been counting his missed calls from Clarissa at the time—she had racked up double digits and had also left him a few voicemails and expletive-riddled texts. The call was from Simpson and she sounded drunk. No doubt she had found Cawley's stash of cheap whiskey and vodka.

"Your wife's here again," she slurred. "She looks pissed off and she brought a big ugly friend."

"But I took her key," Cawley noted.

Simpson made an apologetic noise. "That may have been my fault. I let her in. In my defense, I didn't know it was her—"

"It's okay," Cawley cut in.

He had heard the protestations of Sandra's brother, heard a drunken Simpson turn to him and shush him before saying, "I think you should get here before they rob you blind."

Cawley got there as fast as he could, driving like a madman through the traffic. He didn't need to deal with this right now; he had a solid lead on the case, he was potentially the first police officer in the country to find out where the bandits had spent some time following their robbery and murder, but again his ex-wife was sticking her head in where it didn't belong.

He was furious by the time he arrived at the house. He didn't bother to lock the car after he got out, didn't even pull the keys from the ignition. He was glowering, almost growling, as he stormed his way to the open front door and the broad back of Jonathan Meadows that blocked the path into his house.

"What the fuck is it this time, eh?" he barked.

Jonathan turned around, peering down at Cawley from his thick brow. "No need for language like that," he warned in the tone of a headmaster warning his pupils from running in the hallway.

"It's my fucking house," he spat in retaliation. "I'll fucking swear if I want to."

Sandra slipped behind her brother, using him as a blockade. "What are you doing here?" he asked her.

"I've come for my stuff."

"Again! Really?" He looked around, his arms wide open. "What the fuck else could you possible want? I have nothing left to give you. Here!" He stepped back, ripped off his coat, and threw it to the floor. "You want the clothes off my back, is that it?" He took off his shoes, kicked them across the entrance-way and into the hallway where an amused Abigail Simpson watched on with a smile on her face and a glass of what Cawley assumed was vodka and coke in her hand.

Jonathan tried to object, Sandra didn't flinch. He saw her poke her head out from behind her brother, saw the sniggering look on her face as she watched her former husband lose his mind.

Cawley stripped down to his underwear, the chill of the disappearing afternoon was strong enough to cut through his high blood pressure and flushed skin. "There!" he spat, throwing his arms and legs open, looking like a pudgy Vitruvian man. "Or is that not enough for you, eh? Do you want my dignity as well?"

Jonathan, anticipating what was coming, tried to step forward, to stop Cawley, but it was too late. Cawley ripped off his underwear and tossed them over his shoulder, onto the driveway.

In the living room, Abigail sniggered and continued to drink her vodka and coke, looking from face to face to see who would make the next move. Behind Cawley, beyond his pale, goose-pimpled buttocks, an army of neighborhood voyeurs cracked open their curtains to sneak a peek; some brazenly stood at their front doors, one, an elderly woman who lived a few doors down and had been walking her dog, stopped at the end of the driveway to get a better view.

"You're perverted," Jonathan said, his desperation to stop Cawley from undressing quickly turned into disgust.

"Fuck you!" Cawley thrust a finger at him. "This is *my* house. If I want to swear at the top of my lungs and get butt naked, I fucking will."

"Move that finger away from me before I break it off," Jonathan said, staring at the end of Cawley's accusing digit.

"How about you get the fuck out of my house before I throw you out?"

He saw a flare of anger in Jonathan Meadows's eyes, knew exactly what he had planned before he set that plan into motion. Cawley wasn't strong, he wasn't fit, and he wasn't quick. He had been in his youth, but those days were well behind him, whereas Jonathan was in the prime of his youth. What Cawley did have over the big man was experience. He knew his type, knew that big men like him used intimidation over anything else; they rarely got into fights because they rarely faced a foe who wanted to fight them.

He saw the heavy, inexperienced punch coming long before it had a chance to hit. Cawley simply ducked out of the way, reveling in the rush of air he felt above his head as the big man's fist missed its target. The missed punch threw him off balance, nearly toppled him over. When Cawley straightened up, he saw the shock in Jonathan's eyes.

He hit him. It wasn't as heavy as his missed punch had been; it wasn't as strong. But it was quick, effective, and on target. Jonathan crumbled like he was made of precariously placed paper cards. He lay at Cawley's feet, still conscious, but with no idea what had just hit him.

"Get the fuck out of my house," Cawley told his ex-wife. "And if you come back again—"

"Then what?" Sandra snapped, an edgy nervousness to her voice, not for fear of what Cawley would do—she knew he wouldn't lay a hand on her—but because he had fought back and hadn't bent over and let her fuck him, like she'd done every day since the divorce. "You'll hit me? You'll beat me?"

He shook his head calmly. "I'll arrest you."

"What?"

"This is not your house anymore, Sandra. I'm no longer a part of your life. Do you think it's acceptable behavior to bring thugs to peoples' houses so you can intimidate them and steal their stuff?" He shook his head. "I've let you off in the past, not just because of what we went through, but because I didn't really give a shit. I let you have what you wanted because you seemed to want it more than me, but now you've gone too far." He paused to prod Jonathan with his toes. Now that the anger had gone and his blood pressure had settled, he suddenly felt very exposed; he hadn't looked down but he doubted the cold air would be very flattering.

"Take your thug and piss off," he told her.

She gave him a long and angry stare, like a wolf eyeing up its prey before tearing it to pieces. Then she hung her head, kicked her brother angrily in the back, and barked at him, "Get up, you pussy! We're leaving."

Jonathan dragged himself to his feet and meekly scuttled away without a glance in Cawley's direction.

Abigail sidled up to Cawley, and they both watched the pair leave.

"Well," Abigail stated with a long sigh. "That was certainly interesting."

Cawley stared at her, looked at her glass, now nearly empty. Simpson wasn't the sort of woman who drank her spirits with coke; she liked them neat and hard. The coke was probably for Cawley's benefit, a weak attempt to hide her boozing.

"You've certainly cheered up," Cawley said.

"Like I said," Simpson said, draining the last dregs in her glass. "I feel good lately."

Cawley nodded slowly, his eyes on the empty glass. He thought about commenting, but he didn't want to drag his friend's mood down, didn't want to draw attention to something that would only serve to depress her.

"Good for you," he said. "Now, what do you say we have a drink, eh? You can join me for a little one, right?"

Simpson's eyes nearly popped out of her skull. "Sure," she was quick to say. "I mean, if it's just a little one."

Cawley grinned. "Help me find my clothes first. I think the neighbors have seen enough."

25

She hadn't eaten, hadn't drunk. She had been tied to a bed for what felt like a lifetime. The rotten stench of her own body odor and dried urine clogged her nostrils. Her hair matted to her forehead, grasped at her face like the spindly legs of a lethargic spider.

She didn't know how long it had been, but the darkness had given way to light again. She was either being tricked, like a blanket draped over a bird's cage to simulate time shifts and stimulate silence, or it was morning again and she had spent an entire day on the bed.

The man hadn't raped her yet, not that she could remember anyway. It was possible that she had fallen asleep and he had fondled or entered her. The thought sickened her and forced her dry stomach into a gagging heave. She reasoned that he would probably want to clean her up before he did anything; a part of her doubted he would get his kicks from sleeping with a woman who had bathed in her own piss and sweat, but a much larger part of her, the rational part, knew that if he got his kicks from watching her piss herself then it wasn't much of a push to suggest he preferred her dirty.

She didn't think of Dexter, didn't want to ponder what he was going through. She knew he would be suffering more than her.

He had been through a lot in his life, half of which he never talked about, but she could sense it every time he spoke of his father, his family, his upbringing. She was sure that he could take whatever torture and sadistic games they threw at him, but she knew that what he couldn't take, what would gnaw away at him like an infestation, was the uncertainty of what was happening to her. He couldn't do anything to save her, couldn't do anything to help her, didn't even know if she was dead or alive, comforted or suffering.

"Are you there?" she asked the room beyond the blindfold.

She heard a shuffle, the sound of a squirming man who hadn't expected his presence to be realized.

"What is it you want from me?" she pleaded.

"It's better if you don't know," he answered.

"Better for who?" Pandora croaked, her voice grating in her throat, which hadn't felt the lubricating touch of liquid for a long time.

He didn't answer.

"What are you going to do with me?"

She heard a soft laugh, a heavy breath she felt crawl up and down her spine. She shivered, snapped angrily against the restraints, and then quickly softened. She didn't have the strength to fight.

"If you're going to rape me, get it over with."

"You *want* me to rape you?" he asked.

She sensed the smile on his face when he asked, as if he got a kick out of the possibility of her answering affirmatively.

She thought about telling him that anything was better than being tied to the bed to wait for the inevitable, but then she pictured what that *anything* could entail and she quickly decided against it.

"Is it money you want?" she asked, pushing the images of his sweaty and desperate body out of her mind, shooing away the thoughts of him forcing his way inside her. "We have money, all the money you want—"

"Is that all that matters to you?" he asked bitterly. "*Money.* Is that it? Is that the height of existence for you?"

"Excuse me?"

"Is that why you did all of this?"

"All of *this?*"

"Robbery. Murder."

She shook her head violently from side to side, sensing the bitter hatred in his voice. "We're not murderers. It was one man and it was an accident."

He found that amusing. The sound of his laugh made her blood run cold, pricked up the hairs on the back of her neck and arms.

"An accident?" he recited, amused. "Well, that's okay then."

"Please—"

"He had a daughter, you know."

"What?"

"The man you killed. He had a daughter. Thirteen she was. An aspiring writer. Sweet little thing."

"Please," Pandora begged. "I didn't know, we didn't mean—"

"She killed herself—"

"Oh god," Pandora moaned.

"Her life, taken away, just like that." She could hear him make a tut-tut-tut noise. "Imagine what she could have become. What she could have done. And him, he was young too. But thanks to you . . ."

He trailed off, Pandora didn't need to hear anymore anyway. She tried to turn her head toward him but couldn't twist her neck more than a few inches. The muscles between her shoulder blades and at the base of her neck seemed to split with the movement.

"Who are you?" she asked, looking in his direction. "What do you want?"

She heard him stand up. She snapped her neck back to her body, tried to make herself as still and as small as she could.

She heard him advance across the room, his feet creaking on the floorboards, thumping against the thin carpet. He stopped above her; the orange light that burned through the edges of her blindfold was eclipsed by his looming shadow.

He bent down. She could feel his hot breath on her naked torso, could smell the scents of coffee, cooked breakfast, and a deep, sinful lust as he moved his head slowly over her stomach, her breasts, and then settled on her face. He leaned in close to her ear. She jerked when she felt his desperately quivering voice whisper warmly into her ear, *"What do you think I want?"*

* * *

Cawley spent the night drinking with Simpson, celebrating his victory over his ex-wife and her brother. They both drank more than a little, which, by Cawley's calculations—as Simpson had already been drinking before his arrival—meant that his former partner had knocked back enough alcohol to drown a horse. Simpson was clearly more experienced, though, as she didn't seem to be suffering the next day, when Cawley woke with a splitting headache, feeling like he needed to simultaneously vomit and defecate his internal organs.

"Feeling any better?" Simpson asked as they clambered out of the car, bracing a rush of cold air that nearly knocked them off their feet.

Cawley pressed against the wind with a grimace and nodded. His stomach still felt like it was in battle with his throat, and he wasn't sure he could hold down its contents much longer. He didn't feel better. Simpson had been in high spirits all morning and had cooked them both a fried breakfast, which Cawley regretted eating moments after swallowing the last chunk of fat-drenched bacon, when the crispy shards of meat instantly began to repeat on him.

"Still settling," he said, tapping his stomach with his fist.

Simpson grinned back, looking pleased with herself for having cooked a breakfast that was still, nearly two hours later, fighting digestion in Cawley's stomach.

Cawley regarded his friend warily as she rounded the car. He hadn't seen her so happy for a long time, couldn't remember the last time he had seen his friend smile. He knew it was all fake, of course, the smile and the happy attitude wasn't genuine, but Simpson herself didn't seem fully aware of that. She had tricked herself into believing that it was okay to hide her own misery.

"So, remind me why we're here again?" Simpson said as she glanced up at the dilapidated facade of the Stubbies pub.

The door to the building swayed gently in the breeze. A jagged piece of glass poked menacingly out from the rotting wood, catching the gun of the morning sun. As Cawley watched, a strong gust of wind sent the door clattering into its frame, where it seemed to lodge itself, as if Mother Nature was trying to keep the detectives away.

No attempt had been made to fix the door, which screamed of laziness and procrastination, but the off-white patches on the otherwise black tarmac, along with the distinct lack of broken glass and other detritus on the ground underneath the door, suggested to Cawley that someone had spent time cleaning up.

"The owner is up to something," Cawley said eventually, his eyes still on the door. "Something doesn't add up."

"But you think he definitely saw Bleak and Bright, right?"

Cawley nodded. "That's the problem. If he did, and they got away like he said, then why be so coy about it? The only thing that made sense was that he was lying, making it all up for the notoriety, but if he's telling the truth, as I'm sure he is, then what the fuck is he hiding?"

"And the door?" Simpson said, nodding toward the boarded-up bottom.

"Another piece to the puzzle. He said they smashed it up,

but he's lying. If he did it himself, why hide it? Not illegal to smash your own door, and it seems trivial to do it for the insurance. There's something he's not telling us."

Simpson nodded in agreement.

"Thanks again for coming out," Cawley said, giving his friend a meek smile. "It's good to be back on the job together."

"I'm here as a friend," Simpson reminded him. "Not a partner."

Cawley nodded. "Here for the day, gotcha," he said. "And maybe afterward I can take you to the cinema, buy you a meal or—"

Simpson glowered; Cawley grinned and nodded toward the pub. "Come on. Let's see what this guy has to say for himself."

The pub was quiet, empty but for three patrons gathered around the bar, the bartender on the other side seemingly directing them. They all turned as Cawley and Simpson entered; the newcomers gave them welcoming nods, they received confused and alerted stares in reply.

The patrons exchanged glances, swapped a stare with the bartender and then tried to disperse, breaking off into menial conversations in a vain and obvious attempt to hide the fact that they had been talking about something they shouldn't have been talking about. Cawley and Simpson recognized the situation; they had seen it on countless faces of drug dealers, trying to hide their blatant dealing in the face of the law.

He held up his badge, although they already knew who he was. "Detective Inspector Cawley," he said. He nodded toward Simpson, spoke almost instinctively and then stopped himself, "This is—"

Simpson finished for him, "Detective Inspector Simpson."

"We have some questions to ask about the other night," Cawley directed his attention to the bartender, keeping the others locked in his periphery. He rested his elbows on the bar, looked into the bartender's eyes and saw him twitch, an involuntary spasm. The bartender diverted his eyes, flicked them around the bar, and then dragged them back to Cawley, immediately looking away when he saw that Cawley hadn't even blinked.

"Again?" he asked, unable to hide the quiver in his voice.

Cawley held his eyes a moment longer. He glanced at a notepad. "Mr. Sellers, right?" he asked.

The bartender nodded.

"And these three?" Cawley wondered, gesturing to the other three.

"Nothing to do with 'em," Sellers was quick to interject. Too quick.

"Excuse me?" Cawley said, elongating every syllable.

"They don't know anything; they weren't 'ere."

Cawley hadn't been interested in the other three. He figured that the bartender was the key, but after noting their reactions when he interrupted their meeting, he became very interested. He turned to look at them. One of them had some heavy bandaging down the side of his face, a visible cut at the top of his nose and matching black eyes.

"What's your name?" he asked.

"None of your concern," the third one, the one who hadn't flinched under Cawley's stare, answered. He was younger, much younger. Cawley recognized him as the kid from the bar during his last visit, the one barely old enough to ride on the big boy attractions at the theme park, let alone old drink.

"Not you," Cawley said. "Zorro here," he gestured toward the man with the black eyes.

"I don't know nothing," the wounded man answered.

"Really?" Cawley said, looking interested.

"Really. I wasn't even here."

Cawley grinned. He could hear the bartender sigh. "You weren't?"

"No," Zorro opened his mouth to add more, then he noticed

the looks of disgust he was receiving from the others and he silenced himself.

"You weren't here, you don't know anything, and yet you clearly know what I'm here for." Cawley opened his notebook and took some notes, nothing more than a few doodles, but enough to keep the wounded man worried.

"I—I . . ."

"I told 'im," the bartender jumped in. "Of course I told 'im. I told everyone. Not every day you get some famous criminals in 'ere, is it?"

"Isn't it?" Simpson chimed, looking around. "Looks like just the sort of place they'd want to hang out."

"What's that supposed to mean?"

Simpson grinned, shrugged, and was immediately disliked by the bartender.

"So, what do you want to know?" Sellers quizzed. "I told you everything."

* * *

He hadn't slept. It was hard to sleep in the dark, cold basement, but it wasn't just because of his discomfort and his pain.

He was waiting.

He had drifted off—staring into nothingness and trying to retain focus—when he heard her descend the stairs again. The same chubby legs tapping softly on the creaking rungs, the same pudgy toes poking through dust-covered sandals.

She also wore the same smile, but now he could see through it. He knew that there lay a sadistic and devious woman behind that red, joyous face, something sinister behind her Stepford charm. He'd always said that the worst evils rested in the quietest places. Sadism and deviousness wasn't at home in the slums, the dilapidated, poverty-stricken tenements; the true evils hid behind suburban smiles and middle-class ideals. There waited the perverts, pedophiles, serial killers, and other sick individuals who wore neighborly masks for the world and exposed their secrets in the shadows.

This woman, with her checkered apron and her beaming smile, was the sickest kind. Rosemary West, Myra Hindley; the women behind the men; the women who displayed innocence to the world while mastering their husbands' sickening games behind closed doors.

This time she didn't offer him an ammonia-drenched sandwich, but she did come bearing treats. She had a tall glass in her hand, which she held in front of her. Another offering.

"I came to apologize," she said, sounding genuine. "What I did was wrong." She tilted her head to the side like a begging dog, gave him a sorrowful smile that sucked in a dimple on her cheek. "It wasn't my idea."

"Really?"

She nodded fully. "It was my husband. He's a good man but . . ." she allowed herself to trail off thoughtfully. "Anyway," she said, returning from a momentary trance. "I brought you this. I figured you must be thirsty."

She offered the glass. Dexter took it and raised it to his lips, noticing her eager stare as she watched him purse his lips and prepare for a drink. He halted before tipping the glass; she looked disappointed.

"It's good," she said. "It's freshly squeezed," she told him, adding, "orange juice," almost as an afterthought.

He looked into the frothy liquid. It certainly had some orange juice in it, but he doubted that was all it contained. It was so tainted that it didn't even smell of orange juice and had lost most of its orange color, which was probably why she'd chosen to pour it into an opaque tumbler.

"Thanks," he said with as much enthusiasm as he could. "Could you loosen my leg first?" he asked, gesturing to the aggressive red welt around his ankle. "You don't have to remove it, just loosen it. Please."

She was smiling at the glass, at his face. She turned to the leg, stared at it, then back at the orange juice, waiting for him to take a drink. "Okay," she relented. "But you drink up, you need your strength."

He nodded, smiled, pursed his lips as she took a long key from her kangaroo pouch, her eyes on him all the while.

She put the key in the lock and adjusted the shackle, staying out of range of his free foot, in case he decided to swing it at her. He watched as she readjusted the shackle, loosening its tight grip on his ankle without freeing his foot.

She turned toward him when she had finished, ready to insist he drink his juice. He lashed out. He threw the tumbler as hard as he could, aiming for her face. The base of the tumbler hit above her right eye, splintered a spider web fracture down the sides of the glass.

She toppled backward; the glass fell at her feet and shattered into deadly shards. He crawled over them, ignored the sharp pains in his shins as the glass dug into his flesh.

She saw him coming and tried to scramble away, to get out of his limited reach, but he quickened after her, fighting against the tide of the heavy shackles and his tired body. He grabbed her by the foot, tried to pull her into his radius, tasting revenge.

She kicked out like a wounded animal, aimed her free foot at his head and landed a few shots. Her sandal came off in his hand; he threw it away, clawed at her naked feet as she continued to kick. She caught him on the bridge of the nose with her heel, he felt the appendage break, heard the snap, felt an instant rush of blood pour down his face. But he didn't stop. He knew that if he let her go then he could be signing his and Pandora's death warrants.

She didn't scream but she squirmed. Dexter grabbed at her shins, her thick calves grasped so tightly that the flesh bulged out of his fingers like dough from a baking tin. He clawed further up as she struggled to get away. He worked onto her thighs, onto her groin. He was rabid, growling and spitting like a broken, desperate dog. He reached out for another handhold, grabbed a large breast. He squeezed, pulled himself further up.

She was petrified, her face a picture of horror. He looked into her eyes, reached his hands onto her throat. Then he saw the fearful orbs shift upward, looking at something, someone, above her, above him. The anger and the desperation deflated when he realized that someone was standing above them, then he felt the foot in the side of his ribs, strong enough to fracture a few of the bones and knock him off her.

He rolled over, clutching at his chest. He tried to roll further away, sensing more attacks, but the chains stopped him, forced him to stay where he was. He was kicked again and again, pummeled like a boxing bag.

Through the haze of his own fading anger and the rush of his agony, he saw the grinning faces of his abductors standing above him, both of them delighting as they kicked his beaten body. They took turns, spurred each other on, even stopped to regain their breath a few times. Eventually they left him a beaten, broken mess on the floor.

He groaned, pushed himself upward through gritted teeth. He could hear their footsteps above him. They moved on, back to their warm house, their innocent lives—the monster in the basement now reduced to a wreck.

But Dexter wasn't alone and hopeless anymore, his kidnappers had forgotten something.

He scrambled over to the broken glass. The liquid, a sickeningly pale orange juice that had been cut with some sadistic poison, probably from the woman's own body, had spilled everywhere. It seeped into Dexter's clothes as he dug through the mess of glass for the biggest, thickest shard he could find.

He was in agony, he was desperate, and he didn't have many choices left. He looked down at the shackle around his ankle. They had taken the key, pocketed it after delivering their own form of vengeance, but he still had a means of escape. He gritted his teeth, readied the shard above the welted skin on his ankle, and prepared to hack off his own foot.

26

Cawley consulted his notepad. "You said they arrived at around twelve—"

"I never said that," Sellers was quick to interject. "I said one, mebbies two."

Cawley eyed him momentarily and then nodded. The fact that he remembered his earlier story didn't prove it was real. If the lie was important enough, there was a good chance he had rehearsed it to perfection.

"Okay," he continued. "They saw the report on the television, smashed up the place, and then left?"

"That's right."

"Were you here?" he asked, quickly turning to Zorro, who stood at the bar anxiously nursing a pint of cider.

The bartender answered for him, "No, he wasn't 'ere," but Cawley had already seen the beginnings of a nod from Zorro, already knew that the bartender was lying for his friend because he didn't trust the dim-witted individual to lie for himself.

"You look pretty beaten up," Simpson offered. "How did you manage that?"

Zorro looked from Cawley to Simpson and then at the bartender before turning his attention back to his cider and saying nothing.

"He doesn't have to talk to you," Sellers said.

"Did you do that to him?" Cawley wanted to know.

"Lovers' tiff?" Simpson offered.

"Fuck you," Sellers spat.

Cawley couldn't hide the grin. "What about you, kid?" he said, turning to the youngster.

"He was 'ere," the bartender began.

"I wasn't asking you."

"I saw it all," the kid said cockily, clearly more confident of his lying than his injured friend.

"You saw the fight?" Cawley asked.

"What fight?" the kid answered suspiciously.

"You're trying to catch us out," Sellers noted. "It's not going to work."

Cawley laughed. "Catch you out?" he repeated. "When you're telling the truth, what's there to *catch out*?"

The bartender looked momentarily stumped, a reply whirred its way around his head, but Cawley interrupted him before it could form. "Look, whatever dodgy side-line you have here, I don't give a shit. You're hiding something, that's obvious, but I really don't care. I just want to catch these guys."

"We're not—"

"Don't bullshit me." Cawley leaned on the bar, crept his face closer to the bartender. "You're not telling me something. What is it?"

The bartender paused, seemed to be weighing something in his head. For a moment, Cawley thought he was going to spill the beans, open up to him, but then he lowered his head defensively and said, "I've told you everything I know."

Cawley sighed tiredly. "Fine."

He took out a few cards, handed them to each of the patrons. "If you remember anything that might help, *anything*, give me a shout."

176

* * *

Cawley felt like screaming. He kicked his foot angrily into the floor, balled his fists and ground his teeth. He took out a cigarette, lit it with a hand that trembled with rage, and took a deep drag that burned half of the stick.

"I see what you mean," Simpson said. "They're hiding something."

Cawley inhaled deeply, gave an open-palmed shrug.

"We could get a warrant. Search the place."

Cawley shook his head. He didn't want to get into the details with Simpson, didn't want to inform her that there was no way he was going back to work and no way that he could ask any favor from Clarissa, even if it was integral to him doing his job.

"We could just break in," she offered.

Cawley blew out a long line of smoke, raised his eyebrows at his friend, a twisted smile tweaking the corners of his lips.

Simpson nodded slowly, her eyes wide with excitement.

"Seriously?"

"Sure. What do you say?" she said. "Tonight. Look at this place, it wouldn't take a group of elite criminals. Hardly Fort Knox is it?"

Cawley regarded the dilapidated building. It was only one storey, accessed through front and back doors. There were no shutters, no heavy locks, no security systems. The pub didn't take in much money and probably didn't store any of it on the premises, and besides a few bottles off cheap booze and a handful of barrels too cumbersome to shift, it had nothing worth stealing.

"You're serious?" he asked.

Simpson merely nodded.

"Okay then," he said, cheering up.

* * *

Dexter's hand shook as he held the glass over his wound. The tip of the shattered glass pricked his skin, exposed a pinpoint of bright red blood that was almost lost against the angry red flesh beneath.

He'd heard stories of desperate people hacking off their own limbs in a bid to escape certain death. He was sure he was in such a situation; he doubted that the sadistic couple upstairs would keep him alive very long, and if they did prolong his life, it would only be to torture him further. Then there was Pandora: he didn't know what they had done to her, what they were *doing* to her, but something told him that she would be suffering even more than he was and he doubted that she had long left.

The glass was thick, strong. It wouldn't cut through bone, but he didn't need it to. Bone could be broken, he could easily shatter it against the stanchion to which he was tied, but the glass would easily sever his flesh and muscle. He was weak and wasn't sure he would be able to maintain consciousness throughout the ordeal, and then what, what did he do if he succeeded and managed to escape? He would have to escape the basement, find Pandora, and escape the house and town, all while he slowly bled to death.

He closed his eyes tight, tried to force away the doubts. As complicated and morbid as it was, it was his only chance of escape. He clenched the glass so tightly in his fist that it cut into his palm and into the base of his fingers, the abrasive surface grazed against the open wounds, which bled torrents of blood around his knuckles and the back of his hand.

He pressed it against the welt, harder this time, hard enough to break the top few layers of skin, hard enough for the injured flesh to scream a stabbing pain through his leg. He closed his eyes, gritted his teeth, lifted the blade up, and prepared to hack his own leg off.

He couldn't bring himself to do it.

He tried again but he couldn't force his hand into action.

"*Come on*," he hissed to himself, a trickle of sweat running down his face. "You can do this."

His hand was bleeding heavily; it refused and eventually he relented. He dropped the glass to the floor, keeping it in reach—it would make a useful weapon—and threw himself backward. His spine struck the cold hard floor and he straightened out, threw his bloodied hand to his head.

He cried exasperated tears of anger. He shifted onto his front, twisting and turning through his own mental torment, and then hissed when he felt a sharp pain strike his thigh.

At first he thought he had rested on a shard of broken glass, but when he looked there was nothing on the floor. The pain continued, felt like a persistent insect was clutching at his leg. He reached inside his pocket with a confused grimace and pulled out the offending item.

It was Pandora's brooch, a bronze emblem of a butterfly. The pin had unlatched itself from the back and had forced its way into Dexter's leg.

The grimace faded and he smiled at the brooch, images of Pandora swimming into his mind. She said it gave her an air of innocence, which her usual attire didn't allow for. He grinned, closed his eyes, and held the brooch—possibly the last piece of Pandora he would touch—tightly in his bloodied hand.

He opened his mouth to issue her memory his well-wishes, to tell the empty silence that he loved her and that he was sorry for letting any harm come to her, but he stopped, snapped open his eyes, and glared at the pointed metal pin with renewed hope.

He wasn't an expert lock-picker but he had toyed with a few locks in his youth. He had mixed with the wrong crowd, spent a lot of time with one particular tearaway who was an expert at petty delinquencies. Dexter had watched him pick a few locks. With most locks there was a skill to it, it required the right tools and the right knowledge; Dexter was halfway there on both accounts and this lock was old, basic.

He thrust the pin inside the keyhole and jiggled it around until he found the pins. He slid a smaller shard of glass into the bottom of the lock, waiting until he heard the pins fall into place before he turned it.

He paused when he heard shuffling sound above him, heavy footfalls—the husband—shifting across the room. He darted his eyes instinctively toward the staircase and then concentrated back on the lock, moving his hands more hastily.

He turned the pins, nearly opened the lock, but lost his nerve; his bloodied hand slipped on the bronze brooch. The footsteps pounded heavily above him, he heard the door at the top of the staircase open. He tried to ignore it but the sound caused his hand to shake even more. He lost control, nearly dropped the brooch.

He muttered to himself, urged himself on as he heard the heavy footfalls begin to descend the stairs. They'd probably remembered the broken glass and had come to claim the pieces, making sure he didn't try to hide them and use them as weapons. They would search him, remove the large shard he intended to use as a weapon and take the brooch.

He nearly lost his nerve as the brooch slipped again. The man was on the middle stair, his descent slow and methodical.

"*Come on, come on,*" he whispered desperately, wiping away a line of sweat that traced from his forehead to the bridge of his broken nose.

The man was on the final steps, Dexter heard him, could sense him, but didn't want to look up and see him. The pins clicked in place. He twisted the lock open, reveled in the feeling of relief as he heard it click and felt the pressure on his ankle ease, the reddened skin exposed to the air.

He quickly covered up his activities, slipping his leg, and the undone shackle, underneath his body and plastering an expression of innocence on his face. He hid the brooch and the glass behind his back, slowly worked them up his shirt as he saw the tip of the man's feet pop into view beyond the wall.

A shout from upstairs stopped the man from going any further. He groaned the groan of a married man being shouted at by his wife. Dexter found it strange to hear such a common, human exchange between two people who were far from human.

He saw the man's head appear around the corner of the wall; he leaned forward and grinned at Dexter. "Just checking up on you," he said. "How are you?"

"Fuck you," Dexter spat.

He chuckled. "I'll be down soon." He disappeared behind the wall and turned to climb the stairs. "Don't go anywhere," he mocked.

27

Cawley wasn't averse to breaking the law in an effort to uphold it. It wasn't that he thought he was above the law—as he knew some members of the force believed they were—he just didn't appreciate the red tape that stopped him from achieving what he felt needed to be achieved. He didn't want to contemplate the legal route, didn't want to jump through any hoops, and certainly didn't want to grovel to his boss. Breaking into Stubbies was the perfect solution.

It wouldn't be the first time they had broken in somewhere. A few years previous, they were on the case of a suspected drug dealer—a middleman to some nasty kingpins who pumped large parts of the district with heroin, cocaine, and cannabis. He was a career criminal, had spent the majority of his thirty-three years behind bars, and the rest in rotten poverty of addiction and petty crime.

They saw him driving around in fast cars, splashing his cash on fancy jewelry, clothes, and even a quad-bike that he used to tear up the local school field. He was stupid enough to blow his ill-gotten gains on obvious purchases but not stupid enough for Cawley and Simpson to catch him. They suspected he was involved in large drug deals but, despite following him around for weeks, they never saw anything.

At their wits end, sick of his lavish exploits, which they perceived as bragging, they waited until he was on vacation and broke into his house. They discovered he was shipping pounds of product into the country from contacts on the continent. He ran everything online, rarely got his fingers dirty, and if not for their illegal intervention, they wouldn't have known and might have never found out. They couldn't use the evidence they found but had enough to set him up. They made a few phone calls, gave some suggestions to customs as to which shipments should be checked, and he was locked away for fifteen years. They didn't take the credit, but they enjoyed the result nonetheless.

Now it was different, but Cawley was hoping for similar results. He didn't know what he would find, didn't even know where he would begin to look, but something told him that Sellers, and the others at Stubbies, were up to something.

They planned to head back to the pub later that night. It closed its doors at eleven, at which point Sellers would retire to his flat above the bar and they could discover what he'd been hiding.

"And if he's not hiding anything?" Simpson inquired as the two drank whiskey to calm their nerves in preparation.

"He's hiding something. It might not have anything to do with our suspects, but he's up to *something*."

Simpson nodded in agreement.

"What do you think he's not telling us?" Simpson asked. Cawley could sense his partner's intrigue and excitement grow, knowing she hadn't had enough of either over the last few years.

"*My* guess? Probably tried it on with the woman, may have been fighting over her, with the bandaged one taking the brunt of her refusal."

"Not technically illegal," Simpson noted. "You think he would hide that?"

Cawley nodded confidently. "Creeps like him like the world

to think they're not creeps. So if he tried it on with her, tried to do something he shouldn't have been doing, he wouldn't admit it."

"Doesn't get us anywhere though," Simpson noted. "They try it on, get the shit kicked out of them by a woman and then our fugitives piss off, just like he said."

Cawley couldn't help but smile at his friend's suggestion they were *our* fugitives. Whether it was a slip of the tongue or not, he could sense that a part of Simpson was missing the job. He shrugged. "We'll see."

28

His limbs were tired, but they felt like his own again; unrestrained by the iron grip of the rusted shackles. He stood, stretched, and shook away a lackluster weariness that poisoned his blood.

He didn't want to fight, didn't know how much of a fight remained in him, so his heart attacked his chest, his hands moistened with his own unease, and his blood ran cold with a sense of trepidation as he used his limited time to search for an exit in the basement. He hoped for a window to street level, or a door besides the one at the top of the stairs, but he found nothing.

His focus had been limited when he was shackled, his visibility restricted, but there was little else to see that hadn't been seen except the stairs themselves, which served as his only escape.

The staircase looked old and rickety but felt sturdy underfoot. He'd heard his abductors track up and down a number of times and hadn't noted any creaks or noises. He was confident they wouldn't be able to hear his ascent, but not so confident that they wouldn't open the door at the top and stare straight at him as he was making that ascent.

He contemplated hiding and pouncing on them but not for

long. He was younger, stronger, and he had the broken shard of glass to use as a weapon, but he was weak, tired, and beaten. They had done a number on him, and if he tried to fight them they would finish the job; he struggled to move, struggled to lift his feet, to shift his aching ribs that pulsated with a painful throb every time he breathed.

He exhaled in short, sharp, staccato breaths as he took in the stairs. He wiped his sweaty palms on the seat of his blood-stained pants, closed his eyes to say a silent and reassuring prayer, and then planted his injured foot onto the bottom step.

A loud thump from above interrupted him. He looked down at his foot, planted firmly, and told it to move. It didn't shift an inch.

Another thump. A heavy sound absorbed by the floor above.

He squeezed his eyes shut, tightened his jaw, and listened in the silence for another series of thumps, for the door to open and an angry face to glare down at him.

He heard a shout, softened through the walls, and then nothing. He waited, still stuck in a half-step, until he couldn't hear anything through the sound of his own blood rushing in his ears. Then he took his first step.

* * *

Pandora had heard the ruffles of her kidnappers' conversations a number of times. She had listened to their faded voices dribble through the thick walls and closed doors, deciphering little more than a few words. But now she could hear them clearly.

The woman had been in to tease her with food, waving it in front of her face, letting her smell it, telling her what it was and how good it would taste, before taking it away. She had been interrupted by the sound of a doorbell. She hesitated at first, waited for a few seconds and cursed at her absent husband, before leaving to answer it herself.

In her rush, she left the bedroom and hallway doors open. Pandora could hear everything that followed.

She recognized Dorothy's voice, the pleasant and sinister tone. "So, where are they?"

"The girl is upstairs," the woman replied. "The other is downstairs."

It pleased Pandora to know that Dexter was still alive but worried her that he was referred to as *the other*. Did that mean he wasn't as important as her, and, if so, what important thing did they have planned for her?

The woman called to her husband at that point. He shouted something back; she heard a door being closed.

"He's excitable," the woman said, excusing her spouse.

"That's understandable," Dorothy said, a sliminess to her tone. "So," there was a long pause, at which point Pandora could imagine Dorothy looking around eagerly and rubbing her hands together. "When do we get to see them?"

Pandora's heart skipped a beat as she thought about Dorothy torturing her the same way the sadistic woman had. For some reason, it disgusted her more. The woman was a stranger—a sick, sadistic stranger—but she had liked Dorothy, she reminded her of her grandparents, of *all* good people. She swallowed thickly, thought about all the sick things that such a smiling, sociopathic mind could conjure.

A door slammed. Pandora felt the vibration kick up through her, rocking her cold and hungry body. Another door slammed shut and then she heard the booming voice of her male abductor as he greeted his guests, followed by his Jekyll and Hyde wife who excused his loud banging and then offered his guests tea before promising to show them *the victims*.

* * *

Dexter lost his balance, nearly toppled over. He grabbed hold of the banister—his cold hands sliding against the partially rusted iron—and stopped himself.

It felt like he had been climbing for an age. Every step was slow and methodical, an inch by inch encroachment toward the door at the top which was both a goal and a fear. He held the glass in his free hand, ready to use it if need be, but he doubted he could land any deadly blows in his state.

He wanted to be silent, to make sure that he didn't make a sound, but he struggled to hear his own footsteps. His head rushed with a wave of blood; a whining sound screeched out of his ears. He knew he had to keep going, had to get to the top, but he didn't know how long he could maintain consciousness. He was weak, he was tired, he was hungry and thirsty, and he was in pain. He hoped his survival instincts would kick in and force him to continue, but he'd forgive his body if it gave up, packed in—a part of him felt like doing just that.

The thought of Pandora pushed him upward. They had been through a lot together, from their days as a penniless couple who got by on lust and money made from odd jobs, to their days as famous outlaws evading the law, hiding in drug dens, running away from the police, and meeting their insane fans. Their relationship had been mocked by her friends and misunderstood by her parents; it had been questioned by the media and had become a target for countless online trolls. But throughout all of that, they remained the most important people in each other's life. They had barely spent a day apart since they'd fallen for each other, and if he had it his way, he would never spend another minute apart from her. But despite all of that, he felt that he'd let her down, that he was on the brink of losing her, if he hadn't already.

That was what kept him going, that was what helped him fight through the pain and the tiredness. That was why he made it to the top of the staircase.

The keyhole was blocked; there was no way of knowing what was on the other side of the door. He had images of his abductors waiting for him, wondered if they had somehow been watching him all along, laughing at his struggle, waiting to push him back down to the bottom again. He stuck an ear to the door, pushed a bruised lobe up against the cold wood.

He heard talking, a multitude of voices. He would have dismissed it as a television, or even a radio, but he hadn't seen either device since his arrival in Fairwood. He strained until he could pick up the voices more clearly, until he could differentiate the voices, could tell that there were at least four people in the house.

The clarity increased as he listened, he even picked up a few words. Then he realized that his hearing wasn't improving, his focus wasn't clarifying; the noises were just getting closer.

They were on the other side of the door.

Dexter sprung backward, shot a worried glance over his shoulder and instantly knew that there was no way he could make it back downstairs quick enough. He could fight, give them everything he had, hope to take at least one of them out before they inevitably overpowered him.

He turned to face the door; ready to accept his fate.

"*Fuck*," he whispered under his breath.

* * *

They left the hallway, moved into the living room. She heard their muffled excitement as they walked through the house and tried to pinpoint their location. She knew they weren't coming to see her, so they were probably going to Dexter.

In the silence of the bedroom, she strained to hear every noise she could from downstairs. She struggled with the female voices but could pick up the heavy bass tones of the two males, one—probably the creepy, slimy man—clearly more enthusiastic than the other.

Then she heard the woman scream, a rattling sound that echoed throughout the house and was followed by a loud thud and a shout from one of the men.

She didn't hear much else, couldn't pick up any words, but she knew something was wrong.

29

Dexter wobbled unsteadily, shivers of pain coursing through his body as he stood on the stairs. He held his head, his fingers clasped behind his neck and pressing against the top of his arched spine. His eyes were closed; a series of stars blinked and disappeared in the reddened darkness beyond his tightly squeezed eyelids.

He had never feared for his life, or his own safety, as much as he had over the last few days. He enjoyed the thrill of robbery, thrived on the adrenaline rush of being on the run, but this was different. This was sordid, this was deep. It strangled a nerve that had never been touched, activated an innate fear that had never seen the light of day.

He had been clenching his teeth, didn't realize it until he released the tension in his jaw and felt a sharp pain spread around his head, from his neck to the back of his skull.

He looked up through the gap in the door, a bright, vertical window into the room beyond. His abductors, along with Dorothy and her husband, stood in a cramped circle, still giggling hysterically.

He pulled away from the light, ran a hand through his hair.

He had slipped out of the basement before they'd entered the kitchen; he hadn't wanted to fight them on the stairs, didn't want to face them at all if he could avoid it. He had staggered out, dragging his feet, bent over like a crippled hunchback. He expected to be caught but they hadn't seen him. In the safety of a closet under the stairs, he watched as they prepared to enter the basement. His female abductor had gone first, only to play a joke on the others, pretending that Dexter had grabbed her and pulled her into the basement.

She screamed, pulled the door half shut behind her. Her husband nearly had a heart attack and told her so afterward, right before they all chorused a nervous laugh.

Now they were standing at the half open door and Dexter was waiting for them to enter. He needed to find Pandora and had a whole house to search; he doubted he had more than a minute before they realized he wasn't in the basement and began to look for him.

The husband went first, holding the door open for the others. Dexter saw his needy eyes pass over the closet door and for a moment his heart was in his mouth, sure he had been seen. He ducked into the darkness, waited in the silence and then slowly leaned forward, expecting the homeowner to be waiting for him with a knife and a grin.

He saw his broad back disappear down the stairs, leaving the door to close silently behind him. He heard their steps through the door, heard their excitement and knew he didn't have long. He prepared to dart through the house. If he couldn't save Pandora, couldn't get her out in time, then at least he could join her.

He slipped out of the closet, nearly bolted for the living room, then stopped short. He remembered the blocked keyhole on the other side of the door, remembered not being able to see into the kitchen.

He crept backward towards the door and cracked his first smile in a long time when he noticed that, as suspected and hoped, the key to the basement door was in the lock.

The homeowners had laughed and mocked as they beat him; Dorothy and her husband had giggled like school children as a harmless joke was played at his expense. Dexter felt like laughing himself when he turned the key and locked them all in the basement.

* * *

He didn't need to rush—there was no way the four elderly sadists were getting past the basement door anytime soon—but he did. He checked every corner of the living room and scanned the kitchen and the dining room for any sign of his partner in crime, the love of his life. He couldn't find her, couldn't find anything indicative of her location or her state.

The house was clean, prim and proper, just like the couple that owned it. He hadn't expected anything else; he knew that the sickest and darkest individuals kept their skeletons in the closets, or in the basement, hidden away from the world.

The decor reminded him not just of his grandparents' house but of every grandparents' house. It was floral vomit, a mismatch of dense flowery patterns, flowery cushions, and landscape paintings on the walls. A screen door led out into a back garden that was home to an army of gnomes and fairies; a beaded door led from the living room to the hallway, clinging to Dexter's face and shoulders as he strode through. He brushed it off, imagining all the times those beads had clung to the bodies of his captors. The thought disgusted him.

The stairs creaked as he climbed, wearily and painfully at first, then taking them two at a time.

"Pandora!" he called when he reached the top. He listened intently in the silence that followed, praying he would receive a reply, any reply, so that he would know she was still alive.

When he didn't hear anything, he refused to let his heart sink, refused to let it get to him. He staggered across the hallway, peeked into the first door he saw: the master bedroom, decked out with enough tat to stock a seaside gift shop. A dozen faces, from porcelain teddy bears on the dresser to lifeless masks on the walls, grinned vacantly at him.

He backed away, left the door open. "Pandora!" he called again, tracking further across the hallway. His heart skipped a beat when he heard something in reply. It wasn't a voice, wasn't coherent, but it sounded human.

He pushed open the bathroom door, disregarded the light blue interior and the linoleum floors, moved quickly on. He could hear banging from downstairs, angry fists on an impenetrable door.

His foot sunk on a loose floorboard that squeaked with a vengeful creak. He heard a mumbled call, louder, clearer—and bolted forward, through the door ahead of him.

He saw Pandora tied to the bed. She looked terrible, hungry, thin, dirty, but his spirit lifted at the sight of her. He was just happy that she was alive.

"Pandora," he said softly.

She squirmed at the sound, kicking out against her restraints when she recognized his voice.

"It's okay," he assured. "We're getting out of here."

He ripped off her blindfold. She flinched as she laid eyes upon his beaten face, an expression of pity crept onto her gaunt features.

"It's okay," he said with a grin. "You should see the other guy."

He took out her gag. It peeled away painfully from her face, taking with it a line of dried skin from her lip and a strand of saliva that hung like string from the gag to her bottom lip.

He pressed his head against hers, feeling her breath against his face, her skin against his. "I'm so sorry," he said.

He pulled back, looked her over, desperation and agony in his voice. "Did they . . ."

She shook her head. "No," she said. "But they did everything else." Her voice was rough and dry, forced out of her throat.

"Bastards," he said through gritted teeth.

"Did you kill them?"

He shook his head, she looked a little disappointed. "They're locked in the basement."

"Dorothy?" Pandora asked as Dexter untied the rope from her arms.

"You heard her?"

Pandora nodded, keeping her eager eyes on him.

"She's in there as well."

He used the shard to free her arms, severing the tight rope that wrapped around her wrists. He left the makeshift weapon on the bed; he couldn't carry himself, Pandora, and that. He was confident he wouldn't need it, sure that he wouldn't be able to successfully use it if he did.

They embraced before he planted her on her unsteady feet. "You think this was her doing?" she wondered.

They held a stare. They had both been taken in by Dorothy's charms and had both suffered because of it; they hated her, even more than they hated their kidnappers.

"I don't know," he said. "But we'll find out."

He wrapped her arm around his shoulder and helped her out of the room. She peeled away from him, told him that she could handle herself and that he didn't need to escort her out, but he stayed close regardless, fearful of losing her again.

Their former captors banged, kicked, and screamed—the sound of their mocking, vicious tongues reverberating throughout the house. They called her a slut, a whore; they called him a killer, a demon. Dexter blocked it out easily, but he knew that Pandora would struggle to be as calm. Outside the room that had become her prison, he planted his hands over her ears, stared into her eyes, and kissed her on the forehead.

"Wait here," he said. "And don't let those assholes get to you."

He ran into a nearby bedroom, clean, well-kept, but devoid of the trinkets of life. He grabbed a pair of jeans and a hoody from the closet, some underwear from a bedside drawer, and took them back to Pandora, who happily changed into them.

After changing, she grasped his hand tightly.

"Come on," he said. "Let's get the hell out of here."

The banging increased as they descended the stairs. They heard shouting, male voices at first, threatening them with repercussions if they didn't open the door. Then Dorothy offered them idle promises in a motherly tone that shot bile up Dexter's throat, sickening him.

At the bottom of the stairs, he felt Pandora pull away from him, realizing that the old woman's words had had the same effect.

"Where're you going?" he pleaded as she headed for the kitchen. "Leave it. Ignore her."

Pandora wasn't listening. Dexter followed her as she half-ran half-hobbled to the source of the noise, reaching the door just as Dorothy was piling on the faux charm and trying to convince them that it was all a big game.

Pandora listened with an ear to the door; waiting patiently, measuredly, before slamming her fist hard into the wood. Dorothy screamed in shock and moved away from the door.

"You're going to rot in hell for this, you bitch!" Pandora told her.

Dorothy regained her composure. "Just open the door, dear. This has all been a big—"

"*Fuck you!*" Pandora spat. Dexter put a hand on her shoulder, squeezed gently, and tried to usher her away. "We're going to go to the police, tell them all about your sick little games."

Dorothy laughed. The motherly tone gone from her voice. "The police? Are you also going to tell them who you are, that you're wanted for robbery and murder?"

"We'll let you rot," Pandora said, changing tact.

"Or we'll burn this place to the ground and cook all of you fuckers alive," Dexter chimed in.

He expected a horrified response. They were wanted for murder, after all, and if Dorothy knew that, then she surely wouldn't put the deed past them, but Dorothy didn't sound shocked at all. She laughed.

"What the fuck are you laughing at?" Pandora spat.

"You'll leave us here?" Dorothy said in a menacing tone that cut through the thick door and reverberated through Pandora's soul. "You can't leave," she stated simply. "You'll never win."

After the laughter subsided, after the silence that followed, Pandora opened her mouth to offer something in reply, anything, but Dexter pulled her back before she could regain her composure.

Dorothy and her sadistic friends were still laughing when Pandora and Dexter left the house.

30

When the night came, it brought a cruel chill with it. Cawley zipped up his jacket until he could feel the cold zipper pressing against his larynx. He dug his chin inside the felt-lined interior, breathed in the musty smell of a coat that hadn't been worn in three weeks and hadn't been washed in three years.

He stretched his eyebrows to peer at Simpson, standing in front of him with a wide grin on her face. She had knocked back a few whiskeys, saying she needed some Dutch courage. Cawley couldn't believe the difference he was witnessing in his partner and didn't know if it was down to denial, her current freedom, her constant inebriation, or a combination of all three. He didn't mind, he liked the new Abigail Simpson—her random, almost bipolar swings and her sudden lust for life was intoxicating.

He turned away from her, toward the back window of the building. He'd seen something shift across, something black moving quickly out of his periphery. He lifted his head from his cocoon and gestured toward Simpson, who immediately stopped trying to pick the lock on the back door.

The window was heavy with dust, an almost impenetrable layer that blocked any light from entering the building. He saw the movement again and realized it was his own reflection, the movement of his hands as he stuffed them in his pocket and then used them to pull his friend back.

"What is it?" Simpson whispered, her wide grin switching into an alert and darting glance.

Cawley released his grip on Simpson's elbow, shook his head to indicate it was nothing, not wanting his former partner to know he was scared of his own shadow. He'd always been the forward and reckless one of the partnership, not because he was crazy, mainly because Simpson had been so withdrawn and distant.

He heard a click, a sound that echoed like a heavy-handed clap in the silent night. Simpson turned to him, the smile back on her face. She pushed the door open, and it swung on the hinge with an awkward grating noise that Cawley was sure had been heard by everyone within a two-mile radius.

Simpson gestured for Cawley to enter.

"You sure about this?" Cawley whispered as he pushed past and sucked in a breath of air from inside the pub.

Simpson shrugged casually. "Bit late to turn back now, isn't it?"

Cawley threw a quick and concerned glance over his shoulder, toward Simpson. He was ready to react but silenced his objections when he heard muffled noises filtering through the dust inside the dark interior.

He threw a finger to his lips, gestured for Simpson to follow him. They both crept inside—wary of each footstep, cautious not to make a sound—and pinned their ears to the air, listening to the occasionally frantic and constantly worried voices from within.

* * *

The scenes of Fairwood were painted with an ominous brush when night set in. The once picturesque trees, standing tall and proud before expanses of green fields, stretched like skeletal fingers over the landscape; the houses, grandiose and imposing in the daytime, loomed like malevolent castles against the grayed backdrop.

Dexter and Pandora stumbled out of the house and onto the street, lit by the halo of a stuttering streetlight. He held onto her for support, she held onto him. The blind led the blind on a wavering line, down the street and around a sharp corner that ushered them away from the house that had held them captive.

The cold wind froze Dexter's throbbing ears, probed into his spinning head. He struggled to maintain a clear mind but knew he had to keep going, even if he didn't know exactly where he was heading. They weren't safe in the town, couldn't turn to anyone nearby. He doubted he would be able to find his car or make it very far on foot, but he didn't let himself dwell on that, didn't want to face the consequences.

They couldn't go back the way they came in. They didn't want to track past the houses and out in the open. They needed to find another way, preferably through the green expanse where no one could see them leave.

Pandora watched Dexter with bleary, bloodshot eyes as they scuppered away from the street, into the shadows of a line of trees that bordered an embankment. He looked at her, exchanged a brief smile in which he tried to hide the futility of their situation.

He slipped, lost his footing. His hand still gripped hers, he didn't want to let go and his instinct forced him to keep hold even when he felt himself fall. His feet kicked out and he hit the ground backside first, feeling a volley of moist earth splatter the back of his pants as the bottom of his spine shuddered under impact. Pandora fell to her knees beside him, her kneecaps sinking into the earth.

He moved to stand and she followed, but he stopped her, held her down. A flashlight beam danced a dozen yards ahead of them, skipping and whirling like an obese and merry firefly. He held a finger to her lips, gestured for her to be quiet and still.

They pricked their ears to the air, tried to listen beyond the sound of their own trepidation, the beating of their own heavy hearts. They heard the rustling of cautious feet, of someone careful of each step they made, checking their surroundings intently after they made it.

The trees were thick above and around them, the torchlight wouldn't be able to pick them out of the darkness if it happened upon them, but after a few seconds, Dexter motioned to Pandora to stand. They needed to leave quickly; the torch carrier was headed straight for them.

* * *

A beam of light broke underneath a slit in the door ahead of them, stretching a radiant yawn onto Cawley's feet and ankles. The voices, filtering through with more cohesion than before, came from the other side.

He recognized the voice of the owner, Sellers; he seemed both annoyed and worried, two emotions that pleased Cawley when he recognized them in his abrasive tone. There was a good chance he was on the right track, a good chance he had rattled his cage. There was also a good chance that the current conversation had nothing to do with Cawley or the case, a notion that the detective soon dismissed.

"The pig knows," Sellers said with disgust.

"You're paranoid." Cawley recognized the whiny voice of the youngster, the same one who had been there earlier in the day. "He don't know nowt," he said.

"You sound confident," Sellers said with a hint of derision.

"I got a good read on 'im, 'es just like the others, don't know shit."

"The kid has a point," someone piped up, Cawley didn't

recognize the voice. "So what if he knows something's up? What's he going to do?"

"Exactly," the cocky youngster chimed.

Cawley nearly jumped when the silence was interrupted by a loud crack, followed by the hasty movements of a chair scraping on the floor.

"What the fuck!" the kid screamed. "*You hit me!*" he said, answering Cawley's unasked question in a high-pitched tone of disbelief.

"You're pissing me off," Sellers stated simply. "You're not taking this seriously. I don't think you understand," his tone took on a serious note. Cawley imagined him leaning forward, drawing a sinister smile on his face and aiming it at the arrogant teenager. "If he *does* suspect something, if he *does* have any reason to think we're bullshitting him, he'll be on us like hair on soap. This is a big case, the whole world has eyes on Bleak and Bright and every copper in the country wants their name on the front pages. If he's onto us, he'll stop at nothing to get answers."

Cawley flashed a curious look toward Simpson, who replied in kind.

"This is all *your* fault," Sellers continued. "If you hadn't flapped your fucking mouth to your idiot friends and inbred family—"

"Hey! Don't talk about my—"

Another crack, this time followed by a loud thump as the youngster toppled off his chair and crashed to the floor.

Cawley reached forward, eager to see something, anything. He needed to know who was in the room, needed to confirm the mental images of a conversation that could prove vital to the case. He grasped the door handle; it felt cold and stiff in his hand. He squeezed down in small increments.

"You're a fucking liability." Sellers was furious, his voice filled with a fiery aggression and a wetness that indicated he was spraying his target with spittle as he loomed over him. "I knew I should'a killed ya, if it wasn't for you then—"

The sound of a squeaking door stopped Sellers short. Cawley released his hand from the handle, cursed under his breath, and gave his partner a worried and regretful stare.

A few seconds passed before the conversation started up again.

"Anyway," Sellers was saying, "that's all done now, we have to forget about it and move on."

"Agreed," the youngster said.

Cawley scrunched his face as he listened, something didn't sound right.

"So," someone else jumped in, their voice sounded strangely distant, "anyone watch the game last night?"

Cawley turned to Simpson, but before he could arch his eyebrows in curiosity, the door ahead of him was yanked open. A bath of light washed over him and he stood, rooted to the spot like a rabbit caught in the headlights, staring at the three figures. The one in the middle, the only one he hadn't seen before, was pointing a shotgun at his face, smirking over the top of the barrel.

"Detective Cawley," Sellers said, appearing from behind the three men. "Good to see you."

Cawley gulped, stared at each menacing face in turn, lingering on the youngster to the right of the gunman. His right eye was quickly swelling shut and his nose leaked blood onto the top of a swollen lip, but the smile on his face suggested all his Christmases had just come at once.

* * *

Dexter had Pandora's hand gripped in his as he scuttled sideways, keeping low and strafing through the trees. He squeezed tightly, needing to keep her close. Her hand became slippery and clammy as a coating of sweat from both their palms lubricated their grip.

The flashlight bobbed with greater rapidity, dancing and weaving in the night. They couldn't see who was holding it, couldn't even make out a silhouette in the darkness beyond the sphere of light, but they were sure he could see them. The beam had passed their way a number of times and now lingered on them.

He felt Pandora stop behind him, felt the resistance as he tried to tug her onward. She made a small yelping sound as the light stayed on her, looked down at the beam on her legs like someone glimpsing the laser dot from the sniper rifle that would, very soon, cause their demise.

"Come on," Dexter hissed.

The light traced up her legs, to her stomach and then to her neck, lighting up her worried expression, which pleaded with Dexter. He tugged harder, yanking the chain on a disobedient dog.

"Let's go!"

The light moved from her face and seemed to concentrate on the floor in the distance. She watched it illuminate a pair of feet, walking at first but quickening to a jog.

"Quick!" Dexter said, tugging her again.

This time she allowed herself to be led away.

31

"Please," Sellers stepped aside, motioned for the men to allow Cawley through. "Come and join the party."

He stepped through into the warm orange glow, emitted from a single light above the bar. The rest of the bar dark. The tables and chairs were still out; empty glasses and filled ashtrays littered their dusty tops.

They showed him through and then slammed the door shut behind him; the gust of wind propelled him forward. He turned a curious eye toward the door, noticing that Simpson hadn't followed.

"Where's ya friend?" Sellers, like Cawley, wanted to know.

The detective shrugged. "She couldn't make it."

Sellers held Cawley's stare and slowly nodded, then he turned away, gestured to the others who had returned to the bar, clustering under the light. All except for the man with the gun, a bulbous, ugly, bald man, who stayed near Cawley—his finger edgy as it toyed with the trigger.

"These are my friends," Sellers said. "Two of them I think you've met already. The other . . ." he said, playing with the word on his tongue as he surveyed the big man with the shotgun. "May be new to you."

"What're you up to?" Cawley demanded to know.

205

"Us?" Sellers thrust his hand to his chest, taking in the faces of each of his comrades. They all looked on with equally fake expressions of bemusement. "We're just sitting 'ere enjoying a quiet drink."

"True dat," the youngster said, holding up his pint.

Cawley caught a sneer on Sellers's face as he regarded the youngster.

"I heard you," Cawley said. "What happened here that night? What are you hiding?"

"I don't know what you're talking about."

"Bullshit," Cawley spat, flashing a brief and instinctive glance at the gunman to make sure his cursing wasn't going to get him killed. "You're up to something."

"I'm not telling you nothing."

Cawley turned to the man with the bandages on his face. He looked nervous, unsure. He wore a large-brimmed Stetson hat that shaded his black eyes, but Cawley could still make out the unease in them. Cawley knew he was the man who would provide him with the answers.

"You're Martin, right?" he said, throwing a random name into the mix.

He received a curious arched eyebrow in return, followed by a brief shake of the head.

"No."

The others looked on, too interested in the strange line of questioning to halt the questioner.

"Mark?"

Another gentle shake of the head. "No, what—"

"Are you in on this?" Cawley asked quickly. "Are you hiding the suspects?"

The man with the bandaged face gave another instinctive shake of his head, only a slight horizontal shift before he interrupted it with another refusal. It was enough to give Cawley the answer he needed.

"What the fuck are you playing at?" Sellers snapped.

"I just—"

"We have the fucking gun, dickhead. We'll ask the questions here."

"Be my guest."

Sellers opened his mouth, closed it again, looked unsurely from face to face.

"What happened to Prince Charming over there?" Cawley asked, gesturing toward the beaten kid.

"I walked into a door," the teenager said simply. "What's it to you?"

"You walked into a door?" Cawley said with a smile and a nod. "You must be as stupid as you look."

He stood up, slammed his pint down on the bar. "Fuck you, copper!"

Cawley laughed, amused at the outburst, reminiscent of a toddler tantrum.

"What the fuck're you laughing at?" He screamed at the top of his lungs. He bounded over to Cawley with the cocky and lopsided gait of a kid trying, and failing, to perform an intimidating swagger. He stuck his face up against Cawley's, close enough for the detective to smell his breath—a hermitic concoction of beer, cigarettes, and the plaque from a dozen dirty meals.

"Not laughing now, are ya pig?" he said, twitching his nose as he spoke.

"'cause your breath is making me sick."

The youngster took a step back, threw a punch that Cawley had seen coming before he even thought about throwing it. He didn't move, didn't try to block it. It landed below his ribs, absorbed by his stomach, which he tensed before the impact. It had no force, no power. Cawley doubled over regardless, leaving the grinning idiot to treat himself to a smile and a look of pride.

"Told you, pig," he said, looming over Cawley with the pose of a confident boxer—his arms down by his side, his fists clenched. "Don't fuck with me."

The others at the bar were shocked, including the man with the shotgun, who lowered the weapon to get a better look at Cawley and his attacker, trying to figure out how a man he considered feeble managed to floor someone who had clearly seen his fair share of fights.

The shock was all that Cawley needed. When the youngster was still flaunting his success, receiving attention for doing so, Cawley snapped upright and rushed at the man with the gun.

He grasped the shotgun, one hand on the barrel, the other on the butt, and pushed against it, forcing his strength into the weapon and then into the holder. The big man sprung backward, releasing his grip on the gun and nearly toppling over his heels.

Cawley thrust the weapon at him, took a few steps back, into space, and waved it around, gathering everyone into his sights. The youngster's confident stance crumbled into a hunchbacked defensive pose and he hobbled to the safety of the bar. Sellers didn't seem to be bothered.

"Now," Cawley said, slightly out of breath from the rush of the ordeal. "How about you tell me what the fuck is going on before I shoot you all?"

32

They made it to the river; Dexter nearly fell in, dragging Pandora with him. The moonlight sparkled a reflection off the still water, enough for him to see his own horrified face as he stopped himself from toppling in.

The person who had been following them was behind them, beyond the line of trees and down the hill. They probably had over a hundred yards on him, but he knew where he was going and had a light to aid in his search; they were lost, guided in their blind stumbling by nothing but the moonlight, which barely allowed them to see a few feet in front of them.

They walked along the edge of the river. They were both breathless and sickened, felt like keeling over and opening their lungs and stomachs to the world, but they had to keep silent, had to keep going.

Dexter stopped abruptly and held out a hand to keep Pandora still. He thrust a finger to his lips, nodded to the other side of the river where a long field stretched into nothingness. He waited in the silence, watching keenly, before tugging at her and setting off again.

It felt like they were walking for hours. Their energy had already been sapped, sucked out of them throughout their tortuous ordeal. They had made it to where they were now on adrenaline alone, but that adrenaline was drying up, and their agonized, weakened bodies were ready to give up.

Pandora winced at every twig she heard crush underneath her foot, every leaf that crunched and rustled. She looked back a number of times, at first she saw only darkness but her eyes were adjusting, growing more accustomed to it. She began to pick out the shape of the trees, the line of the riverbank. She began to feel better, more confident now that she was regaining her senses, but then the tired orbs picked out something else: the man with the flashlight was back. And she knew it as a man now, because she could see his face as he emerged from the trees, could see the glaring anger, the sadistic smile as the torchlight—flickering and wavering, catching everything as its operator rushed and pushed his way through the trees—lit up his face.

She gasped and hopped forward, straight onto Dexter's heels. He lost his shoe, lost his balance. She felt him fall, felt herself tumbling over the top of him, and then she felt a cold shock as she broke the silent river and sunk under its peaceful waters.

* * *

Cawley kept an interested eye over his shoulder, wondering what had happened to his partner. The others noticed his fleeting glances and apparent paranoia but didn't register that he was looking for his friend.

"You scared o'the dark, old man?" Sellers sneered mockingly.

"Shut the fuck up."

Sellers laughed one short and mocking laugh. He looked at his friends, seeking and getting their approval like the chief delinquent of a group of idiots.

"Tell me," Cawley said. "What happened here?"

"Why would we tell you anything?" the youngster wanted to know, stepping forward and displaying intimidation despite the gun in Cawley's hands.

Sellers gave his dim-witted accomplice a derogatory look, grabbed him by the shoulder, and tugged him backward. "*Nothing* happened 'ere," he clarified.

"Whatever happened, I'm sure it's nowhere near as bad as what'll happen if you don't end this now," Cawley told them. He waved the shotgun at the man with the bandages. "You," he said, pointing with the barrel, "how did you get those wounds?"

The man gave Sellers a look, begging for confirmation. The youngster answered with the confirmation that none of them wanted. "Don't tell 'im anything, 'arry."

Sellers snapped his hand around the kid's face, knocking his head into his pint glass, which toppled over on the bar. "Idiot!" he snapped.

The youngster held a hand to his head, an ugly grimace on his ugly face. He sneered at the bartender, a look of threatening intimidation, but his true feelings exposed themselves when he took an instinctive step backward.

Sellers was still glaring at him, oblivious of the show of simultaneous intimidation and submission. "What the fuck are you playing at?"

"I'm holding the gun now," Cawley reminded him. "I'll ask the fucking questions." He played his finger over the trigger, aiming the gun directly at the bartender. His threat didn't have the desired effect. Sellers shifted out from behind the bar, moved toward the detective with a confident swagger.

"You're also a copper," Sellers told him. "And ya not going to shoot me. Have you ever even fired a gun before?"

"Aim, pull, and watch your miserable life end. How hard can it be?"

"And then what, plead self-defense?" Sellers threw his head back, aimed a laugh at the grimy ceiling that stared back with a veiled scowl. He turned to the big man: the one Cawley stole the weapon from. "Get him," he said, nodding apathetically at Cawley. "He won't shoot."

Cawley really wanted to shoot, just to prove the cocky git wrong, but he didn't have it in him. His life was bad already; if he pulled the trigger he'd be able to add at least twenty years in prison to the long list of misery tagged to his soul.

Self-defense with a shotgun against an unarmed man didn't hold water, but the law would allow him some leniency, something he kept in mind as he drove the butt of the weapon across the big man's face, forcing enough power into the blow to stagger the attacker and send him sprawling.

A couple of seconds dragged by before Sellers, the youngster, and the bandaged man all rushed him. He aimed the gun to the ceiling and squeezed off two shots, enough to shower a hail of plaster at his attackers and force them all to their knees in a desperate and instinctive act of defense. Then he turned and ran, back the way he came.

He threw himself at the door, slapped a desperate hand on the handle that had deceived him earlier, and tugged. It didn't budge, it was stuck.

He tried again but his hands, moist with sweat, slipped from the handle. He didn't turn around, didn't want to see how close they were to gaining on them, but he could feel them near, could sense their presence behind him.

He dropped the weapon to the floor, its barrels now empty. He grabbed the handle with both hands and tugged with all his might. It still didn't move. It wasn't stuck; it was locked.

He felt a hand on his shoulder, felt the fingers pressing deep into his flesh. He spun around to face the big man who had clambered to his feet and was grinning at Cawley, his nose bent and bloody; his features forming bruises.

He looked over the man's shoulder, saw Sellers grinning and dangling a set of keys. Then he looked back, catching the glint in the big man's eyes just before he drove a heavy fist across Cawley's temple.

33

Dexter hit the ground, his outstretched hands stopping him from eating the dirt and weeds on the river bank. He felt Pandora falling over him, her feet clipping his ankles, heard the splash as she hit the water, the gasp and gurgle that followed. He shot a look over his shoulder and saw that the person following them was now less than fifty yards away and gaining quickly. He could sense the eagerness in their hurried steps, could practically feel their desperation.

Dexter clambered upright, threw himself to his knees at the water's edge, felt the rippled water lap onto his pants and soak through his shins and his backside. He reached down just as Pandora managed to flap her way above the surface. He grabbed for her, felt his fingers brush her soggy clothes, and then lost control as she struggled and slipped under.

She couldn't swim. She could keep herself afloat, could stop herself from drowning in her right mind, but she was weak, panicked, and fighting against an unseen threat in the dead of night. She was far from her right mind.

She lifted her head above the surface again, coughed a splutter of water, and shouted something to him before dipping under.

The man with the flashlight was so close that he didn't

213

need a torch anymore. He was lit by the moon, his smiling features grayed. He was young, tall, and gaunt. Dexter recognized him but wasn't sure from where. The man slowed to a sinister walk; like a masked madman in a slasher movie, he knew it was inevitable he would catch his prey.

Something to the right of the man caught Dexter's eye, he turned to see a stream of flashlights flicker their way out of the trees, buzzing into life through the thick darkness like an army of merry fireflies. He gulped; his quickened heart skipped a beat. Behind the approaching man, appearing in their droves, was an entire search party. It seemed that everyone in Fairwood was there.

Feeling that he had no other choice, watching Pandora still struggling in the still waters, Dexter threw himself into the river. He had braced himself for the cold, braced against the feeling of icy water seeping into his wounded flesh, but it still shocked him, jumping his weary heart into near submission like a defibrillator jolt.

He fought through the water, felt like he was fighting through a thick oil that threatened to hold him back and keep him from the one he loved. Every stroke was agonizing, every movement of muscle and mass. He found his way to his soaked and gasping lover, who immediately threw her arms around him and dragged them both under, into the darkened depths of the peaceful water, through which the dizzying lights and the threat of reality didn't penetrate.

The sounds of the night disappeared. The gasping of air, the rushing of water, the sound of a dozen quickening footsteps were all replaced by a serene nothingness; a gentle lolling of water inside his own head, accompanied by the sight of Pandora—her face inches from his, her eyes and cheeks bulging. He was ready to give in, ready to give his body the submission it screamed for, but she was tugging at him, a gentle urge that turned into a desperate pull.

She opened her mouth. Little bubbles of water escaped, rose to the surface and popped into the night. She tried to scream at him. He didn't hear anything through the sound of the water in his ears but he nodded, urged his body into one final push. He kicked his legs, threw out his arms and spread his way to the surface with Pandora holding tightly onto his waist.

The breath he took upon surfacing was relieving, welcoming, but it came with another rush of panic, another rush of desperation as the world returned to a chaotic, noisy, and desperate place. The bank of the river was quickly filling with eager spectators, peering over the ledge and shining their lights onto the water, onto the couple who clung to each other for dear life.

They saw many familiar faces. The man they'd met on their first day in town; the shopkeeper; the couple who had kidnapped them; Dorothy and her husband.

The tall man, the first to follow them, was nearly in the water, so close they could splash him. Dexter blinked away the beams that bore down on him and looked into the gaunt face, and this time he recognized it. It was the clerk at the petrol station—the apathetic, distant kid who served them before they entered Fairwood, before their nightmare began. He didn't look distant anymore and his apathy had transformed into a blood lust.

Dexter felt Pandora gripping tighter onto him, trying to pull him away, toward the other side of the river. No one was swimming after them; no one bothered to try to follow them as they clambered to the other side, flopped onto the opposite embankment, and climbed the muddy slope.

They were tired, beaten, bruised, and struggling for breath; their ravaged lungs rattled with sprays of river water, but they were both smiling as they looked back over the river, back onto the nightmare they had left behind.

They expected to see a field of light, a row of pissed-off faces staring back at them, but they saw nothing but blackness and emptiness. Dexter turned to Pandora to voice his confusion, and what he saw over her shoulder stripped any remnants of a smile that remained on his face.

The torchlights, the expectant faces, were all there—hovering behind Pandora. He looked to Pandora, ready to direct her attention, but she was preoccupied, staring, horrified, behind him. He spun around, came face to face with Dorothy and her friends, a smiling army of sadists.

"I told you," she said, standing at the head of the group and moving confidently toward them. "You can't leave."

34

A bigail Simpson stood motionless, shocked. She couldn't believe what she was seeing. This was one of the main reasons, if not *the* only reason, she quit the job. This was what she was trying to get away from, what she had gotten away from and why she was happier. She was still drinking and she still had a few personal problems to deal with, she knew that, she wasn't in denial, but this . . . she never thought she would have to see this again.

She shook her head slowly, took a small step backward.

She had been on the force for six months before she saw her first dead body. The kids were the hardest to deal with and she'd never been comfortable around the elderly ones either; there was something so helpless and innocent in the very young and the very old. They depended on people, they needed the rest of the human race to help them survive—seeing them dead through neglect or violence was a sign that the world had failed them. The fact that her first body had been a man in his twenties should have made things easier, but she still couldn't forget his face. He was an addict, a down-and-out with little to live for. A man whose legacy in life wouldn't live past the few minutes it took the coroner to pull the needle out of his arm and mark his death certificate with the black lines of self-abuse.

That had been a turning point, but they hadn't stopped coming after that. The rich and the poor; the young and the old; the hopeful and the hopeless.

Simpson swallowed deeply, stopped shaking her head. She didn't know how hopeful or hopeless this one was, but she doubted that this image—of his blue body propped up in this cold, dusty room, among the old beer barrels and spent boxes—would ever leave her.

She hadn't heard the conversation in the main room, hadn't heard the commotion, but she finally snapped out of her melancholic trance when she heard the door snap open and listened to the sound of men trundling out.

The door had been locked behind Cawley, and Simpson hadn't wanted to jeopardize her location by trying to open it. She decided to try another access point, to try to help her friend. Then she stumbled upon the body in the storeroom. At that moment, she knew why the bartender, and the others, had been so reluctant to talk to the police: they were murderers and probably had the body stashed all along.

Her legs refused to allow her to move, but eventually she dragged them forward, regained control. She hid in the storeroom, slipping behind a stack of empty boxes—the stiffened dead body within touching distance—and listening as the men approached the other side of the door.

* * *

Cawley watched the world through blurry eyes. He didn't see much after the big man hit him but he certainly felt a lot. His whole world had exploded out of the back of his head; a whining ring, like the shrill call of a banshee, erupted in his ears and refused to let up. He was dizzy after that, as pliable as if he were on sedatives. He felt them move him, felt them half-carry half-drag him out of the room, but he wasn't able to stop them.

They took him away from the light and into somewhere dark, dumping him there and slamming the door behind him. They left him there to stew in his own misery, to listen to the banshee in his ears and to breathe in an awful scent that clogged his nostrils and seemed to burn through his skin like acid. He hadn't moved, hadn't reacted. They knew he was barely conscious but they knew the job wasn't done. He heard them talking—their voices drifting and fading, leaking through to him as if through a heavy filter. He knew what they had planned.

He felt around. The floor was cold, hard. There was a stack of boxes to his left that felt soft, almost soggy. To his right, he grasped something cold, stiff, and palpable. He had been around enough dead bodies to know what he was touching, had seen death enough times to link the sour stench invading his nostrils to the clammy touch at the end of his fingertips. He squeezed his hazy eyes shut, removed his fingers from the corpse. When he opened his eyes, they had turned off the lights in the hallway and left him alone, in the dark, with the body.

35

Dexter had no fight left in him, he was prepared to give up, to let the residents of Fairwood do to him as they pleased, but Pandora had a different idea. Dexter felt a rush of air beside him, saw a blur of flesh and anger fly straight into Dorothy's face.

Pandora's punch connected perfectly, smacking into Dorothy's nose and contorting her sinister smile into something far less amused. She was weak, her arms were tired, their energy sapped from being tied up for so long, but Pandora didn't waste any time in launching herself at the woman. She knocked her to the ground and punched her repeatedly, projecting every fearful thought, every moment of anguish she'd experienced since entering the town, into the owner of the bed and breakfast.

The young clerk tried to help the elderly woman but Dexter, feeding from Pandora's spirit, blocked him, first with his shoulder—which sent a juddering bolt of agony through his crippled body—and then with his fist. When the youngster was caught off-guard, Dexter delivered a swift kick to his groin. It was dirty, but it did the trick. He dropped to his knees with a squeal and then twisted toward the ground.

Others came but Dexter was ready for them, able to block the pain and let the adrenaline take over. Dorothy's husband

and the man that had kidnapped him both rushed him. He hopped over Pandora—climbing off her injured, barely breathing foe—and charged straight for them with his head down and his shoulders out. The corner of his shoulder connected with Eric's stomach, sucking out his breath and throwing him off guard. The kidnapper absorbed the charge but couldn't absorb the kidney punch that followed.

Dexter was hurting but he used the pain as a fuel, thought of the searing agony as an electricity that bolted through his body to provide life to his aching muscles. He barely had time to catch his breath before three more charged him. He fought one off with a lucky punch to the jaw, knocking the weakened, surprised man to his knees, but the others grabbed him, each taking an arm while Eric regained his composure and prepared to sucker punch Dexter into his open and exposed chest.

Dexter opened his mouth to spit at Eric, the only assault he could manage with his arms restricted, but Pandora acted first. She took out the man to Dexter's left, driving the heel of her foot into the back of his leg, which gave way under the impact. Dexter ducked out of the way of Eric's slow and weary punch and then drove a fist into his ribs and another against the side of his head.

He turned around, ready to help Pandora, but he stopped when he saw that everyone was rising to their feet. They were all beaten and bruised, but none of them looked concerned, let alone hurt. Pandora was breathless, finishing up her assault on the man who had held Dexter. She stopped when she saw his expression, turned, gave Dorothy a look of disbelief.

"What the fuck *are you*?" she asked softly.

Dorothy smiled, looked around. Everyone was surrounding them, some shining their flashlights, all smiling. Dorothy met each of their stares, the whole town of Fairwood at her back, and then she nodded toward Dexter and Pandora.

"Get them."

* * *

The dead body grabbed him; Cawley nearly screamed.

"It's me, Max!" it hissed.

He wasn't sure how the dead person knew his name or what business it had in frightening the life out of him, but then he recognized the voice. He turned toward his former partner's voice, squinted as Abigail Simpson sparked up a lighter and illuminated her face.

"Are you okay?" Abigail asked.

The blow had knocked him for six, but he was slowly regaining his senses. He still had blurred vision and his ears still rang with an incessant scream, but his body was slowly shaking off the knock.

"I'm good," he said, looking away from the bright light, seeing its embers dancing in the corner of his eyes.

"You see that?" Simpson said.

Cawley knew his friend was talking about the body. He turned toward it but couldn't make much out. It was male, that much he was sure of, but it had been beaten badly and decomposition had set in. He tried to get a better look but his own form blocked the light from Simpson's lighter and the body was doused in darkness.

"You think it's them?" Simpson asked.

"Them?"

Simpson hissed, the light went out. Cawley listened to her whispering curses in the darkness as she shook her scalded hand before turning the light on again, this time with her sleeve tucked over her thumb to protect against the prolonged heat.

"The bandits."

Cawley frowned. He hadn't thought of that. He looked at the body again, gave the blackened outline a brief once-over and then shook his head. "I don't think so. And there's only one. Something else is going on."

"What?"

Cawley rubbed his head, slowly climbed to his feet. "I don't know, but we've got to get out of here quick." He glared at his friend as the light went out again. When it came back on, Cawley was still glaring.

"They're coming back," he said sternly, "to finish what they started."

36

They beat them, hogtied them, and tied ropes to their feet. Then they were dragged along the riverside by half a dozen men and women, with more ahead and behind. The sound of their feet beat a rhythm into the cobbled roads that vibrated through to the two fugitives as their heads, backs, and legs bobbled over the hard ground.

Dexter turned sideways, taking a few heavy knocks to his cheek as his head bounced over the ground and slammed back again. He watched Pandora with a sinking heart as she struggled against her restraints, trying unsuccessfully to wiggle her way out. He closed his eyes, turned back toward the skies. He didn't even try to protect the back of his head from the hard ground. He had given up, he had failed not just himself, but the one he loved.

Dorothy walked close by, he could see the tip of her head as his own head rocked up and down. He caught her stare once; she was smiling, the same smile she had given them when they first arrived in town, the smile that they had found to be warm and friendly.

* * *

Cawley and Simpson were waiting for them when they returned, one on either side of the door. They couldn't see much in the dark, but they used the lighter to get into position, shivering in the pungent cold of the flickering flame, passing directions through glances.

When they came through the storeroom door—their footsteps heavy, kicking dust and vibrations from the floor outside the room—the experienced officers pounced.

Cawley hadn't entirely regained his senses, but he had enough strength and experience to call on. He grabbed the youngster, twisted his feeble arms behind his back, pulled until he felt the vibration of a shoulder dislocating, until he heard the scream and the childish whimper, then he turned him around and shoved him against the wall, face first. The whimpering stopped immediately, the youngster slid down, smearing the wall with a long streak of blood before crumpling into a human heap at the bottom.

The bandaged man was next. He looked unsure, had witnessed his friend being beaten, his other friend currently wrestling with Simpson. He didn't know whether to run or fight. He chose the latter, launching at Cawley like a madman, his arms up in the air, his features twisted to aid a roar which erupted from his lungs and sounded more like an anguished moan.

Cawley jabbed him in the face. A simple, soft punch into an exposed, open area. His moaning silenced, he paused to glare at Cawley and then he changed his mind, deciding to turn and run, save himself from more bandages. Cawley stopped him before he could get away. He threw out a boot, tripped up the escaping patron who flew across the floor and skidded to a stop against a stack of bottles, like a bowling ball hitting the pins.

He moved toward him, wrestled his arms behind his back, felt the strain as the bandaged man fought to save his limbs. He was stronger than the youngster, he had more experience, more muscle, had been in a lot more fights, but Cawley had seen more than his fair share of violence. He won the struggle.

"Please!" he screamed, sensing that his shoulders would go the same way as the youngster's. "I won't fight, I won't do anything, please don't—"

Cawley held onto his arms, placed a boot in his back and pushed until his shoulders popped. It was cruel and it was brutal, but it was also the only safe way to immobilize them without handcuffs. He knew he was dealing with killers; he couldn't afford to take any risks.

Simpson was still wrestling with the big man when Cawley looked over. She managed to win the battle, landed a few quick punches on his chin and his temple. When he was weak and disoriented enough to give up the fight, Simpson took his head and slammed it against the wall. Cawley opened his mouth to object, closed it slowly when he saw the big man slide to his knees, his face grazing the wall on the way down.

Simpson rubbed her hands together, gave Cawley a proud smile. Cawley looked around quickly, his eyes darting back to the room. "Where's the gun?" he asked his partner.

Simpson shrugged but Sellers, who had heard the commotion from the bar, answered it for him. He appeared through the doorway, pointing the gun at the detective as he scanned the damage to his pub and his friends.

* * *

The night was clear, the stars were beautiful. As a child, Pandora liked to stare at the stars and lose herself in them. She liked to make shapes and faces from them; she never understood the constellations and preferred to think up her own. They were always a place of wonder, of distant worlds where everything was possible and anything could happen.

When she had given up the fight, when her neck muscles

tightened, weakened, and gave way, and she couldn't hold her head up any longer . . . when her brain had taken so many knocks that she struggled to retain consciousness . . . she stared into the night sky—into that beautiful abyss of magical worlds and endless possibilities—and she escorted herself away, away from Fairwood, away from earth.

She shed a tear for those worlds; for those lives; for those possibilities. She shed a tear for herself and Dexter, for what they'd lost. She shed a tear for the life they had taken, for the lives that they'd failed to create. She loved their life in the fast lane, but as much as she hated normality, as much as she despised the nine-to-five monotony and the limited ambition of family, house, and home, she still wanted to settle down at some point. They both did.

She turned from the stars to look at Dexter and she shed another tear for him, because she didn't know if she would ever be able to hold him again.

* * *

Cawley had a shotgun to his face, a shotgun held by someone who had killed in the past, but he liked his odds. Sellers was alone, the bandaged man was the only other conscious friend, and he was reluctant and unable to raise a hand.

Cawley caught Simpson's stare, saw a glint in his partner's eyes that suggested she also liked the odds. They tried to keep their distance from each other, making sure Sellers was in the middle of them. He was unable to train the gun on both of them at once, but he realized what they were up to and ushered them back into the room; a room occupied by his two unconscious friends and one dead enemy.

He told them to stand by the far wall and then he snapped the light on, his face twisting into a sadistic smirk when he realized he had two police officers at his command. Cawley didn't like that smirk; the smirk of an idiot and a madman, never a good combination.

"What's your game?" Cawley asked. He tried to lower his arms, but Sellers thrust the gun at him, placed his finger on the trigger.

"Keep 'em fucking raised," he snapped venomously.

Cawley did as instructed, sensing an envious look from the bandaged man as he lifted his arms high above his head.

"So, what is this?" Cawley asked. "Are you in the drugs game?" He made a point of staring at the gun. "Weapons?"

Sellers seemed confused and he slowly shook his head, keeping his eyes on Cawley. "You don't get it, do ya?" he asked methodically, explaining something to a child.

"Get what?"

A smile slowly formed on Sellers' face, a wide-mouth grin of stupidity and psychosis. He nodded toward the wall, to the corpse that sat slumped near Cawley's feet.

"Take a look," Sellers said.

Cawley and Simpson twisted around to look, keeping their arms in the air.

"Jesus."

Cawley barely believed what he was seeing. In the light he recognized the face; he knew the dead man.

"Now do ya get it?" Sellers asked.

Cawley nodded, keeping his eyes on the corpse's face. He looked up, about to ask to another question, but Sellers answered for him, nodding his head to the right.

Another corpse lay against the opposite wall, slumped in a similar pose to the one by Cawley's feet. He strangled a chunk of saliva down his throat, began to wish that he had never broken into the pub. Beside him, Simpson was wishing the same thing.

37

They passed all the beauty of Fairwood: the rich and pleasant rivers, fields, and trees, the postcard-perfect houses and vibrant gardens. The people, the dark and ugly side of the town, watched on.

All the houses were empty. Every resident, young and old, was on the streets baying for the blood of the fugitives. A small girl hovered back to see, to witness their blood-soaked faces bob along the ground. It was the same girl Pandora had spoken to on the street; she recognized her through the crimson blur: the same dress, a different expression—intrigue and delight.

They dragged them to a large garden at the back of the pub. The ones that had gone on ahead were already inside, sitting and waiting eagerly, the rest rushed in behind them, some helping to strap the lovers to the stockades that had been set up in the center of the yard.

They didn't put up a fight as they were locked inside, their wrists and heads bolted into place. They struggled to remain upright, could barely stand, but the stocks stopped them from slumping, forced them to use what little strength they had in their legs.

Spotlights screamed bright lights onto them from the back of the pub. Pandora couldn't lift her neck, couldn't shift a single muscle, but Dexter managed to crane it upward to look at the sea of expectant faces.

It took him a few attempts, first to speak over the silence, then to find his voice, but Dexter finally managed to ask, "What is this, what do you want?"

The crowd hushed. Dexter felt like an alien brought to a distant world, a backward backwater where everyone hated him but longed to know where he was from and what he had to say. It didn't surprise him that it was Dorothy who answered. What did surprise him was that she looked completely unharmed, unaffected from her earlier beating.

"We want you to suffer," she told him.

He slumped, unable to hold his head. "Please," he whimpered. "Leave her, let her go. You can do what you want to me. Kill me if you want. She doesn't deserve this."

"You're both to blame," Dorothy disagreed.

He raised his voice, annoyed and desperate. "She didn't do anything wrong. It was mostly me. The robberies, the murder. I shouted the orders; I pulled the trigger."

"It doesn't matter who held the gun," Dorothy told him. "The blood is on both of your hands."

Dexter groaned, tried to drop to his knees but couldn't with the shackles of the stockade tight against his throat. "Just kill me," he told her. "Get it over with."

Dorothy seemed to enjoy that. She laughed and, after a few seconds, the others joined in. Before long, a chorus of laughter was pilfering the silence from the night.

* * *

The gun was still trained on him, but Cawley wasn't paying any attention to it. He was more concerned with the corpses, struggling to understand what he was seeing.

"Why?" he asked eventually, keeping his attention on the

male corpse that lay slumped just a few yards from him, his decaying scent clogging his nostrils like some sickly summer pollen.

"You really wanna know?" Sellers said cockily, a laugh tweaking the corner of his mouth.

Cawley held his stare, saw the lack of remorse behind his eyes. It didn't matter how or why he had done it. He wasn't a sociopath, didn't get a kick out of killing like a serial killer would, he was just an apathetic idiot. Someone who could easily, and without regret or a second thought, kill for money, fame, or just because the other person annoyed him. He had met plenty of those types in his time on the job, and he had wanted to do to all of them just what they had done to their victims—see if their apathy would remain when they were staring death in the face.

"Well?" Sellers spat, begging to unleash his story.

Cawley looked at Sellers, almost forlornly. Sellers looked ready to talk, but before he could speak, Simpson was upon him. She moved in a blur at the corner of Cawley's vision, barely seen by him and not seen at all by Sellers.

Simpson tackled him against the wall, taking out his gun-arm first and smacking his elbow against the door frame. The fragile bone rattled and juddered, forcing him to drop the weapon and unleash a surprised and feeble scream.

Sellers wasn't as strong as the big man Simpson had taken out earlier, but he was craftier. He kneed Simpson in the stomach just as the former detective tried to swivel around his back. The strike incapacitated Simpson, dropped her to her haunches. Sellers put her in a headlock, squeezed until the air and color drained from Simpson's face.

He reached down with his free arm—keeping Simpson locked in the other—and grabbed at the gun. The steel handle brushed his fingertips but he failed to grasp it. He repositioned himself, bent down further. It was taken away from him before he could pick it up. He straightened up, stared down the barrel of his own weapon, the gleaming eyes of Detective Max Cawley glinting above it.

"Let her go," Cawley said softly.

Sellers released his grip and Simpson pulled herself free. She took a few deep and satisfying breaths. She looked toward the doorway, saw the bandaged man trying to exit silently through the back door.

"Don't you fucking move!" Simpson snapped, throwing out her hand as if cradling an invisible gun. The threat worked, the bandaged man tried to lift his hands to the ceiling, didn't even turn around to see who was threatening him or what they were threatening him with.

Simpson took some ropes from the back of the storage room where they had been used to tie down a few boxes. Sellers was quiet as they tied him to a chair, didn't flinch or attempt to fight them.

When Simpson finished restraining him, Sellers looked up at Cawley, the smile faded from his face, replaced by apathy.

Cawley nodded to the back of the room, to the female corpse; once a beautiful, radiant young woman. Her arms had been tied behind her back when she was alive, and she had died in the restraints, suffering the indignity of rape and torture, unable to throw out a hand to protect herself.

"Is she what it was all about?" he asked. "Did you kill them because you wanted to have fun with her?"

They all turned slowly to face her. Her once striking blonde hair was mattered to her face, covered in blood. Her clothes had been torn; a pale breast—dotted with dried blood around the nipple—was exposed.

Sellers grinned, seemingly thinking about what he had done. He turned away from Pandora's corpse, gave Cawley a brief and delighted nod.

"She was a pretty little thing though, right?"

Simpson couldn't help herself. She spat in Sellers's face. The thick glob of saliva hit him above the right eye, dripped through his eyebrow before running a course down his cheek. Sellers didn't flinch.

"She was worth it," the barman said surely.

"There was a big bounty on their head," Cawley noted. "Why didn't you take it?"

A wrinkle tweaked in the corner of Sellers's eye, a thin line above his right eye that cut a distasteful furrow toward his temple. "I wanted to, believe me," he said, lowering his brow and staring at Cawley through the top of his vision. "But they put up a fight. You saw what they did to Harry." He nodded toward the bandaged man in the Stetson hat. "Poor fucker ain't been the same since, gonna be scarred for life, might never want to take those bandages off."

The bandaged man remained quiet, averting his eyes shyly. They hadn't tied him up, didn't think he posed a threat. His arms lay loose and useless by his side, his head was slumped onto his chest. He was breathing heavily and looking mournfully at the floor, contemplating a life of regrets behind bars.

"The fuckers pulled a gun on us; they nearly got away."

"But?" Cawley pushed.

Sellers shrugged apathetically. "They didn't," he stated simply. "Car wouldn't start. After a few minutes, we all went out to 'ave a look, 'cept for 'arry 'ere who bled his shit all over my bathroom."

Harry looked up just as Cawley turned to him. He was contemplating escape, on getting up and sneaking away while they were distracted with Sellers. Those contemplations were cut short when he saw the glare in Cawley's eyes; the shotgun in his hands.

"We stayed back at first, watched him struggle. He still had the gun on us, still threatened to shoot us if we went near, but eventually . . ." Sellers shrugged. "We stopped giving a shit. Rex wanted the girl," he nodded to the youngster, murmuring in his unconscious state on the floor, drooling a sticky mess down his cheek. "We all wanted the money. Rex rushed 'im first, none of us followed, we figured 'e would shoot. He'd just killed someone at the bank with the same gun after all, but 'e didn't. He seemed scared, cautious. Rex ripped open the door, tried to rip the gun right outta 'is 'and, he didn't succeed, skinny fucker can barely 'old 'is own tiny cock to take a piss, but that was all that everyone else needed to rush 'im."

"Just you three?" Cawley asked.

Sellers shook his head, a long, tired gesture. "There were others, just a couple. They didn't 'ang around, didn't want anything to do with it when it got 'eated, but they 'elped us get 'em out of the car."

"Heated?"

Sellers nodded slowly, looked at Cawley, at Simpson, and then turned to look at Pandora. "We beat 'em up pretty bad in the struggle. Rex was trying to kop a feel o'the lass, her fella wasn't too happy about that. He took some stopping. Left him near death by the end, her too. She was one 'ell of a fighter." He cleared his throat, echoing a dry, stuttering noise through the room.

"We tied 'em both up, then we had a little argument. The others wanted to phone the police. Us three wanted to have a little *play* first."

The way he emphasized the word sickened Simpson. She turned away from the man in the chair, only to face Dexter's dead, decaying body. "That's enough," she said, turning back, looking shaky on her feet. "We get it."

"What happened to the others?" Cawley wondered, wanting to know more.

"They scarpered when we started on the girl. Said they wanted nothing to do with it."

"And Bleak?" Cawley asked, nodding toward Dexter.

"We let him watch. What was left of 'im anyway."

Simpson hit Sellers. Hard. Cawley saw the relief, the delight on her face as she watched him snap back. He looked at his friend, at her bitter smile, at her fist, which she held tight to her chest. "Feel better?" he wondered.

Simpson grinned at Sellers, who was trying to squint away the pain in his head.

"Much better."

Sellers coughed, spat a glob of blood onto the floor. "You got what you wanted, as well, right?" he said through a slanted smile.

"What the fuck are you talking about?" Simpson spat.

Sellers turned to Simpson, then to Cawley. "You got your killers," he clarified. "You caught the Bleak and Bright bandits. Dead or alive, it don't matter. You'll be famous for this."

Cawley didn't reply, he kept his eyes locked on the sadistic killer in front of him.

"So will I," Sellers said with a wide grin.

Cawley turned the gun around, struck the killer across the side of his head as hard as he could. He felt the vibration through the gun, felt the impact reverberate from Sellers's skull, through the weapon, and into his wrist.

"Bastard," he hissed silently, stepping back and smiling as he watched Sellers's head slump unconsciously onto his chest.

He looked around—at Dexter and Pandora, dead and decaying; at their unconscious killers, scattered around the room; at the bandaged man, looking grim by the exit; at Simpson, looking sick as she stared at Sellers.

"Now what?" Simpson wondered.

"We should burn the lot to the ground," Cawley said simply, hearing a barely audible squeak from the bandaged man in the corner.

"Should?"

Cawley nodded, shook it off. "Should, but can't. There's a phone in the bar," he said with a nod. "Phone it in, let someone else clean this mess up."

38

"You're already dead," Dorothy said once the laughter had faded and the bemused expressions remained creased on Dexter and Pandora's face. They both strained their necks, finding the energy to fight against their weakened muscles.

"You're mad," Dexter told her simply. "All of you." He flicked his eyes around the room, taking in as much of the insanity as he could. "You've lost your minds."

Dorothy smirked, raised and dropped her eyebrows.

"What is this place?" Dexter asked, finding his voice. "What has happened to all of you? *Who the fuck are you?*"

"We're nobody," Eric said, stepping forward, standing beside his wife.

The clerk at the petrol station, the one who had led the chase, moved alongside him. "Because of you," he noted.

"*Excuse me?*" Dexter felt angry, bitter. He had given up but was finding some fight again. He didn't want to go down to a gang of weirdoes, didn't want his life to end because of inbreeding and crossed wires—because a small-town mentality, similar to the one he had grown up with, had morphed into something obscene and psychotic.

"You stopped us from living," someone added from behind

him. He strained to see them but couldn't twist his neck muscles enough.

A child, a young girl, no more than ten or eleven, stepped forward. "You killed my great granddad," she said soberly.

Dexter felt her words touch him. They didn't sound as crazy as the rest.

"The guard at the bank?" he asked, his voice breaking as the fight faded again. "That was your great granddad?"

She nodded, held his stare with eyes that despised him.

His face creased as the memories returned. Something wasn't right. "But he was young, he couldn't have been more than thirty-five. He couldn't have great-grandchildren. He couldn't even have grandchildren."

A woman in her early thirties stepped forward, planted a motherly arm on the young girl's shoulder, stared at Dexter with despicable eyes. "He *didn't* have them; but he would have."

He stared at her for a moment, waited for an explanation. His face dropped when one didn't come. He turned to Dorothy, to Eric, to anyone that would make any sense.

"What the fuck is going on here?"

Dorothy was hailing the others, gathering them around the front of the stocks so they could witness the humiliation for themselves. They knocked them, slapped them, and ran curious eyes over them as they passed and huddled around. Pandora winced as she felt a few hands on her face and her back, a couple of them ran through her hair, against her cheek. She could feel their heat, smell their odor. She tasted the sour sweat on the hand of one as he trailed a finger across her cheek and lingered for a moment on her lips.

Dexter heard her squirm, tried to see what was happening, but couldn't maneuver himself enough.

"If you touch her I'll—"

"You'll what?" Dorothy suddenly snapped, snarling as she stepped to the head of the huddle. "You'll kill us?" she grinned. "I told you. We don't exist. *You* don't exist anymore. Look around you." She threw her arms over her head, gesturing to the throng of people—packed in like revelers at a festival, all looking at Dexter and Pandora with eager, desperate and vengeful eyes. "We are the descendants of the man you killed. The ones who didn't get a chance because *you* took him away."

Dorothy pointed to the young girl. "The man you killed had a daughter, Annie, her name was. She doted on her father. She lived for him. But she also idolized you two, you—" Her face was suddenly a picture of disgust. "—Scum." She spat at him. "She found out what had happened, she blamed herself. She thought it was her fault. She was too young to know better, too young to know that scum like you will exist regardless of what she does, what she thinks, what she writes."

"I don't understand," Dexter said, turning to the little girl.

"That little girl would have grown into a strong woman. A journalist, a mother, a grandmother. Maggie here," she pointed to the young girl, "would have been her great-great-granddaughter. This sweetheart here," she pointed to another, a woman in her forties, "Her daughter. And this strong, loving, handsome fellow—" she pointed to the clerk. "Her son. You took a life, one warm, kindhearted person, and in doing so you stopped all of us from living."

"This can't be real," Pandora said, her mouth agape as she studied the faces that stared back at her.

"Oh it is, my dear. Or at least, it is for you."

"And where does that leave you?" Dexter asked. "What is your relation, or are you just the little cunt they put in charge of everyone?" he laughed, hoping to anger her, even though the action caused his lungs to ache.

"Annie was my sister," Dorothy explained. "Or she would have been. She was an only child who dreamed of having siblings and she would have had those siblings, three of them in fact, if you hadn't killed our father and left our mother distraught and alone."

"Bullshit," Dexter spat. "This is insane. All of you from one family? If you're going to go the crazy route, at least make sure it makes sense."

He could see that his words angered Dorothy, that they got through to her. Her saw the corners of her mouth twitch, saw her eyes flash madly. But she stopped herself short. She looked away, shook her head and laughed, as if to herself. Behind her, a few complaints rose from the crowd, people eager to have their pound of flesh, eager to silence Dexter. Dorothy rose her hand as if to silence them, before looking at Dexter once more.

"Craig!" she barked, her eyes still on Dexter. "Come forward."

A young boy, shy, timid, walked forward. Dexter recognized him as the youngster who had spied on them the day they walked to the river. He stood next to Dorothy, his hands cupped together in front of him, his head held low.

"Craig here was Maggie's brother. He was shy, but she saw herself in him. She doted on him. She taught him everything she knew and when he was just seventeen, he became the successful artist she had always wanted to be."

Dorothy patted the boy's head, held up her hand again. This time a woman strode forward, one Dexter hadn't seen. She was tall, confident, beautiful. "Susie here would have been a doctor. She would have helped to save thousands of lives, including her own daughter—" Dorothy paused as another person stepped forward, this time a woman of no more than twenty-five— "who had a sudden heart attack during a family gathering."

Dorothy looked around her, seemingly giving signals, and as she turned back to Dexter and Pandora, more people approached from behind her, silently sidling up alongside her.

"Amber here—" A woman in her mid-twenties, with scars on her face and beautiful brown eyes "—was an amateur stuntwoman. She wasn't accomplished and wouldn't have lived long,

but she burned bright and made many people happy. Michael—"
a buff man in his forties, one of the many who had helped to
hold Dexter down in the bar "—was a champion bodybuilder.
Mary—" an equally buff woman of a similar age "—was his
twin sister. They would have competed together. Eddie and
Marie—" the two that had 'won' them in the pub "—were also
twins. It runs in the family, you see, or at least it *did*. Julie—"
another little girl, another sweet face "would have—"

"Stop!" Pandora screamed. "We get it!"

Dexter looked at Pandora, saw the remorse on her face,
the tears streaming down his cheeks, the helplessness. He still
wanted to scream and shout, to kick and squirm, but in that
moment, he was paralyzed by guilt. He had pulled the trigger,
he had led them here. It was his fault.

"So you see," Dorothy continued. "This is our home. This
is where we'll always be: stuck in a place that doesn't exist in a
time that doesn't exist. But now none of that matters, because
now you're here with us."

She moved forward, until she stood in between Pandora
and Dexter, who both craned their necks to see. She lowered
her voice, bent over, her hands on her knees, turning her head
to look at each of them in turn.

"This may be our home, but this is *your* hell. You're forced
to live with your mistakes, forced to repeat them while we
watch and make things as hard and as miserable as possible."

They didn't hear anymore, didn't comprehend anything
else that was said.

The riot started, the torture began.

The town had their fun with what was left of Dexter and
Pandora. They tortured them, humiliated them. Everyone had
their turn, and when they finished, when Dexter and Pandora
were left in barely human guises—lifeless and bloodied on the
floor—the town of Fairwood returned to their homes, ready for
another day.

39

Sellers was still grinning when they removed the ropes, replaced them with handcuffs, read him his rights, and bundled him into the van. The others had regained consciousness by then and didn't share his apathy. The youngster was close to tears; he didn't express any remorse for the deaths of the two fugitives but did seem very concerned about how his stepdad would react to the news of his impending imprisonment.

The bandaged man and the big man went silently, taken away in separate vehicles.

The press was already arriving; someone had tipped them off and they were crowding around the pub in their droves, the flash of cameras fused with the lights from the police cars to create a carnival atmosphere.

Someone had the sense to erect a line of tape before the throng arrived, and a few officers held back the excited gaggle of journalists and cameramen who tried to snap their pound of flesh.

Cawley ignored the calls from the press, tuned them out completely. He felt Simpson's hand on his shoulder, felt her fingers dig into the flesh.

"Looks like that's my call to leave," he heard her say. He

didn't know what she was talking about at first, didn't react when he felt Simpson brush past him. He watched her scuttle away to mix with the other officers who gathered around the scene, looking complacent and bored as they tried to look busy. Then he heard a shrill and annoyed female voice and he understood why Simpson had left.

"Cawley!" the harpy snapped. "I've been looking everywhere for you, what the fuck have you been doing?"

His heart sank. He lowered his head, turned to face the wall of high-pitched noise.

"Cawley! What's wrong with you?" Superintendent Clarissa Morris asked, her face askew, her bony hands on her bony hips. "I've been trying to phone you all day. Again!"

Cawley sighed. He had left his phone at home. He didn't need it ringing during the break in and had no desire to talk to his boss, the only person likely to try ringing him.

"Have you been avoiding me?" she barked.

Cawley raised his head, couldn't stop the sly smile that wormed his way across his face. He nodded, slow and long.

"Excuse me?" Clarissa snapped, her eyebrows raised so high that they disappeared under her fringe. "You *were* ignoring me?"

"Yes, sir," he said with an assured nod.

He saw her nostrils flare, saw her hands tighten into fists and grow white under the pressure as she pushed them tighter into her hips. "May I ask why?" she said through a clenched jaw, the words squirming out of her mouth.

"Because I can't stand you," he said simply.

"Excuse me?" she stuck out her jaw as she spoke.

"You heard me," he said, his head now raised. "You annoy the hell out of me. You're evil and manipulative and I despise every moment that I'm forced to spend around you."

She opened her mouth to object but he hadn't finished.

"You're a horrible, demonic witch and no one likes you." He

was shouting now and the throng of people around him, the officers in close proximity, and the press, who were pushed further back, all silenced their activity to hear what he was saying. "I know this all boils down to me rejecting you at the Christmas party, and for that I'm truly sorry, but there isn't enough alcohol in the world to make me want to sleep with you."

She growled but she'd been thrown from her stride. She tried to react, to regain her control, but he pushed on, now within an inch of her, so close he could smell the sour coffee on her breath.

"You can sack me all you want," he told her. "I don't care. I don't want to spend another day in the same building as you." He left one long stare with her, turned, and departed with three dozen admiring eyes on his back.

"You're fired, Cawley!" Clarissa said as loud as she could, looking around as she did so, making sure everyone had heard just how loud and assertive she was. "You'll never work another day in your life!"

Cawley laughed softly to himself but he didn't turn around. Instead he raised an arm, popped up his middle finger, and left the gesture with her.

40

A year later.

Cawley stared into the still, amber liquid in his glass. He tapped his fingers on the edge of the thick tumbler, stroked a bead of moisture from the rim, and then leaned back in his chair. He ran his hand through his hair; it hadn't been washed for a couple of days and hadn't been cut for much longer. He sighed through tightly pressed lips, looked toward the ceiling.

His mouth was dry; his head was tired, aching. He closed his eyes, squeezed them tight, and then quickly opened them to watch the blue stars dance around his vision. He checked his watch, checked the clock on the wall for confirmation, and then stood.

The barman watched him stand, gave him a curious smile. "Leaving so soon?" he asked.

Cawley nodded in his direction, threw some money onto the bar, dug his hands into his coat pockets, and left.

The day was bright but cold; he sunk his head underneath the lapels of his jacket, kept his head away from the sharp wind.

It was the day of his anniversary, a year since he'd found the dead bodies of Bleak and Bright. He'd spent most of the afternoon in a dark and dank bar, sipping from a glass of whiskey and watching the clock.

He crossed the road with his mind elsewhere and was nearly clipped by a pissed-off boy racer in a flash hatchback.

The youngster stopped the car beside him, rolled down the window, and thrust his angered, pimpled face outside. He formed the beginnings of an outburst, saw and recognized Cawley's face, and then apologized, ducking back inside the car.

Cawley sighed, allowed himself a cheeky smile. He would never get used to that, but he didn't despise it as much as he used to.

"Making more friends, I see?"

He turned at the sound of the voice, allowed the half-smile to contort into one much bigger, much wider, when he saw the woman standing there—a soft smile on her pretty face, a cheeky glint in her blue eyes. "You know me, Mia," he said. "Always a social animal."

"An animal maybe. I've seen your house. But I'm not sure about the social bit." She winked at him, gave him a big hug, and then planted a kiss on his cheek.

"Still struggling with this fame thing?" Mia asked.

He gave a passive shrug. "I could get used to it." He gave her a kiss, looked up at the building in front of them. "This is the place?" he asked, a little unsure at the daunting, impressive facade of the glamorous restaurant and bar.

"I'll admit," Mia said, running her appraising eyes over it. "It's not as impressive as that run-down hole you've been drinking in all day, but it'll do." She gave him a cheeky wink.

"Who told you?"

"The whiskey on your breath."

"I barely finished one glass."

She hooked her arm around his, straightened up. "Don't worry," she said, patting him on the back. "I trust you."

"This place looks expensive," he said before entering.

"This is a special occasion," she informed him. "And you can afford it now," she turned to him, raised an eyebrow. "*Superintendent.*"

He couldn't help but smile; he liked the way that sounded. He'd had the job for a few months but was still settling in. As strange as it sounded hearing his title from his girlfriend, it had been even stranger hearing it from his colleagues, people he had worked alongside for so long. Even Clarissa Morris, his former boss, had been forced to address him as such on a couple of occasions, and that could never be topped.

Clarissa was working the beat again, trying to climb back up the ladder, although no one wanted her at the top anymore. After the bodies of the bandits were discovered, after Cawley had publicly walked away from his boss, Clarissa had given a press conference retaining all the anger and animosity she felt for Max Cawley and unleashing it onto a room of journalists who knew what buttons to press to send the hard-faced superintendent over the edge.

The press conference, filmed live for nationwide coverage, became an overnight hit. It went viral. The video of an angry, abusive woman at the head of an authoritative chain was plastered all over the internet and television. The public loved it; her bosses didn't share the same enthusiasm. They suspended and demoted her.

She no longer talked down to Cawley. She had tried a couple of times but she hadn't succeeded.

Abigail Simpson had moved on, as well. She achieved her own fame. She stayed away from the force but she also stayed away from the drink, sobering up just a few weeks after the ordeal. As half of the duo that finally caught the bandits, she became an overnight celebrity. As current superintendent, Cawley kept his head below ground, kept away from the spotlight. Simpson lapped it up. For the first few months, barely a day passed when she wasn't on the television or the radio, and after that she signed her own book deal. She had enough money stashed away to live it up for a few years and was in talks to become a spokesperson for the force.

The bandits became folk heroes, modern-day legends. Their untimely and cruel deaths only served to expand their popularity, giving them an immortal and worldwide fame. Sellers and his friends became famous for killing them, but not as he hoped. Sellers spent his first few weeks suffering daily beatings from his fellow prisoners and guards before being locked up in solitary and eventually ending up as a medicated drone on the psyche ward.

Rex, the youngster with the big mouth and big attitude, ended up as a bitch to a butch drug dealer inside a maximum-security prison. On his seventeenth birthday, after downing a batch of prison hooch, he picked a fight with his cellmate. The fight didn't last long; the guards found him dead in his cell the next morning, soaking in a pool of his own blood.

Their partners in crime were sentenced to life inside a prison that adored the notorious bandits, whose cooks regularly diluted their food with piss, spit, and any other bodily fluids they can find, whose population took their showers with extra shanks.

For Cawley, life wasn't perfect. His ex-wife was still on his tail, berating him for whatever she could get, but she was losing patience with him. She knew she wasn't getting to him anymore, wasn't affecting him as she once did, and that was forcing her to give up. She had never wanted his money or his possessions; she had always wanted to deprive him of his life, his soul, and when she saw just how happy he was becoming, how comfortable he was in his new life—with his new job and his new girlfriend—she experienced a depression of her own and had all but given up on hounding him. On more than one occasion, she even tried to rekindle their relationship, drunk dialing or texting him with apologies and desperation which

Cawley promptly ignored. He still hadn't told her what he knew, and he didn't intend to, but that knowledge continued to fuel his hatred toward her.

Max and Mia sat down at their table, stared at each other over a single red rose that sat solitary in a crystal vase.

"So," Mia said, holding Cawley's gaze with a radiant and cheeky smile that lit up her face and his. "What's new?"

* * *

The radio fizzed with a static wail, a banshee screaming through resisting airwaves. Pandora released the knob and sighed. She reached into the glove box, dug around through the dated collection of CDs, but failed to find one she liked.

"No decent music in there?" Dexter glanced across at her, his eyes half on the road, his thoughts back on the present.

She shook her head.

"I could sing for you if you want?" he offered with a dimpled grin.

She sniggered, shook her head. "I'll pass, thank you."

"You're missing out."

"I'm not. I've heard you in the shower," she giggled as he turned a grin toward the road. "Where are we going then?"

"Like I said and like we planned: somewhere to lie low."

"But, where?"

He shrugged, scrunched up his face. "There's bound to be somewhere around here."

"Another place like the bar back there? With a dozen dumb-fuck locals looking for rape, torture, and reward?"

He shrugged again.

"Hm," she glared at him.

"I wouldn't trust anyone to hole us up with such a big reward hanging over us."

"There must be somewhere we could go," she said hopefully.

Dexter turned to her. "I don't know what you want me to say."

"How about, 'I've arranged a flight out of here,' or 'I have a friend who's going to let us stay at his place until things blow over.'"

"Unless you have a light aircraft that I don't know about then we can't fly, not when every security checkpoint in every airport is looking for us." He sighed and then added, "And I don't have any friends."

A smile fought annoyance on her face and eventually won. "Fair enough," she conceded. "A drive into nowhere it is then."